# WARRIORS OF THE FORGOTTEN FRONT

*By*

*L. Craig Johnson*

# PREFACE

This book, while a work of fiction, is based on actual events and real people. Inspired mostly by my father's first-hand accounts of his memories while serving in Italy during WWII, this story also includes experiences told to me by other members of his unit, Company G of the 339th Infantry Regiment. I had the good fortune of meeting these men when I became a member of the 339th's reunion group. In this way I came to count as beloved friends the very men of whom my father spoke so often. Without their acceptance of me as a junior "Polar Bear" (the knick name given the 339th because of its service in Russia during the harsh Archangel Campaign of WWI) and their willingness to share their personal experiences, the book would have omitted a number of important occurrences.

Aside from the events concerning Monte Cassino and the debacle of the Anzio beachhead, the war in Italy is often dismissed by many as a mere "holding action," implying that only limited engagements of minor importance took place there. This view overlooks the brutal combat that occurred not only at Monte Cassino but also that in the Apennine and Dolomite Mountains, where the Allied Forces fought a constant uphill campaign against some of Germany's best and most determined troops.

It is my hope that in telling the story of my father and the men in his unit some greater attention and appreciation might be brought to the brave men who fought there and especially to those, like Lieutenant Robert Waugh and so many others, who died there. Readers may also be interested to know that, according to published data, the Allies suffered more casualties in Italy than in any other European Campaign except for the Russian Front.

This book is dedicated to all who served in Italy during World War II and especially to the men of the 85th Division and especially to those in the 339th Infantry Regiment. My special thanks go out to Hoy Shingleton, Worth Haynes, Arthur Ferdinand, Charles Bradley, Jack Claytor, Harry Klutz and Frank Ruth, who are indeed outstanding examples of our country's finest generation. Also, though I was never able to locate him or any member of his family, I am personally indebted to Private Francis Furlong for the influence he had on my father. It is a great tribute to him that when the men of G Company meet at their reunions the names most often mentioned are Robert Waugh and Francis Furlong.

In addition I can't give enough thanks to Lauran Strait and all members of her writing courses who provided instruction, critiques, and helpful suggestions to me as I wrote. Among this group, Frank Lawlor kept me honest on matters military, Valerie Wilkinson and Jean Hendrickson provided insightful comments, and Sharon Poch, Sandy Everton, and the late and dear Barbara (Bobbie) Hartin, gave me encouragement and assistance during those times when I thought I might never complete this work.

L. Craig Johnson
August 2010

# CHAPTER ONE

"Car's been followin' us ever since we crossed the county line," Aaron said as he glanced into the rearview mirror of his '33 Chevy.

"Prob'ly just somebody on a late date—like us." Maggie snuggled closer to him.

He caressed her knee and smiled. Maybe later…

"Mary Lou got a letter from John this week. He said his unit is shipping out soon—probably to the Pacific. How much longer is this war gonna last? It's been almost two years already."

"Yeah—well, there's—"

The trailing headlights flashed bright in the mirror. "Uh-oh--he's really comin' on fast."

Maggie twisted in the seat and looked out the rear window. "You think it's a cop?"

"Dunno. I'm gonna get over so he can pass." Aaron pulled to the shoulder.

The approaching vehicle swung left and slid to a stop beside them. Aaron peered through the dust that enveloped both cars. It was a black '40 Ford coupe—not a cop. Who—what was the guy—

"Look out!"

Aaron pushed Maggie toward the floorboard as a shot rang out. The bullet streaked past, barely missing their heads and smashing the passenger side window.

Maggie screamed. Aaron jammed the accelerator to the floor. The man in the Ford aimed, ready to fire again. Aaron roared away as a second shot sounded.

"Who—" Maggie yelled above the sound of the Chevy's revving engine.

"Your old boyfriend! The bootlegger—I thought you told him to get lost!"

"I did!"

Aaron checked the mirror. The headlights were gaining. Rounding a curve, he headed down a dark straightaway and dropped his speed as the Ford's headlights drew closer.

"What are you doing? He's gonna catch us!"

"I can't outrun that V-8—gotta try something else."

The Ford sped up beside them. When it was almost even with the Chevy, Aaron swerved sharply toward it. The driver cut hard left, fishtailed, and ran off the road, ramming into a small pine tree.

Aaron skidded to a stop in a cloud of red clay dust. He jerked his door open.

"Aaron, don't!" She grabbed his arm.

Aaron broke free and dashed to the wrecked Ford. Smoke poured from the hood. Behind the wheel, Charley Simpson, reeking of alcohol, rubbed his forehead and groaned. Aaron jerked the door open. A blue-steel revolver tumbled onto the ground as he pulled Charley from the car, shoved him against the fender, and grabbed his shirtfront.

"What the hell do you think you're doing? You coulda killed us!"

"I told her if I couldn't have her, I'd—" His right fist came up in a roundhouse swing.

Aaron blocked it with his left arm and punched him in the face with his right fist. Blood gushed from Charley's nose.

"Goddamn you! You broke my nose!" Charley cupped his hands over his face. "Shit!"

"Yeah, I oughta break your stupid head open."

"Charley Simpson, I told you to leave me alone!" Maggie stood six feet away, fists clenched, dark eyes glaring. "You make me sick!" She snatched Charley's gun from the ground and held it in both hands, pointed at Charley's head. "I told you we were through, and I meant it. Now—"

Aaron wrenched the pistol from her. "Jesus—give me that! Go sit in the car!"

Maggie's eyes flashed. "You tell him—you tell him—"

She began to shake. Tears streamed down her face.

Aaron put the pistol in his jacket pocket and then placed his hands on her shoulders. "Maggie—please—go wait in the car. I'll be there in a second."

Maggie sniffed, squared her shoulders, and marched toward the Chevy.

Aaron turned to Charley. "Listen, you. Maybe you haven't heard. We're married. We eloped two months ago. Now—leave us alone. If you ever come around us again, I'll fix you good. Understand?"

"Married? You're married?" Charley mumbled through the handkerchief he held to his bleeding nose.

"You heard me." Aaron stepped closer. "And you better heed me."

"Yeah—yeah." Charley waved him away. "Get outta here and leave me alone."

Aaron stepped back. "You got any way to get home?"

"There's a station just up the road. I'll walk and get somebody."

Aaron nodded. He took the pistol from his pocket, broke open the cylinder, and threw the bullets into the darkness. He tossed the gun inside the wrecked car. "I suggest you lock that thing away somewhere before it gets you in trouble."

Back in the Chevy, Aaron started the engine and pulled away. Maggie sobbed quietly beside him. He took her hand. "It's okay, honey. He won't bother us again."

"I know he won't. I'll be okay."

Aaron took in a breath. "Look—there's somethin' I have to tell you. This might not be the best time, but I gotta tell you."

Maggie lifted her head and looked at him.

He sighed. "My draft notice came today."

Two weeks later Aaron kissed Maggie good-bye as a big blue and silver bus pulled into the station. "I'll write as soon as I can," he said. "You take care of your momma and Lloyd."

Maggie lowered her head and nodded. "Momma said to tell you she'll pray for you every day."

Aaron snorted. "Yeah, my momma said the same thing—said God loves me and will look after me. I told her if God really loved me, he wouldn't let me get drafted."

The uniformed driver stepped down from the bus. "Let's go, fellas. Uncle Sam is waiting for you."

Aaron kissed Maggie again, squeezing her tight.

"I don't want you to go—it's not fair," she said.

"It'll be okay—don't worry. Take care of your folks. I'll write when I get there."

He turned and boarded the bus with fifteen other Alexander County men, all headed for Fort Jackson, South Carolina. Other wives and sweethearts stood waving as the bus pulled away. Aaron stared out the window at Maggie, watching her waving white-gloved hand until it and she faded from sight. Then he closed his eyes and rubbed his brow.

What would basic training be like? Maybe the Army would let him be a mechanic, like in his civilian job. Let him work in a motor pool. Maybe it wouldn't be so bad. Maybe.

Maggie watched until the bus was out of sight. She walked slowly toward the car where her father, and her younger sister, Juanita, waited. Both of them looked like blurred outlines because of the tears that rolled down her cheeks. So many things to worry about. Aaron gone. Would he have to fight? What if... She dared not think the worst. And now her mother was sick and didn't seem to be getting any better. Moving back home would help hold down expenses, and she could help tend to her mom and Lloyd. Juanita would help too, but she had a right to enjoy her last year of high school.

Nothing was what she'd imagined it would be when she and Aaron ran off a few short months ago to be married. They'd had it all planned out. They'd rent a little house in town. He'd keep his job as a mechanic at the Chevy dealership. She'd get a job so they could save for their own house. All that would have to wait now. There was one other thing, too. Aaron didn't know he was going to be a father.

# CHAPTER TWO

"Men, welcome to Fort Jackson, South Carolina. I'm Lieutenant Michaels—the commanding officer of your basic training company. Over the next several weeks, you will receive instruction in the art of soldiering." He turned slightly and gestured to a tall, uniformed man beside him. "This is Sergeant Donovan. He and the other members of the cadre will take good care of you. Now, if you'll excuse me, I have work to do. There's a war on, you know."

Michaels and Donovan exchanged salutes. The lieutenant walked away and disappeared around the corner of a flat-roofed one-story building.

Aaron waited on the grass where he and the others had exited the bus. His eyes narrowed as he took in the well-tanned Donovan. He reminded Aaron of Mr. Ingold, the principal of Taylorsville High School. A man he'd never gotten along with very well.

Donovan turned to face the new arrivals. He scanned the group from left to right. After a full thirty seconds, he smiled.

Sweat rolled down Aaron's face. Why did he feel so uneasy?

Donovan put his hands on his hips. "You men are in the United States Army now, and you belong to Uncle Sam, Lieutenant Michaels, and me. Nobody else. Forget your mommas and poppas and your wives and girlfriends. I'm gonna do my best to make soldiers out of you sorry lookin' excuses of humanity."

Donovan spat and glared at the group. "Now, the first thing I want to tell you is that Lieutenant Michaels is an officer and a gentleman. All officers are addressed as 'sir,' and when you see an officer you salute him. The second thing I want to tell you ladies is—*get off my grass! Who told you that you could stand on my grass?* Move, move, move—get your shit and your sorry asses down to the platoon area—now!"

Everyone grabbed their bags and suitcases and moved onto the nearby sidewalk. A short, stocky man near the sergeant looked about with a wild expression on his face. "S-S-Sergeant—where is the platoon area, sir?"

"*Sir!* Did you call me *sir?* Don't ever call me 'sir,' you little pissant! I work for a living! These stripes on my sleeve mean I'm an enlisted man, not an officer. Do you understand me?"

"Yes s-s-sir—I mean, Sergeant."

"Are you trying to make me mad, son? What's your name, boy?"

"M-M-McCloud, Sergeant."

"Let me tell you something, McCloud. The sight of you and your pals here makes me damn near sick to my stomach. I don't know how we're gonna win this war with sad sacks like you. Now, drop that bag and give me twenty push-ups, if you can count that high."

McCloud let go of his bag, and the contents spilled onto the sidewalk and grass. He flopped to the ground and began doing push-ups, but after five or six, his arms shook and he strained to continue. Donovan looked down at him and sneered. "We're gonna have fun with you, McCloud."

Donovan stared hard at the remaining members of the group.

"McCloud here thinks he's a smart monkey. Smart monkeys don't set well with me. He thought he could talk to me without asking permission. Let's get something straight. From now on, you do not talk, you do not walk, you do not squat to pee, or do anything else under the sun unless you ask my permission. You will say, 'Sergeant Donovan, Recruit Smith, or Jones, or whatever the hell your last name is, requests permission to speak, eat, crap—whatever.' Do you understand me?"

No one spoke.

"I can't hear you! Do you understand me?"Donovan yelled.

Aaron swallowed. "Sergeant, Recruit Johnson requests permission to speak."

Donovan spun around. "Who said that?" He stepped toward Aaron. "Was that you?"

Aaron blinked. How was he supposed to answer?

"Sergeant, Recruit Johnson requests permission to speak."

Donovan smiled, revealing a row of tobacco-stained teeth.

"Well, well, well—Johnson here thinks he's got this figured out, don't you, Johnson?"

Aaron looked into Donovan's eyes but did not speak.

"Take a lesson, the rest of you maggots. Speak, Johnson. What's on your mind?"

"I just want to let you know I heard what you said, Sergeant."

Donovan stepped closer and looked directly into Aaron's eyes. "Well, that's real nice, Johnson. I'm thrilled. There's just one other thing. When I give you permission to speak, I wanna hear you. Nice and loud, like maybe a real soldier—which you ain't—might sound. But humor me. We'll pretend that maybe someday you're gonna be one. So from here on out, when you speak, let me hear you. Now, since you're such a genius, see if you can get these bums to line up. Then follow me."

Donovan turned to the group. "Fall in behind Johnson—now." Donovan glared at Aaron. "You heard me—get 'em movin'." He walked away without looking back.

Aaron helped McCloud to his feet and then turned to the others and whispered, "For Pete's sake, get your stuff and let's get a move on."

The group followed Donovan to a series of white, wood-sided, two-story buildings.

Donovan pointed to one. "This is the barracks where you'll be living during basic training. Understand this—it belongs to the Army, and it's my job to see that you take care of it. In fact, I think of it as my own house. So you'd better keep it in good shape, or you're gonna make me mad. You don't wanna make me mad. Johnson, get these men inside. Each of you pick out a bunk, put your stuff down, and get back out here. You got one minute, and the clock's running—*MOVE!*"

Aaron and the others spent the remainder of the day at different locations where they received uniforms, boots, and haircuts. McCloud looked around. "We all look alike now." Aaron rubbed his head. He sure wouldn't want Maggie to see him now.

Damn, he missed her.

# CHAPTER THREE

Three weeks later, Aaron sat in the barracks and polished his boots while McCloud studied a manual about sanitary field conditions.

"So, what do you think?" McCloud said. "Are we goin' for it or not? We been here three weeks, and that damn Donovan keeps sayin' we'll get a pass someday if we're 'good boys.'"

He slammed the manual to the floor. "My brother said we won't get a pass until we've been here at least six weeks. Me, I ain't waiting that long. I got a girlfriend, and I aim to see her this weekend. How 'bout it, Johnson? Williams over in the next barracks has a car at his cousin's house off-post. He'll take us for two bucks apiece. Are you in?"

Aaron studied his polished boot. "Yeah—but you're sure he can get us back here Sunday night? Donovan's gonna be pissed if we ain't in formation Monday morning."

"Sure, sure. His car's in great shape, and we'll be back here before bed-check on Sunday night."

"What about Saturday?"

"Miller said he and Chapman will cover for us on the weekend detail. I had to give him coupla packs of cigarettes is all."

Aaron nodded.


"I can't get over how funny you look with no hair," Maggie said. "But won't you get in trouble?"

"I don't care, Maggie. I had to get out of that place. And I had to see you. God, I've missed you."

"I miss you too, but you can't take chances like this. Daddy said they could shoot you for going AWOL."

"I didn't go AWOL—I just came home without a pass. I'm going back. Come on, let's not fight about this. There's a dance at the Silver Star—let's go there and forget about the war and the Army. Come on."

"Okay—but first you have to promise that you'll go to church with me tomorrow—and there's something I need to tell you. Sit down."

"See, I told you we'd make it back in time," McCloud said. "Williams's V-8 Ford really moves, doesn't it? And reveille's just now sounding."

Aaron buttoned his fatigue shirt. "It would move faster if the engine had a supercharger—the way we fix 'em for the bootleggers back home." Home. Maggie's news. A baby. He was gonna be a daddy. He shook his head.

McCloud frowned. "Well, we made it back in plenty of time, just like I said we would. And ole Donovan's none the wiser. Let's hurry out—we wanna look like eager beaver little soldier boys for our nice drill sergeant."

Aaron and McCloud rushed from the barracks and lined up with the other men. Donovan eyed the group. Corporal Murtz reported, "All men present and accounted for." Donovan consulted his clipboard.

"Alright—down to the parade ground for calisthenics, then back here. All except Johnson and McCloud. The rest of you, move out."

Aaron groaned. McCloud looked sick.

What would happen now? Would they be shot?

Donovan stepped toward the men. "So, you boys thought you could sneak away and nobody would catch on, huh? Well, I hope you had a good time, you sorry sacks, 'cause you're gonna pay for it. Now get your asses over to the mess hall. You're on KP for the next week. Move it—get outta my sight."

At the mess hall, Sergeant Gaithwright sat Aaron and McCloud in front of a huge pile of potatoes.

"Get busy, you slackers. All these have to be peeled before lunch. Then you can clean the pots and wash the dishes. Then empty the garbage. After that, I'll show you goofballs where the grease traps are—you'll love cleaning them. This place'd better be sparkling when I get back."

That afternoon they reported to Sergeant Donovan.

"You birds look like hell—smell like it too." Donovan leaned back in his chair. "McCloud—I checked your foot locker while you were out. It's a mess. Go put it order." McCloud spun on his heel and left.

Donovan took a drag on his cigarette, narrowed his eyes, and stared at Aaron. "What in the hell are you thinking, anyway? D'you think this is some kind of game like high school or boy scouts?" He leaned forward. "Well, let me tell you, it ain't. This is the real deal, son. I've been in this man's army a good while, and I've been in combat. Still would be if some shithead major hadn't convinced my CO I was too old for it. But I'm here to tell you, you'd better stay in line. The Army's got more ways to beat you than you can dream of. I've seen men smarter than you try it. None of them ever got away with it. You won't either."

"Permission to speak, Sergeant?"

"Speak."

"Sergeant, I just needed to see my wife. She's only a few hours from here. I was comin' back all along. I'm not a deserter."

"Don't be an idiot. The Army sees things its own way. Point is, you might make a soldier if you'll stop fightin' it so much." Donovan leaned forward. "But don't go thinking I like you or that I'm gonna cut you any slack. If you continue to foul up, I'll be on you like stink on dog shit and white on rice. Do you understand me?"

"Yes, Sergeant."

"Good—now get outta my office. You're stinking it up."


One week later, McCloud stopped chomping the gum he was chewing and turned toward Aaron. "Johnson, damn it. I can't believe I let you talk me into doing this again. Now we're only halfway back and Williams's car is almost out of gas. How are we gonna get any fuel with it being rationed like it is?"

"As I recall, I didn't have to talk too hard to get you to come along. And I'm sure we'll find gas somehow. Look, Williams, there's a station up ahead."

Williams braked, downshifted, and pulled into the country station. A lone lightbulb glowed inside. A gray-haired, heavyset man dressed in bib overalls ambled over to the car.

13

"What can I do for you, fellas? Army guys, huh? Outta Fort Jackson I bet. Well, let me have your ration stamps and I'll fill 'er up for ya."

Williams looked at the man. "Look, see, we don't have any stamps. I, um, lost 'em. Can't you help us out somehow? If we don't get some gas, we ain't gonna make it back to Jackson on time, and we'll be in big trouble. Can't you do something?"

"Weeeell, I might have a few gallons I could spare—if the price is right."

"We'll take it," McCloud said, "whatever it is."

The man brought out a dolly with a fifty-five-gallon drum of gasoline. He dispensed the fuel using a hand-cranked pump.

"Okay, fellas. That'll be eleven dollars and twenty-five cents."

McCloud started. "Why, that's double the price—"

Williams stopped him with a stare. "You're the one who said we'd take it. Now, kick in your share."

McCloud and Aaron handed some bills to Williams and then crawled into the coupe.

Williams gave the money to the attendant. "There you go. We didn't give you a hard time, now, did we?"

The man smiled. "Nope."

"And we paid what you asked, right?"

"Right."

"Just so we're clear on that. Now, just one last thing before we go."

Williams landed a haymaker to the man's jaw that almost lifted him off his feet. He fell onto the ground by the gas pumps and moaned. Williams jumped into the car, shifted into gear, and roared out of the station.

"Daggone that ole coot." Williams shook his head. "He coulda treated us better than that. I'll bet he's makin' a fortune sellin' that black market gas to the guys around here. Well, maybe he'll think twice next time."

Aaron sat back and sighed. This was not a good thing. Not a good thing at all.

# CHAPTER FOUR

"Johnson! McCloud! Report to Sergeant Donovan, on the double! The rest of you clowns get outside for morning formation. Move it!" Corporal Murtz spun and walked away.

McCloud looked up from making his bunk. "Aaron, what do you think this is about?"

"I don't know, but I'll bet it ain't good," Aaron said. He gave the blanket of his bunk a final tug. "Let's get this over with," he said.

The two recruits walked to Donovan's office at the far end of the barracks. Aaron knocked.

"Enter," Donovan said.

Once inside, each man snapped to attention and stared straight ahead. Donovan sat at his desk. To his left stood a uniformed civilian law enforcement officer. Aaron drew in a breath and took a quick glance at the lawman. He appeared to be in his midforties, heavy without being fat, and in addition to the badge on his chest he wore a large revolver on his right hip.

"Boys, this is Sheriff Blakely from over in Grisham County. He tells me some soldiers beat up the owner of a gas station in his area recently. Based on the license plate number his wife scribbled down and his description, I think it might be you two birds and that other yokel from the barracks next door—Williams. How 'bout it?"

Aaron sighed. "We stopped for gas. He overcharged us, and Williams—well, he kinda gave the man a little shove before we left."

Sheriff Blakely raised an eyebrow. "A shove, you say? Son, I saw Mr. Gaines an hour after he was smashed in the face. It wasn't no 'shove' that did what I saw. His face looked more like it'd been busted with a shovel, maybe. He also says you three drove away without payin', and his wife and two other customers back him up on the story. That adds a theft charge to go along with the assault and battery."

"We did pay," McCloud said. "He's lyin'. And besides, he should be arrested for selling black market gas—"

Donovan held up his hand. "Shut up, McCloud. You two ain't in no position to be accusing anybody of anything. Now, let me tell you what's gonna happen. I've assured Sheriff Blakely that the Army will take care of this little problem. He's reluctantly agreed to that on the condition that you never pass through Grisham County again. If he catches you there, you'll do some hard time in the county jail—maybe for a year or two. But lucky for you sad sacks there's a war on and we need every man that can fight—even sorry excuses like you two. There will be a court-martial record—a conviction—in each of your files. But to speed things along, Lieutenant Michaels and I worked it out with the post JAG office to dispense with a hearing and all that other red tape."

Aaron winced. A court-martial—how could he ever tell his folks about this? Or Maggie? What would she think?

Donovan leaned forward, resting his elbows on his desk. "I've arranged for you to spend some time in the post stockade for a while. Williams is already there." Donovan turned to look out the window as he lit a cigarette. "Oh, and when you get out, you won't be coming back to my training platoon again. But I'm gonna keep track of you two 'cause I like you so much."

Donovan turned to Blakely. "Sheriff, on behalf of the Army I want to apologize for this and thank you for your leniency."

Blakely stared hard at the two soldiers. "Hmpff. If we weren't at war, I wouldn't hesitate to insist on these guys payin' good for what they done. I'm not a lenient feller by nature." He looked at Aaron and McCloud. "And I mean what I said about what will happen if I catch you in my county again. You'll wish you were in a combat zone by the time my jailers get through with you. And that ain't the worst of it. We've got some ole boys behind bars that would love to have some fresh-faced little guys like you to play with—if you get my drift."

Aaron's face went hot. He swallowed hard and looked at Donovan. "Sergeant, permission to speak?"

Donovan's eyes narrowed. "Speak, Johnson."

"Sheriff, I hope you'll tell the man that we're sorry for what happened. McCloud and I had no idea Williams was gonna do what he did. But we didn't insist we stick around to see if Mr. Gaines was okay, either, so we're to blame for that."

"And just as guilty as Williams in the eyes of the law," Blakely said.

Turning to Donovan, the sheriff nodded and strode from the room.

Donovan sat for a few moments without speaking. Then he rose and walked around his desk to face his trainees. "There'll be some MPs here in a few minutes to take you down to the stockade. Take my advice. Do your time. Don't make any more mistakes, or so help me you'll regret it every day for the rest of your lives."

A knock sounded at the door. Donovan swung it open to reveal two MPs wearing white helmets and pistol belts with billy sticks and holstered side arms.

"We're here to take the prisoners, Sergeant," one of the MPs said.

"Take 'em. Get 'em outta my sight."

Aaron and McCloud stepped outside the office. Donovan slammed the door behind them.

The taller of the two MPs smiled. "Let's go, you two. We'll introduce you to Sergeant Fuller. You're gonna love him."

The other MP stifled a laugh as he took Aaron's arm and guided him toward the door. The other MP followed with McCloud.

Aaron's stomach tightened.

# CHAPTER FIVE

"Well, well, new arrivals, huh?" Sergeant Fuller smiled before spitting a brown stream of tobacco juice onto the ground. "I've been expectin' you two ladies. Welcome to my humble establishment."

The taller of the two MPs chuckled. "They're all yours, Sarge. Take good care of 'em."

Fuller appeared to be in his midforties, maybe a little older. About five nine. Stocky, powerful build. Fat face—little pig-like eyes. Crooked, yellow teeth.

"You guys are just in time to join the morning formation. Follow me."

They fell into ranks with about thirty other men, Williams among them.

"What do you think they're gonna do with us?" McCloud asked under his breath.

Aaron shrugged.

Fuller faced the assembled men. "Corporal Evers, are the men ready to proceed to the work area?"

A lanky corporal carrying a pump shotgun gazed at the men. "Yes, Sergeant Fuller."

"Very well, proceed. I'll be along shortly."

"Company, left face!" Evers shouted. "Now, double-time. No talking."

The column moved smartly out of the stockade gate and down a dirt road. After a mile and a half, McCloud, moving beside Aaron, struggled, his breathing labored.

"Come on, Henry, you can make it. You don't wanna fall out of this march," Aaron whispered.

A heavy blow to his back stunned Aaron. He stumbled, almost falling.

Evers grabbed his shirt and pulled him upright. A billy club dangled from his right hand. "I said no talking, shithead! Now, keep moving. "

Two miles farther on, Evers called the party to a halt. He pointed to a truck occupied by two additional guards.

"Line up," Evers ordered.

The guards issued picks and shovels to the men.

Sergeant Fuller arrived in a jeep, got out, and walked toward them.

"Alright, you jerkoffs," Fuller said, "as you look closely at this field, you'll notice that it's covered with tree stumps. Now, the post commander, Gin'ral Tomkins, he don't like tree stumps. He wants this field cleared. You will work in parties of two or three, and you will dig these stumps out of the ground and pile them up on the far side of the field for burning." He shifted the wad of tobacco around in his mouth, spat, and then wiped his mouth with the back of his hand.

"Now, as you men know," he continued, "the Army says you have to get a ten-minute break every hour. So, to comply with that order, you will get that break—a break from digging stumps. During those ten minutes, you will either perform calisthenics to keep your muscles nice and loose or run wind sprints to build your endurance. Corporal Evers will decide which of these activities you get to do. Any man who slacks off during the day will be dealt with accordingly. You will get a half cup of water every two hours. Any questions?"

McCloud moved as if to speak. Aaron gripped his arm.

"Permission to speak, sir," a dark-haired man to McCloud's right said.

Fuller stared at him. "Permission denied. Questions upset me. You don't wanna upset me. Evers, see to it that man gets no water at the first two water breaks."

Fuller returned to his jeep and drove away, raising a cloud of dust as the jeep disappeared from sight.

Throughout the day the men dug and pulled at the stumps. Hands already calloused grew new blisters. The summer sun beat down on them. Sweat poured off their bodies.

Aaron and McCloud teamed up with a tall, broad-shouldered man named Harold.

"So, what got you into this luxury hotel?" McCloud asked.

Harold snorted. "I punched out an officer, little fancy-pants ninety-day wonder. Son of a bitch kept riding me. So I gave him a little love tap. Broke his jaw, took out a few teeth, that's all. So I'm four months into a six-month stay here."

"Then what? When you get out, I mean?" McCloud pressed.

Harold looked around before answering. "I'm going home. To Alabama," he said in a low voice. "Damn Army will never find me where I'm going. I've had enough of this shit."

"Speaking of this shit," Aaron said, "when I was cutting timber in heat like this, I saw men pass out right in their tracks. What happens if someone collapses out here?"

"Oh, Fuller loves it when that happens. He takes the poor bastard into a special room at the stockade, strips him naked, and handcuffs his hands to a wire above his head that runs the length of the room. That's after Evers and his goons get done beatin' hell out of him."

"So he just cuffs him and leaves him there?" McCloud asked.

"Well, not exactly. Before they string him up, they make him take a laxative—so he stands there and shits all over himself for a few hours. Then they take him down and have a medic tend to him 'til he can walk again. Then he comes back out here to finish his time. And the time he spends in the sick bed don't count toward gettin' outta here."

"We gotta tough this out somehow," McCloud said, looking at Aaron.

Aaron nodded. Somehow.

"Take your tools to the truck and fall in," Evers called to the men as the sun sank below the horizon.

When the tools were handed in, the men lined up before Evers.

"Double-time. Let's go," he said.

Halfway back, Evers moved beside Aaron. "You got anything else to say today, smartass? Go ahead, my club needs a little more action. Just say a few words to your buddy. Give me an excuse."

Aaron stared straight ahead and remained silent.

Evers smiled. "That's a good boy. Next time I give an order, maybe you'll listen."

Back at the stockade, the men were fed and allowed five minutes to shower. Some grumbled, but most stood mute under the showerheads. From there they entered an open-bay barracks room with barred windows.

Aaron and McCloud searched for places to sleep. McCloud prepared to climb onto an empty upper bunk. Before he could maneuver his way up, a swarthy, muscular man in the lower portion stood and shoved him away. "Nobody sleeps above me!" he said.

"Hey," McCloud said. "Take it easy. I'm just trying to get some rest."

"Well get it somewhere else," the man snarled.

McCloud cocked his arm, but before he could land a blow, the man punched him in the face, knocking him to the floor. Then he jumped atop him and hit him three more times. He drew his arm back again. Aaron grabbed his elbow and pulled him back.

"Lay off—that's enough," Aaron said.

"Says who?" the man said, glaring at Aaron.

"Says me, Jimbo." Harold stood behind Aaron and stared hard at the man. "If you wanna go a few rounds, why don't you give me a shot?"

"You stickin' up for these hillbillies?"

Harold's face went white, and his lips tightened. Stepping around Aaron, he grabbed Jimbo by his shirtfront and pulled him close. At the same time, he placed his boot onto the arch of Jimbo's foot and began pressing down.

Jimbo winced and tried to back away, but Harold pulled him closer and applied more pressure to his arch.

"Where I come from, a man's either a hillbilly or a son of a bitch. Which are you, Jimbo?"

"I—I guess I'm a son of a bitch," Jimbo gasped.

Harold shoved him backward onto his bunk. "That's what I thought."

McCloud, wide-eyed, slowly rose to his feet and rubbed his jaw.

Harold motioned. "You guys come with me. There's a coupla empty bunks near mine."

They followed Harold to the opposite end of the room.

"Watch out for that Jimbo," Harold said. "He's a bully, and he's mean. Just stick close to me. I don't think he'll bother you again."

Fifteen minutes later the guards announced, "Lights out!"

The men fell onto their beds, exhausted.

At four a.m., Evers entered the room, banging his billy club against a metal wastebasket. "Wake up, you sad sacks!" Evers walked between the bunks, rousting the men. "Come on, get up, you lazy bastards! You've got work to do."

Men stumbled from their bunks. Aaron looked at McCloud, whose swollen left eye was already turning black from the previous night's beating.

Following a meager breakfast of bread and lukewarm coffee, the men fell into formation and again marched double-time to the field of stumps. Aaron's arms, back, and legs ached from the previous day's digging. He gritted his teeth. He was gonna make it through this. He had to.

For the next three weeks, the pattern never varied. Each day, including a half day Sunday, was a repeat of the one before. Each day Aaron's determination grew stronger even as his body continued to ache. Several times the first few days, he caught McCloud and helped hold him up as they double-timed to and from the field. Eventually McCloud gained some inner strength and managed to make it on his own. The backbreaking work never stopped, and Evers and the other guards saw to it that no one slacked off. On several occasions the guards savagely beat men who talked or otherwise failed to follow instructions.

On Monday of the fourth week, Evers read off several names at the morning formation, Aaron and McCloud's among them.

"You men report to Sergeant Fuller."

An hour later, Aaron and McCloud stepped outside the stockade fence with orders to report to Sergeant Donovan.

"What are you thinking? You're awfully quiet," McCloud said as they walked toward the company area.

"Sergeant Donovan is right, Henry. I can't beat the Army. They've made a believer out of me. No more shenanigans. I ain't goin' back to a stockade again."

# Chapter Six

Sergeant Donovan growled at Aaron and McCloud. "Did you birds enjoy your stay with Sergeant Fuller?"

"We got a lot of blisters," Aaron said.

"Lucky that's all you got," Donovan replied. "Now, since the platoon you were in is now three weeks ahead of you, you've been assigned to Sergeant Griffin's platoon. Get your gear and double-time it. His platoon's in the third barracks over. Just in time for a forced march. Full field packs. Wouldn't be wise to fall out, neither."

Midway through the ten-mile march, men dropped out like flies sprayed with Flit. Aaron and McCloud moved easily, even with full packs and the heavy M-1 rifles.

"Look at these guys," McCloud said. "What a bunch of—"

"They haven't spent three weeks in the stockade double-timing everywhere they went, not to mention digging up tree stumps," Aaron said.

McCloud glanced around. "I don't like being in a platoon with a bunch of guys I don't know. Our old platoon would never fall out like this."

Aaron hid his smile from McCloud, who was one of the first to fall out in the old platoon. "Yeah, well, they'll toughen up—just like we did. And they won't be strangers long."

At the first break, men sat on the ground and talked or smoked. Sergeant Griffin approached Aaron and McCloud. He turned to address the rest of the platoon.

"These two clowns here—Johnson and McCloud—they're being recycled through basic. Because they thought they were smartasses. They're back from a little vacation in the stockade. Ask 'em about it. Maybe it'll help some of you clods keep your noses clean. Now, I wanna show you how happy I am to have 'em in my platoon. On your feet, you two."

Aaron and McCloud sprang up.

"Drop and give me fifty. Now!" Griffin's face glowed red. "At every break, while the rest of you girls are resting your dead asses, these two will do push-ups or run sprints. If any of you screw up, you will join them." He spun and walked away.

Aaron rapidly clicked through the push-ups. The punishment wasn't over.

After the march, the men fell into formation.

"Get inside and clean up your gear. Tomorrow we go to the rifle range. We'll find out if any of you birds can shoot." Griffin turned on his heel and departed.

Inside, several men approached Aaron and McCloud. "Tell us about the stockade," one of them said.

Aaron shook his head. "Shit. It's a hellhole, man. Training's no picnic, but it beats the hell out of that damn stockade."

The next morning, the men marched the five miles to the rifle range, where they were greeted by the rifle range commanding officer.

"You men have drilled with your M-1s—you've learned how to carry them, how to take them apart and reassemble them blindfolded, how to care for and clean them. Today, you will actually fire these weapons. Targets are downrange at specified distances. When you leave today, your rifle will be adjusted to your zero and you will have knowledge of marksmanship skills.

"Believe me when I say this part of your training is critical. When you are in battle, the only real friend you have is your rifle. Your ability to use it is crucial to your survival—and the demise of the enemy you face. Sergeant Albright and the other members of the cadre will now instruct you."

Albright stepped forward. "When you are on the firing line, you will obey immediately the commands of the range officer. You will be told when to load your weapon and when to fire it. Prior to every firing sequence, you will hear the following: 'Ready on the right? Ready on the left? Ready on the firing line?' Following that, you will be given the command to commence firing. If at any time you hear the command 'cease firing,' you will immediately stop firing, make your weapon safe, and remove your hands from it. Anyone who does not obey the orders will be dealt with accordingly."

Throughout the morning and afternoon the men received instruction in sight alignment, different shooting positions, breath control, and trigger pull. Several groups of three rounds were fired at targets, and the sights were adjusted to fit each individual.

"Damn, it's hot out here," McCloud said.

"Yeah, but I'd still rather be here than diggin' up stumps," Aaron said.

The men marched back to the barracks and cleaned their rifles. Aaron stuffed a cleaning patch down the barrel of his disassembled M-1. "You know, McCloud, it's funny. For the first time, I almost feel like a soldier."

Following calisthenics the next day, a recruit named Fox approached Aaron and McCloud.

"Our platoon gets busted at inspections every time we have one. Some of the guys are getting tired of it. Sergeant Griffin, well, he's okay, I guess, but we've been watching some of the other DIs. They seem to care about how their platoons are doin'. But Griffin—well, rumor is he's got a girlfriend downtown. He don't hang around at the end of the day like some of the sergeants. We get the feelin' he's just going through the motions. We're all willin' to play ball, but we just can't seem to get the scoop on things. Do you two have any ideas on how we can do better and maybe get some weekend passes instead of KP?"

Aaron looked at McCloud. "Maybe. Get some of the guys together and let's talk."

Ten minutes later, Aaron and McCloud sat before the assembled men.

"Look, guys," Aaron said, "it's hard to get everything done and get outside for the morning formation. You've been gettin' your butts kicked over not having bunks squared away and not having the floor cleaned, among other things.

"You have to stretch the rules a little to get by. Henry and I have an idea. He's squared away at putting things in order. If you look at his bunk, you'll see it's A-1. His footlocker is perfect. His mom taught him well."

Henry turned so red, he glowed.

Aaron continued. "Tomorrow, Henry and—who else is good at housekeeping? You, Coleman? Okay, you two stay inside and fix any bunks that aren't made up tight. Run the dust mops over the floor to make sure it's clean. While we're out front, shake the mops out the back of the barracks. You should also have time to see if anything else needs doing. By then, we'll be filing back in for the morning inspection. Let's see if this helps."

Three days later, Sergeant Griffin called Aaron aside. "The barracks has been in good shape all week. Night and day better than usual. What happened?"

"I guess we're just getting the hang of it, Sergeant."

"I find it curious that this was the worst platoon in the training company 'til you and McCloud got back. Maybe that stay in the guardhouse did some good."

"I really can't say, Drill Sergeant. I just hope we can get some weekend passes. I sure would like to see my wife."

# CHAPTER SEVEN

"Hey, sweetheart." Aaron hugged Maggie close and kissed her. "Boy, you look good. How are you?"

"I miss you so much," she said. "Thank God, you got out of the stockade. You won't do anything to let that happen again, will you?"

Aaron shook his head. "No way. You're all I thought about. I even prayed—but it didn't seem that God was listening."

Maggie took his face in her hands and looked directly into his eyes. "God always listens—sometimes He has a different plan than we do. He had a reason for you being there, strange as that may seem."

"Yeah, sure," Aaron said. "Say—enough of this talk. I can't wait to—you know—be alone with you."

She smiled. "I think we can arrange that."

Later the two sat in a booth at the local diner.

"How much longer in basic?" Maggie asked.

"A few more weeks. I should get some leave time after that."

"But then where will they send you?"

"One day at a time—that's how it goes in the Army."

"I wish I could see it that way. Living with Mom and Dad isn't so good. Seems like I'm tired all the time now that I'm pregnant. Dad's always working or hunting or fishing. Momma just seems—I don't know. She's not herself. I don't think she feels good. But she won't go to the doctor."

"Do you think she's real sick?"

"I caught her bent over the sink the other day. She was holding her stomach, and she looked like she really hurt. I tried to make her lie down, but she wouldn't. Said she had to keep going. It scares me."

"Oh, it's probably nothing to worry about," Aaron said. "She oughta go see Doc Crouch, though. He can most likely give her something."

"I'll try to get her to go with me next time I have a checkup. Oh, we need to get moving. The movie starts in fifteen minutes. I don't want to miss Clark Gable."

"Clark Gable? He's a 4-F if I ever saw one."

"You're just jealous."

Aaron looked into Maggie's brown eyes.

"Don't worry," she said. "I'm not gonna get mixed up with someone else while you're away." She smiled. "Besides, who'd want an old pregnant woman like me anyway?"

"I can think of lots of guys who'd take you any way they could."

She smiled. "Oh, hush. Come on. Let's go."

The next day, Aaron's brother Graydon came to pick him up for the trip back to Fort Jackson. Aaron kissed Maggie good-bye. "I love you. We're gonna be a family now. Take care of yourself—and our baby." He patted her round tummy and hugged her tight.

Turning to her mom and dad, he said, "Thanks for everything, Mrs. Jolly. I sure enjoyed those chicken and dumplings you made. The Army sure don't cook like that. And Lloyd, thanks for letting Maggie stay with you while I'm away. I really appreciate it."

Lloyd smiled. "Anything for the war effort. You know you're both always welcome."

"We need to get moving," Graydon said. "I put your stuff in the Chevy. You wanna drive her? She's still runnin' good."

"Yeah—I'd love to. When we get to South Carolina, there's a little restaurant I know where we can eat. You can drive from there."

Ten miles into the trip, Aaron glanced at Graydon. "So, how's school."

"I don't like it," he said.

Aaron winced. "If I had it to do over, I'd stay in school. Don't be in any rush to get out."

"Even if I do stay in, if this war keeps up, I'm gonna get drafted anyway," Graydon said.

Aaron took a drag on his cigarette. "I hope you don't. How about other stuff? You dating anybody?"

"Oh, first one and then another. Nothing serious. I'm not ready to settle down. Hey, when I get outta school, maybe I could get into the Air Corps. Flake Dyson's training to fly on bombers. That'd be the way to go to war, I'll bet."

"I'd say do anything you can to stay out of the infantry. That's where I'm headed. Carryin' a rifle and livin' in a hole in the ground." Aaron shook his head and took another drag on his Lucky Strike.

"Hey, give me a cigarette," Graydon said. "I've smoked all of mine."

"Here," Aaron said. "Keep the pack."

After a short silence, Aaron said, "Look, if anything should happen to me—not sayin' it will, but if it does, you look after Momma and Poppa, okay? They're getting up there, you know."

"Sure. And Nell's still at home. She'll help out too. But, hey, nothing's gonna happen to you. You're too smart for that."

"I dunno. I'm starting to see that getting hurt just seems to happen. We had a guy in my training platoon fall while running the obstacle course two weeks ago. He hit his head on a rock and it killed him. Just like that, he was gone."

"Hmm—well, you be careful. Maggie's gonna have a baby. You gotta stay around to help her raise your child."

"Yes—and I aim to. Say, now don't run the hell outta my car on the way back home. I expect it to be in good shape when I come home again."

"Oh, I'll try to keep it under ninety," Graydon said, grinning.

# CHAPTER EIGHT

Calisthenics. Rifle range. Forced marches. Night maneuvers, field problems, map reading, constant inspections. Infantry tactics and hand-to-hand combat drills. And marching, marching, marching.

"Today, you jokers will learn the proper use of the bayonet," Sergeant Griffin said. "Sergeant First Class Edwards will be your instructor."

Edwards took command. "The bayonet," he said, "is your weapon of last resort. In a few moments, you will learn how to use that weapon to defend yourself and kill the enemy. Pay close attention as Corporal Waters runs through the bayonet course behind you. Platoon—about face."

Before them was a field with several wooden supports—each with two upright posts and a beam mounted across the top. Crude mannequins made of burlap and stuffed with straw were suspended from the beams by ropes.

"Corporal Waters, proceed," Edwards said.

Waters immediately let out a yell and charged the support nearest him. A bayonet was attached to the forward end of his M-1. He carried the rifle at his right side, pointed toward the dummy enemy soldier. When he reached it, he thrust the rifle up toward its midsection, ramming the bayonet deeply into it. He withdrew the blade and then brought the butt of the rifle around, slamming it into what would have been the head of an actual person. Continuing to yell, he stormed toward the next supported dummy and repeated the drill.

Edwards turned to the platoon. "Fix bayonets."

For the remainder of the afternoon, they practiced. Edwards watched as Aaron completed another charge and destruction of the enemy straw man.

"So, Recruit, what do you think of my little toy, the bayonet?" Edwards said.

"Sergeant, with all due respect, I have to tell you I'm not too fond of it."

"Hmmpff. Just what do you intend to do if an enemy soldier is running at you with his bayonet fixed to his rifle?"

"I'll shoot him," Aaron said.

"If you're out of ammo—what then, smart guy?"

Aaron looked into Edwards's eyes. "Well, Sergeant, as I see it, an enemy soldier might get me with his bayonet, but if he does, he's gonna get me in the ass or the back because I'm gonna be runnin' like hell."

Edwards's eyes narrowed. "Drop and give me twenty."

Aaron completed training at Fort Jackson on September 15, 1943, and received a forty-eight-hour pass and orders to report to Camp Wheeler, Georgia, for more infantry training. He exited the barracks, where he encountered Sergeant Donovan in the process of lighting a cigarette.

Donovan squinted at him through the tobacco smoke. "Well, well. So, you made it through basic after all. I had my doubts about you for a while. Griffin tells me you helped shape up his raggedy-assed platoon."

Aaron squinted at Donovan. "Maybe if Griffin spent more time doing his job instead of banging the waitress downtown, the platoon wouldn't have been so raggedy-assed."

Donovan's eyes narrowed. "Griffin is not your concern. In this man's army, sometimes you gotta figure things out for yourself. Best you watch your mouth. It can get you in trouble—again. You got your orders?"

"Yes—Wheeler."

"There's something you need to know," Donovan said. "If you hadn't screwed up and got your ass in trouble, your assignment would have been a stateside slot as part of a training cadre in Louisiana. But since you messed things up for yourself, you'll be going to a combat infantry outfit after you finish the rest of your training. You're going to war, son. God help you when you go up against the Japs or the Jerries. I hope you're in good shape with the Almighty."

"I don't know that the Almighty cares about me one way or the other, Sergeant," Aaron said.

Donovan started to speak and then turned and walked away.


Maggie waited outside the bus station.

Aaron jumped from the bus and gave her a long, tender kiss. "Let me look at you," he said, stepping back. "Wow, you're really showin' now! How much longer?"

"Mid-January, Doc Crouch says. What happens next? Do you know where you'll be assigned? Will you have to go overseas? Any chance you'll stay stateside?"

"Uhh—no," Aaron said, "I don't think I'll be stateside."

Maggie lowered her head for a moment and then looked up at him. "So what—will you go overseas right away?"

"No, not right away. I'll be going to Georgia for more training. That'll last several months."

"Oh, good," she said. "Maybe the war will be over before you have to ship out."

Aaron shook his head. "Don't count on it. This war's gonna go on for a good while, based on what I've been hearing."

Maggie sat down on the bench outside the bus station and looked down at her hands folded in her lap. "Will they let you come home when the baby's born?"

"I don't know. It depends on where I am and what I'm doing."

She nodded without speaking. Aaron put his arm around her.

"Look, I'd like to tell you different, but the Army is—well, it's just the Army, that's all. But you know I'll be here if I can. You know I will."


On January 17, 1944, Aaron completed his training at Camp Wheeler. He also received a telegram from his brother telling him that Maggie had given birth to a seven-pound baby boy the day before and that mother and baby were doing fine. Aaron read the telegram twice. A pass granting him two weeks' leave was in his shirt pocket. "Wow! I'm a daddy! Look, guys—I've got a baby boy! I've gotta get home. Hey, Talbot—can I catch a ride to the bus station?"

# CHAPTER NINE

"Alright, you knuckleheads. Off your asses and on the trucks. We ain't got all day. Ships are waiting. Move it!"

Troops wrestled with duffle bags and rifles as they boarded the trucks.

"So, where do you think we're goin'?" a soldier named Benson asked Aaron. "D'ya think we're headed to the Pacific? That's the scuttlebutt."

Aaron shook his head. "Nothing's a sure thing. We'll find out soon enough."

At the docks in Newport News, the trucks dumped the men beside a dull gray liberty ship. Finally the order was given to file up the gangplank. The ship's crew directed the soldiers below decks. The strong smell of oil and grease, like in the garages where he'd worked, permeated the air. Other odors, some unpleasant, tainted the air.

Eight hours later, the ship set out down the James River and through Hampton Roads, Virginia, to the Atlantic. Three miles offshore it rendezvoused with a convoy of other troop ships and destroyers, and the convoy headed in a southeasterly direction. Two days later, the word got around. The convoy was headed to Europe.

The liberty ship entered Naples Harbor in the middle of a German air raid. Sirens wailed. The *pom-pom-pom* of antiaircraft batteries firing into the overcast skies filled the air as enemy bombers released their payloads onto the docks and the water. Fires burned. Sailors and soldiers fought the flames. Smoke engulfed everything in sight.

"What a great welcome to Italy," Aaron said to the soldier beside him. "I wanna get off this ole tub before one of those bombs lands on us!"

As the last of the German bombers flew away, the antiaircraft guns grew silent. Later the men were allowed off the ship and herded to a replacement depot just past the dock area.

Two weeks later, Aaron received orders to report to G Company, 339th Infantry Battalion, Eighty-fifth Infantry Division, headquartered just north of Naples.

# CHAPTER TEN

The deuce-and-a-half truck came to a stop outside a small one-story stone building. The driver stuck his head out the window and yelled toward the truck's rear, "G Company headquarters."

Aaron grabbed his duffle bag and rifle and stumbled past the other replacements seated on either side of the truck's open bed. Apparently he was the only one assigned to G Company. He jumped from the truck, almost falling when he hit the ground. The deuce-and-a-half was already in motion.

Aaron straightened and stood for a moment looking after the truck. Over nine months he'd been in the Army. Basic training, infantry tactics and skills, endless drills, firearms instruction, field problems—all that was behind him now. And so, for the time being, was Maggie. And his son. Would he ever see them again? He'd only seen little Barry for little more than a week before he had to ship out.

Aaron entered the doorway and paused. His newly issued uniform contrasted with those of the others in the room, but no one stared. In fact, no one noticed him at all. Clerks hurried around with stacks of files. Others sat at desks, typing or shuffling paper.

Another soldier burst in, pushed past Aaron, and headed toward a tech sergeant on the far side of the room.

"Sergeant Bradley, here's another requisition from First Platoon. Lieutenant Waugh wants more ammo and more rations. And extra canteens for all his men."

Bradley looked up and jerked the stub of a cigar from his mouth. "Oh, he does, does he? Well you tell him—"

"Give him what he wants," a dark-haired first sergeant seated at a desk across the room said. "Waugh knows what he's doing. Too bad the other platoon leaders don't."

Bradley frowned. "But Sergeant Gibbs, Waugh's been a real pain in the—"

"Just do it," Gibbs said.

Bradley took the forms and turned away, mumbling to himself.

Aaron removed his helmet, tucked it under his arm, and moved to the first sergeant's desk. The tanned, stocky man behind the desk looked to be in his early thirties. Deep olive complexion. Dark hair with a touch of gray at the temples.

Aaron cleared his throat. "Sergeant Gibbs, I'm Private Johnson," he said. "I was told to report here."

Gibbs looked up and fixed him with a stare. "That's *First* Sergeant Gibbs to you, *Private*—or don't they teach things like that in basic training anymore? Where's your orders?"

Aaron extended the documents. Gibbs dropped then onto his desk without looking at them. "Where you from, boy?"

"North Carolina—First Sergeant."

"Yeah? Wha'd you do there?"

"Grew up on a farm. After I quit school, I was a mechanic at the Chevy dealership in town."

"A farmer, huh? With that fair skin, I bet you got burned to shit in the sun. Where'd you get that hair? It's plumb white. You an albino or something?"

"No, First Sergeant—it just runs in my family."

"Hmm. How long were you in the replacement depot?"

"Two weeks."

"We're going on the front line in a few days. You'll wish you were still there." Gibbs leaned back in his chair. His eyes narrowed slightly. "How old are you, anyhow?"

"Nineteen—almost twenty."

"Hmpff. You caint be a day over seventeen, if you're that." Turning toward an open doorway behind him, Gibbs yelled, "Hey, Gordon. Get out here. You ain't the baby of the outfit no more. Look what they're sending us now."

The room went still. A sandy-haired corporal stuck his head through the doorway and stared at Aaron. Everyone in the room looked at him now.

Aaron groaned inwardly. Guys who got noticed pulled lots of extra details. He didn't want to get on the wrong side of the company first sergeant. Didn't want to risk any more trips to the stockade.

Gibbs shifted in his seat, cocked his head, and grinned at Aaron. "Son, can you live in a hole in the ground and shit in a K-ration box?"

Aaron's face went hot. "I—uh—I can if I have to."

"Oh, you'll have to, son," Gibbs said with a laugh. "You'll have to."

The room was totally silent as Gibbs leaned forward. The grin faded from his face. "Johnson, can you kill a man?"

Aaron looked directly at him. "If I have to."

Gibbs sat back in his chair. "Oh, you'll have to—you'll have to." He swiveled his chair and motioned toward the tech sergeant. "Bradley, on your way to supply, take Johnson here down to Second Platoon. Give him to Staff Sergeant Palmer."

Bradley headed to the door, motioning for Aaron to follow. "Come on. I'll show you where the mess tent is too. It's on the way."

As they stepped into the sunlight, Bradley said, "So you're from North Carolina? I'm from South Carolina. Makes us neighbors, kinda."

"Is Sergeant Gibbs always like that?" Aaron asked.

Bradley laughed. "Don't worry 'bout Gibbs. He does stuff like that to all the new guys. But hey, he's a damn good first sergeant. Just don't cross him. Do your job and things'll be fine. Besides, once you're in your platoon, you won't see him much."

Aaron shot a sidelong glance at Bradley. "That suits the hell out of me."

# CHAPTER ELEVEN

"Okay, this is Second Platoon's area. There's Sergeant Palmer. See you later." Bradley departed.

Staff Sergeant Palmer looked to be in his midtwenties, medium height, pockmarked face with a crooked nose. He stared at Aaron and rubbed his chin. He asked some of the same questions that Gibbs had.

"I guess I should say welcome or something, but this ain't much of a situation to warrant it. There's a spot in the third tent down the line. Take that. You'll be with Haynes—you two should get along."

Aaron walked toward the indicated tent. What did Palmer mean?

Aaron poked his head inside the small tent. "Sorry to ruin your day—Sergeant Palmer told me to bunk here."

A young private with sandy blond hair grinned at him. "So I finally get a buddy, huh? I was startin' to think I was gonna be by myself for the rest of the war. Make yourself at home."

Aaron looked at the young soldier for a long moment. "Where are you from?"

Haynes laughed. "Somewhere close to where you're from, judging by the sound of your voice. What part of North Carolina you from?"

"Taylorsville—how 'bout you?"

"Down the road from you apiece—ever hear of Mount Airy?"

"I'll say—how about that? We're from the same place almost. Course, Mount Airy's big compared to T-town."

"They still call Taylorsville 'The Apple City'?"

Aaron smiled. "Yeah, still lots of orchards around there—so you have heard of it."

In the next hour, Aaron learned that Haynes's first name was Worth and that their backgrounds were similar. Finally Worth looked at his watch. "Chow time. You hungry?"

"Sure am, just let me move this duffel bag over—"

The flap at the tent entrance flew up. A soldier was silhouetted against the light from outside. "There'll be a Bible study after we eat for any of you who might be interested. We'll meet outside the mess hall." The GI departed to repeat the same invitation at the next tent.

"Who was that?"

"Francis Furlong. Some call him 'Saint Francis.' He's kinda religious."

"I see," Aaron said. Just what he needed. A holy-roller Bible-thumpin' type out to convert everyone he met.

After chow, Aaron arranged his gear, cleaned his rifle, and wrote a letter to Maggie.

> Dear Maggie,
>
> Well, I am here, finally. Did you get any of the letters I sent earlier? You know they won't let me say much with the mail being censored and all, but I want you to know I am okay and in no danger. I sure do miss you. How is Barry? Is he sleeping any better these days? I'm glad the two of you are staying with your dad—Lloyd needs you now that your mom has passed away, and it's good for you to have someone around in case you need any help. I still can't believe how quickly she went. How's he doing? I'm sure he's sad. It has to be tough on him. It's getting dark here, so I'd better close. I hope you get this letter soon. Take care of yourself and Barry—and Lloyd, too. You've got a lot of responsibility now. I wish I could be there to help. Maybe before too long. Good night, darling.
>
> Love,
> Aaron

Two days later, just before nightfall, Palmer came by Aaron and Worth's tent. "You men are going on a patrol with me tonight. Come see me at seventeen hundred; I'll brief you and the other guys then. Tape your dog tags—I don't want no jingle bells out there. And no packs—you might wanna take some extra ammo and a few grenades, just in case."

Aaron and Worth exchanged looks. "I guess this is it—our first mission," Worth said.

Aaron nodded. "Yeah, had to happen sooner or later. Where do we get grenades?"

The two arrived at Palmer's tent as ordered. Four other men were already assembled. The briefing was short. "We're going out to recover bodies. Some of the Eighty-eighth Division guys got caught in an ambush the night before we arrived. I reconnoitered the area last night, so stay close to me once we move out so you don't get lost. There's just enough moonlight to pull this off, but we gotta be careful and stay quiet. Here's a map I drew; memorize it. We'll move out twenty minutes after the moon comes up."

Palmer departed. When he was out of earshot, Patrick Davis spoke.

"Why didn't the Eighty-eighth guys go get their own men? How come we hafta do it?"

"Knock it off, Davis," Bradley said. "Just make sure you don't get trigger happy out there. Our job is to get the dead guys, not to start a shooting match."

"Don't worry 'bout me. Look after yourself. But if we get caught in an ambush, I'm opening up with my Thompson—and I'd better hear that carbine of yours."

Aaron's shoulder muscles tightened. He swallowed hard. Sweat formed on his upper lip. This was the real thing. He sensed that Worth felt as nervous as he. By the time the moon rose, nausea gripped his stomach. He had to get control of himself. Couldn't mess this up.

Palmer returned. A partial moon shone in the night sky. The men picked up their rifles and the stretchers.

"Davis, take point. Bradley, you're in the rear. When we get there, Rogers and Ferdinand, you two move to the far side of the clearing and keep your eyes peeled. If you spot anything, hold your fire unless you're fired on. You all know what we're doin', so no more talking."

The going was hard in the darkness, but Palmer knew the terrain. He led them into a shallow depression that ran out from their lines. They were able to move along it at a crouch for twenty-five yards before Palmer halted the group. He dropped to his belly and began crawling. The others followed suit. For the next ten minutes, the men pulled themselves over rough, rocky terrain.

Surely the Germans could hear them. Hell, they could probably hear his heart beating. Machine gun fire would probably rake them at any moment. He strained to make out the shape of Palmer and the others.

They arrived at a small clearing. Four dead American soldiers lay where they had fallen.

Palmer motioned the men to get the bodies on the stretchers. Aaron and Worth approached one of them. Aaron clamped his hand over his mouth and nose. Worth recoiled as well. Palmer motioned for them to get on with it.

"Gosh, this one's a captain," Worth whispered. Palmer gave him a withering look. No talking.

The moon broke through a cloud, shining a ray of light on the dead officer's face. Aaron stared down at him. He seemed strangely peaceful in death, appearing to be asleep. Is it like that? Is it like being asleep? Were these men in heaven now? Or—the other place?

Worth nudged him. Aaron forced himself to move. He grabbed the captain's shirtsleeve, and Worth grabbed the feet.

Damn, he was heavy. The man's arms and legs lay awkwardly on the stretcher, legs and elbows poking off the sides.

Sweat rolled down Aaron's face in rivulets. His brain told him to hurry, but his actions seemed to be in slow motion.

With all the bodies positioned on the stretchers, Palmer signaled that it was time to pull out.

Aaron and Worth crawled. The dead captain's body was unwieldy, and they struggled to keep it on the canvas. The going was slightly easier once they reached the low spot in the terrain where they could carry the stretcher at a crouch. But Aaron stumbled, and the body fell to the ground. They struggled with the lifeless form. Palmer appeared to be agitated at the delay, but he made no comment.

As they approached their position, a sentry called out in a hoarse whisper, "Halt—apple."

"Cobbler," Palmer whispered back.

"Come on in."

Aaron and Worth followed Palmer, carrying the stretcher past the line of tents to a battalion aid station. A medic told them where to leave the bodies. A sense of relief came over Aaron as he and Worth set the stretcher down and moved back toward their foxhole.

"Some first mission, huh?" Worth said. "I'm glad it's over. It was creepy out there."

"I got a feelin' it could get a lot creepier," Aaron said.

# CHAPTER TWELVE

Palmer stood next to Aaron's tent and lit a cigarette. "Johnson, get a coupla guys together. You're gonna man the outpost down by the river tonight."

"Umm, okay, Sarge. Is there anything in particular we should be expectin'?"

Palmer blew out a stream of smoke before answering. "Other than keeping your eyes peeled for Germans and reporting what you see, no."

"Say, Sarge, is it true what I heard about the guys with the canteens?"

Palmer chuckled. "Yeah. A couple of guys from First Platoon went down to the river to fill canteens for their squad. They were about half finished when they looked up and saw two Germans on the other side doing the same thing."

"Wha'd they do?"

"Looked at each other and kept on filling canteens. Then our guys backed away real slow. The Krauts did the same." Palmer shook his head. "War's funny, ain't it? But if you see any Germans tonight, it's probably gonna be a little different—they'll be tryin' to kill ya."

Palmer departed, and Aaron set off to round up Worth and Harry Klutz.

Harry, another North Carolinian, met them later at Aaron's tent, where he gave them more details on their assignment.

"Sarge said we need to be in position at the OP before dark. We'll have a telephone to report anything we see."

"Are we supposed to open fire if the Germans come across the river?" Worth asked.

"Not unless they shoot first. We're there to watch, unless we get other orders."

"We ain't even seen any real combat yet—this waitin' around makes me jumpy. I almost wish we'd start something," Harry said.

"If the scuttlebutt I hear is true, something's gonna get started soon enough," Worth said. "I'm willin' to wait awhile, I think."

As Worth and Harry departed, Patrick Davis approached Aaron.

"I heard you're manning the OP tonight."

"Yeah. You were out there night before last, weren't you? How'd it go?"

"Nothing that night. But we were ready." He glanced at Aaron's rifle. "How'd you like to take my Thompson out there tonight? If you get into a firefight, it's likely gonna be up close, and this tommy will give you a lot more firepower than the M-1."

Aaron eyed the stubby submachine gun. "Sure, if you don't mind."

Davis handed over the Thompson and a pouch containing several spare magazines. "Have you fired one of these before?"

"Not since basic—and all we got there was a little familiarization."

Davis turned his head and spat. "Well, there's a couple of things to keep in mind. If you fire a long burst, she'll rise up on you and you'll be shootin' straight up in the air. So short bursts are the way to go—you can keep 'er on target that way. Even better if you can get into a kneeling position with the carrying sling under your knee. Other than that, just point and shoot. The forty-five-caliber slugs will do the rest."

Aaron hefted the Thompson and placed it to his shoulder. "Thanks, Davis."

Just before dusk, the men headed out. As they approached the outpost, Aaron signaled for a halt. "We'll crawl in from here."

The OP, a shallow hole situated on a knoll, overlooked a narrow road that snaked up the hill from the river toward the American lines. They relieved Jack Claytor and Art Ferdinand.

"About time you clowns got here," Jack said. "I gotta get back and check on my monkey."

"Your what?" Worth said.

Ferdinand chuckled. "Haven't you seen Jack's monkey? He got it when we were in Africa. The cooks keep it most of the time. They have a heckuva time keeping it out of the rations."

As Claytor and Ferdinand crawled away, Harry shook his head. "Why would somebody want a monkey out here?"

"Beats me," Aaron said. "But I do wanna see it."

The men settled into position. Aaron turned toward the others. "Let's get a good look at the terrain before it gets dark. We don't want to mistake a bush that's blowin' in the breeze for a German. From here on, no talking unless you see something. Then let me know—I've got the phone with a direct hookup to company headquarters. For now, try to get comfortable. You guys get some shut-eye so you can relieve me later."

A quarter moon provided a bit of light. Aaron checked in with company headquarters every hour as instructed. "King One—this is White Knight. Over."

"This is King One—anything happenin'?"

"Nothing."

Shortly before midnight, Worth crawled to Aaron's side.

"Yeah, I hear it too," Aaron whispered. "Down by the river. Make sure Harry's awake."

The sounds grew louder. Dark shapes moved at the water's edge. Muffled guttural voices. An enemy patrol pulled a small boat onto the bank. Several Germans spread out across the road and moved forward.

Aaron blew a low whistle into the voice-activated phone's mouthpiece. Immediately a voice came on the line. "This is King—you got something?"

"White Knight. German patrol advancing up the road. A half dozen or so. What should we do?"

"Stand by—I'll get back to you."

A few moments later, the telephone crackled in Aaron's ear. "White Knight—this is King. Let 'em pass by you. We'll open up on them as they approach us and chase 'em back to you."

"Roger."

The Americans remained still as the Germans passed on the road below. They walked standing upright, the sound of their boots echoing on the hard roadbed. They disappeared into the darkness.

Aaron informed the others of the plan. "Harry, you and Worth get across the road and take up a position there. When they come back this way, we'll let them get just a little past us. When I open up with this Thompson, give 'em all you got."

Minutes later, a firefight erupted from the direction the Germans had gone. Machine gun and rifle fire from the American line was interspersed with answering small arms fire from the Germans. Aaron took a deep breath, pulled back the bolt on the Thompson, and clicked off the safety. A cold chill went up his spine. His heart pounded inside his chest. He swallowed hard. Soon he would fire a weapon at another human being for the first time.

The Germans reappeared at a dead run. As they crested the hill and started toward the river, Aaron focused on their helmeted shapes. As they came nearer, the sound of their boots striking the hard surface of the road filled the night.

Aaron rose to a kneeling position, slid the submachine gun's sling under his right knee, and pulled the weapon's stock tight against his shoulder. Taking aim at the fleeing soldiers, he pulled the trigger. The burst from the Thompson lit up the night.

At the same time, Harry and Worth opened up with their rifles. The noise was deafening. The muzzle flash from the Thompson made it impossible to see clearly. He fired short bursts at first as Davis had instructed—but adrenaline kicked in and he held the trigger back, completely emptying the magazine. When it ran empty, the barrel was pointed to the sky at a forty-five-degree angle.

He reloaded. His hands shook as he fumbled the magazine into place. "Cease fire, hold your fire! Everybody okay?"

"Okay here," Worth said.

"Reload, everybody reload. Worth, come with me to check. Harry, cover us."

Aaron and Worth crawled onto the road. "Some of them hit the water, so we didn't get all of 'em," Worth said. "But we must've hit a few."

"With all the rounds we fired, I would hope so," Aaron said. "I emptied all thirty rounds from this Thompson."

The two crawled forward cautiously. "See anything, Worth?"

"No—d'you?"

"Not yet."

Worth crawled off to the left while Aaron checked farther to the right. When he returned, Worth said, "Nothing!"

"Same here," Aaron said. "We didn't get a one of them! And I don't wanna hear what the ole man's gonna have to say about this. One thing's for sure, though. They were in such a hurry, they didn't bother with the boat—it's right where they left it. I guess they figured it was easier to swim back. Let's get back to the OP. I don't wanna get caught down here on this road if the Jerries decide to send artillery this way."

Daylight confirmed what Aaron and Worth had concluded. No dead Germans. No blood from wounded Germans. No indications of any hits at all. The captain was enraged.

"What the hell were you thinking, Johnson? Why didn't you open up on them before they got past you? Then we'd have had them in a crossfire."

"Captain, I figured that could be confusing as heck. We'd have been firing in the direction of you guys, and y'all'd be firing toward us. The Jerries would have been firing every which way—who knows how many of us would have been hit. And if the Germans decided to send some more men across to help their buddies, me and the guys with me would be sandwich meat. I did what I thought was best. I'm sorry if you don't approve, sir."

Captain Macardo glanced at First Sergeant Gibbs. "Okay, Johnson, get out of here. But I want you and the others with you to target practice every day 'til further notice. That clear? You're dismissed."

"Yes sir." Aaron saluted and left the captain's tent, but he paused just outside to light a cigarette. Getting chewed out by the CO was no fun. Voices sounded inside the tent. He moved to where he could overhear the words of his superiors without being seen.

"What do you think about him?" Macardo asked Gibbs.

"I think the kid's got good sense, Cap'n," Gibbs said. "I'm kinda impressed by his thinking, if you want my honest opinion. After all, there were six Germans but only three of our guys. And we know the German units we're facin' are experienced. Our guys are still green. It woulda been pretty easy for them to flank our guys and take 'em out. I'm not sure I would've done any different."

Macardo frowned. "You've got a point. Maybe he did handle it the best way. But that's some damn sorry shootin'. Have Palmer get them back to the battalion range for more target practice."

"Will do, sir. They'll be okay once they get a little more combat experience, sir."

Macardo sighed. "I hope you're right, Gibbs. I just got word from battalion—we're gonna be makin' a major attack before the week's out. So all our guys are gonna have to come around real quick. You know as well as I do that the brass is concerned about us. This division and the Eighty-eighth are two of the first units made up almost entirely of draftees. They're not sure we'll fight."

Aaron quietly slipped away from Macardo's tent.

# CHAPTER THIRTEEN

Aaron and Worth were cleaning their M-1s following the morning round of target practice when a slightly built, dark-haired second lieutenant with a boyish face approached them. Before they could salute, the officer motioned for them to stay seated.

"At ease. I'm Lieutenant Waugh from First Platoon. Are you Johnson and Haynes?"

"Yes sir," they answered in unison.

Aaron squinted at Waugh. What was coming? The lieutenant talked funny. A Yankee, no doubt. Not a large man, but he seemed pretty sure of himself.

"Lieutenant Slade said I'd find you here. He tells me you guys had a little firefight with a German patrol a few nights back."

"Umm—yessir," Aaron said, dropping his gaze.

"Sounds like you handled yourselves okay—except for not hittin' any of 'em." He smiled. "But don't worry—you'll have lots more chances."

"We've been shooting every day since," Worth said. "We'll be ready next time."

Waugh smiled. "I wanted to meet you men. I think it's important to know everyone in the company. Especially those who'll shoot when the time comes. You men in Second Platoon will be in good hands with Lieutenant Slade when we make our attack. He's a fine officer."

"What do you hear about that, sir?" Worth asked. "The rumor's been goin' around for days that we're gonna attack soon. Can you tell us anything?" Worth kicked at a clump of dirt lying at his feet before looking up at Waugh.

"You know as much as I do. I've got a feelin' we're gonna find out pretty soon. We gotta do something to break the stalemate at Monte Cassino and link up with the guys at Anzio. It won't be long."

Waugh pushed his steel helmet back off his forehead and looked around. "Keep up the target practice, men. I gotta get back to my platoon."

"What do you make of that? And him?" Worth said, nodding toward the departing lieutenant.

"I don't know. Never had an officer make a social call before. The only ones ever talked to me just wanted to chew my ass."

"Yeah—you think the old man sent him to size us up or something?"

"I wouldn't think so," Aaron said. "Lieutenant Slade could tell him anything he wanted to know. Sure is strange—platoon leader comin' over just to meet us when we ain't even in his platoon?" Aaron shook his head. "There's something different about him."

"Maybe. One of the guys in First Platoon said Waugh's been in a lot of trouble. Almost washed out of OCS, likes to hit the bottle. Apparently the battalion commander didn't even want to let him come overseas—but Waugh talked him into it somehow. His men like him a lot. Say he really looks after 'em."

"Hmm," Aaron said, smiling. "A Yankee-rebel, huh? Well, he seems like an okay guy to me—for an officer."

Aaron crawled from his tent to pull his turn at sentry duty. He crept up to the shallow foxhole where Private Donohue lay. Donohue's rifle was pointed into the darkness.

"Hey, Donnie," Aaron whispered. "What's up?"

Donohue placed his finger to his lips. Aaron tensed and then crawled into the foxhole.

"I thought I heard something just now. I'll stick around a few minutes just in case," Donohue whispered.

Aaron nodded and stared into the darkness. What was out there? He tightened his grip on his M-1.

"There," Donohue said a few seconds later. "Did you hear it? On our right."

Two shots rang out. Bullets zinged above their heads.

"We're taking fire!" Donohue yelled. He snapped his rifle to his shoulder and fired off three rounds in quick succession.

"Take that, you bastards!"

Aaron raised his rifle and aimed in the direction of the fire. Before he could pull the trigger, two more shots rang out.

This time the bullets kicked up dirt to their left.

What was it the rifle range officer at Jackson said about an M-1? *Sounds like the slap of a heavy leather belt when it's fired.*

Aaron grabbed Donohue's arm. "Cease fire! That's an M-1—it's one of our guys!"

"Huh? You sure?" Donohue said.

"He's right, you idiot," Staff Sergeant Palmer hissed as he crawled up behind them. "You're firing at Third Platoon's sentry. He must have heard you jabbering and started shootin'. Christ almighty! The Germans must be laughing their asses off listening to us try to kill each other. Keep your heads down 'til we can get that other genius to stop shootin' over here. Donohue, report to me in the morning. I got a feeling we're gonna be seeing the old man. You better come too, Johnson." Palmer crawled away.

Aaron cursed under his breath. In trouble again. And this time it wasn't even his fault.

The next morning, Aaron and Donohue reported to Palmer as ordered.

"We're going to see the old man," Palmer said, shaking his head. "Just as I suspected."

At Macardo's tent, Third Platoon's Sergeant Ross and the other involved sentry, Private Stottlemire, joined them. Stottlemire was a tall, skinny, freckle-faced kid who looked to be no more than seventeen. At the moment, he looked green around the gills.

First Sergeant Gibbs stood smiling just outside the tent. "Step right in, gentlemen," Gibbs said. "The captain's expectin' you."

Inside the tent, they stood at attention before Macardo's makeshift desk and saluted.

Macardo slammed his fist onto the desktop. "What in the hell were you men doing last night? Can somebody tell me that?"

Private Stottlemire stepped forward. "Sir, I heard some noise to my left and thought it might be German infiltrators. So I fired."

"And which one of you clowns decided to shoot back at Private Stottlemire here?"

"I did, sir," Donohue said.

"You can't tell the sound of an M-1 from a Mauser, Private? That what you want me to understand?" Macardo sat back, eyeing Donohue.

"Sir, I guess I was a little excited. I didn't recognize the sound at first."

"Obviously not," Macardo replied. He turned his gaze on Aaron. "And what was your role in all this mayhem?"

"Sir, I was there to relieve Donohue."

Palmer stepped forward. "Captain, Johnson figured out it was an M-1 and told Donohue to cease firing just as I got there."

Macardo looked at Aaron again. "Don't I know you? Haven't you been in to see me before?"

"Yes sir." Damn, he'd hoped the old man wouldn't remember him.

"Well, what for?"

"Umm—sir, I was one of the guys at the OP when the Germans raided us a few nights ago."

Macardo narrowed his eyes. "Oh yeah, now I remember." He sighed and turned to Stottlemire.

"Did you hit Donohue or Johnson when you fired your weapon, Private?"

"N-no sir. As you can see, sir, they're fine."

Macardo nodded. "And you, Donohue, did you hit Stottlemire?"

"No sir!"

"Well why the hell didn't one of you hit something, for Chrissake! God, first Johnson and his crew shoot up the whole Italian front without killing any Germans, and now you two blast away like hoodlums in a bar fight, and nobody's hit anybody yet!" Macardo ran his hand through his close-cropped hair. "Goddammit, can't somebody in this outfit show me some marksmanship? God help us when we meet the Krauts."

Macardo slumped back.

Gibbs studied his fingernails, obviously bemused by the entire affair.

"I'll tell you one thing," Macardo said. "You men are gonna have to shoot better if you're gonna kill Germans. Palmer, Ross—get Stottlemire and Donohue to the range. Target practice every day 'til they can hit something. Johnson, are you still practicing?"

"Yes sir, every day, sir."

"Alright. Dismissed. All of you. The next time you men pull the trigger, I expect you to hit something. Now get outta here."

# Chapter Fourteen

Second Lieutenant Robert Waugh entered First Platoon's area. First Sergeant John Strickland looked up.

"How are the men, Sergeant? Any problems today?"

Strickland pushed his helmet up and looked around. "Couple of guys at the aid station with sore feet—nothing serious. Everyone else is doin' okay. They're gettin' a little antsy, like we all are."

"Yeah, well, we're gonna be in it soon enough. And I'd guess sooner rather than later. Anything else goin' on?"

"No—oh yeah, one thing. You missed mail call. You got a letter." Strickland pulled an envelope from his shirt pocket.

Waugh glanced at the return address and placed it inside his shirt. "Thanks, Sergeant. Let me know if you need anything."

Inside his tent, Waugh opened the letter.

Dear Bob,

I hope you are well wherever you are and not too uncomfortable. I'm sorry I haven't written in a while, but I've been really busy at work. Bob, I may as well get right to it. We both know it isn't going well between us. I've met someone since you've been away. Bob, I want a divorce. I know it's a bad time to tell you, but I can't go on pretending. I don't want to hurt you, but I have to do this. We can work out the details later, but I wanted to let you know before you heard it from someone else— like your sister, who's been doggin' me ever since you left. I'm sorry, Bob. Good luck.

Mary

Waugh returned the letter to the envelope. He sat back and blew out a long breath. Damn. After all this time. She has to do this now?

Double damn. He dug inside his pack and took out a small flask, took a long pull, and stared into the distance. "I wish we were attacking tomorrow," he said aloud.

Sergeant Strickland approached. "Sir, you don't look so good. Anything wrong?"

"Nothin' a night in Naples with a coupla bottles of Cognac won't cure," Waugh said.

"Sir, like I mentioned—some of the guys, well, they're really jittery. About the attack and all."

"We all are, John. Anything specific?"

"No, not really. I think we've made all the preparations we can. The men are trained. We got extra ammo, grenades, canteens, and rations issued all around. It's just the waiting, sir."

"Yeah, tell me about it. Waiting is always a bad thing. But sometimes after the wait is over, it gets worse."

"Let's hope that won't happen with First Platoon, sir."

Waugh looked at Strickland. "The men will be fine, Sergeant. This morning I met some of the guys in Second Platoon. The company's gonna do fine."

"Yes sir." Strickland turned to go.

"John?"

"Yes sir?"

"Are you married? I never asked before."

"Yes, I am, sir. Four years. Two kids."

"You're a lucky man, John. I'm sure your family will be glad to have you back home when all this is over."

"I'll sure be happy about it, sir. What about you, Lieutenant? You got a girl back home?"

Waugh looked at his hands for a moment. "No—nobody. Just myself to worry about."

"Are your folks…?"

"My father's dead. I haven't seen my mother in over a year and a half. I've got a sister in Maine. She writes to me once in a while."

"You going back to Maine after the war?"

"I dunno, Sergeant. Maybe."

Strickland stared into the distance.

"What is it, John?"

Strickland picked up a handful of dirt and let it trickle through his fingers. "Sir, I think I speak for all the men when I say we feel good about you being our platoon leader. We'll follow you, sir."

"I know you will." Waugh turned to gaze at the terrain in front of the American line. "You see those hills out there, John?"

"Yes sir."

"It's obvious we're gonna be attacking them. I'll tell you something. When the time comes, I'm taking our platoon up one of those hills. And I'm either gonna win a medal for it, or I'm gonna die. Either way, we're gonna accomplish our mission. You can tell the men I said so."

"I think I'll just tell 'em the part about accomplishing the mission. None of us want to see anything happen to you, sir."

# CHAPTER FIFTEEN

"Men, the rumors you've heard about G Company spearheading an upcoming attack are true. Tomorrow night the entire Fifth and Eighth Armies will attack the German's Gustav Line." Captain Macardo turned from his assembled company staff officers, platoon leaders, and senior NCOs and walked to a map pinned to the company headquarters wall.

"As you know, the Gustav stretches all the way across Italy. The central point in the German defenses is Monte Cassino, here," he said, tapping the map. "I don't have to tell you about the damage the Krauts have been able to do by holding that high ground. They can see every move we make. This will be our fourth attempt to get the Germans out of Cassino and break this stalemate. This time we're gonna push 'em out of their positions, head north, and link up with our guys from the Anzio beachhead.

"Our objective is here—hill seventy-nine, directly in the center of the German line facing us." He moved his pointer to the left of Monte Cassino and rested it on the marked location. "Taking seventy-nine— and holding it—is key to this attack for us. There is an intermediate ridge we have to take before we can get to the top. The whole area is full of pillboxes and dug-in infantry, and you can bet their artillery is zeroed in on every square inch of ground. Once we start, we can't stop. We have to move fast and hit 'em hard."

He moved the pointer again. "Now, while we go after hill seventy-nine, E and F Companies will attack hill fifty-eight on our right flank. K and L Companies will take out hills sixty-six and sixty-nine respectively on our left, here," he tapped the map again, "and here. Other battalion elements will attack the town of Scauri, securing our left flank.

"An artillery barrage will begin at twenty-three hundred hours. Lieutenant Waugh with First Platoon will move out as soon as the barrage lifts, followed by Lieutenant Slade's Second Platoon. Third Platoon will advance shortly after."

Waugh shifted slightly in his seat. How would his men react? They had the training—they were capable. Would they follow him? And how would he hold up in battle? Was he fooling himself to think he had what it took to endure combat and look after his men?

Macardo put down his pointer and turned to face the group. "It's gonna be rough, men, but this is what we've been waiting for. Quite frankly, the top brass is concerned since we haven't seen any combat yet. They're not sure we can do the job. But I know you'll do your duty—I have complete confidence in you. If there are any questions, come see me. If not, go brief your men and make sure they know how important this is. Dismissed."

Waugh's mind raced. Tightness gripped his chest. Was he afraid? Sure. Concerned? Certainly. The moment he and his men had trained so hard for had arrived. What more could he do? What last-minute preparations needed to be made? He would dwell on that later—briefing his men was the immediate task.

As Waugh entered the First Platoon area, Sergeant Strickland and the other noncommissioned officers stopped talking.

Waugh took a deep breath. "Men, we're jumping off tomorrow night. It's the big push we've been expecting. There's no turning back—we've gotta push through the German positions in front of us to flank the Jerries at Cassino so they have to withdraw.

"We'll be the lead platoon in this sector. I want every man to study the maps and the terrain. Memorize every depression, rock, tree, and shrub. It's gonna be dark when we jump off, so the more familiar we are with the ground the better chance we have. Make sure everyone takes the extra ammo, rations, and canteens I ordered."

Sergeant Elder, one of the squad leaders, said, "Sir, what about the mines? Will they be cleared by tomorrow night?"

"I've been going out with the engineers the last few nights to clear a path through those minefields. Just make sure you stay in formation and follow me. There's barbed wire, too. If the artillery barrage doesn't destroy it, we'll have Bangalore torpedoes to blast a way through. I think our biggest concern is going to be the enemy artillery and the machine gun emplacements. It's a cinch they have multiple bunkers with overlapping fields of fire. That's why we've gotta move fast before they can get all those guns into action.

"Men, I assume no one's surprised by this. The captain trusts us to be the lead platoon, so he obviously has confidence in you. So do I. For now, rest up, write letters home, double check your gear, and then get some sleep. We're gonna need it."

Waugh and Slade talked later that day.

"You nervous?" Slade asked.

"Hell yeah. Aren't you?" Waugh responded.

Slade finished wiping down his .45 automatic and replaced it in its holster. He picked up his carbine, removed the magazine, and opened the bolt. "You show me a man on this whole Italian front that ain't scared, nervous, or both, and I'll show you a fool."

Waugh nodded. "But it's what we've trained for. Gotta do it."

"Yep," Slade said. "It's been a long time, hasn't it, ole buddy? OCS at Benning. Camp Shelby. Desert training. To Africa—too late to fight. All that to get here for this little party."

Waugh reached inside his field jacket and drew out a flask. He offered it to Slade, who shook his head.

Waugh took a swig and put it away.

"You know that stuff gets you into trouble," Slade said. "Almost kept you from getting here at all. Don't know how you talked the old man into letting you come overseas with us. He was really sore." He finished inspecting his carbine, reinserted the magazine, and set it down. "You busted that bar all to pieces. Fighting with the MPs didn't help any."

"It was just a little misunderstanding," Waugh said. "After I explained it to the old man, we worked things out."

"And now you've got a platoon. Even though he said you'd never hold a command under him. If Wilson hadn't gone down with dysentery, you wouldn't have, either."

"Knock it off, will ya? I wanted a platoon, and I've got it. How it happened don't matter to me."

"I heard about Mary," Slade said.

"Yeah, she found somebody else. I got the ole 'Dear John'."

Slade turned his gaze away from Waugh. "I'm sorry, Bob."

"Me too. Real sorry. I love—loved—her."

"Damn poor timing on her part," Slade said.

The two sat in silence. A moment later, Waugh stood and looked toward hill seventy-nine for a full minute without speaking. Then he spoke over his shoulder to Slade. "Ole buddy, I'll tell you something. I'm goin' up that hill tomorrow, and nothing's gonna stop me. Nothing."

# CHAPTER SIXTEEN

At exactly 2300 hours, May 11, 1944, every Allied artillery piece in the Fifth Army fired salvo after salvo at the German lines. Flashes from the exploding shells mixed with flares and mortar fire, turning darkness into near daylight. The ground shook from the impact of the exploding shells. The noise was deafening.

"How long did you say the barrage is gonna last?" Sergeant Strickland shouted into Waugh's ear.

"Forty-five minutes. Tell the men we're moving out in fifteen!" Waugh said.

Strickland raised his eyebrows. "Fifteen? I thought we're s'posed to wait for the barrage to lift."

Waugh shook his head. "If we wait 'til then, we'll never get across the open ground between here and the base of the hill. It's a walking barrage—we'll be movin' on the back side of it. We go on my signal."

Strickland gazed at the terrain ahead. "I'll tell the men."

Fifteen minutes later, Waugh raised his arm and looked to his left and then his right. He brought his arm down fast. "Let's go!"

He leapt from his foxhole. "Move it, move it!" he shouted.

Waugh ran toward the base of hill seventy-nine over five hundred yards away. His men followed close behind. No enemy fire. He ran faster. "Come on! Move it!"

Allied artillery shells fell farther up the hill as he came upon the first German bunker, a machine gun emplacement fortified with logs and sandbags. Two soldiers inside the bunker hovered over the gun. Waugh raised his Thompson submachine gun and fired a burst of automatic fire through the bunker's view slit.

The Germans fell back. Waugh yelled over his shoulder to Sergeant Strickland, "Have somebody grab that gun and ammo."

Waugh continued on. Thank God they'd moved out earlier than planned. If the Germans had gotten that machine gun into action, they could have slaughtered the entire platoon.

Dirt flew up in front of him. Another machine gun. Where? On his left! Waugh fell into a shell hole; Sergeant Strickland dove in beside him.

Waugh poked his head up. "Sarge—there's at least two more machine gun bunkers ahead. Tell the men to lay down covering fire. I'm gonna see if I can get closer." He wrenched a grenade from his belt, pulled the pin, and hurled it in the direction of the nearest enemy machine gun. When the grenade exploded, he rose to his knee, fired a burst in the direction of the enemy gun, and ran in a zigzag pattern toward the emplacement.

A German soldier struggled to reload the gun. Waugh tossed another grenade into the bunker and fell to the ground. After the blast, he ran to the opening and fired a long burst into the bunker's interior. Two down.

Waugh peeked around the side of the bunker. Another machine gun blazed wickedly—ahead and to his right. The gun fired down the hill, pinning the platoon in place. Waugh reloaded the Thompson and then sprinted to the bunker as bullets whizzed around him. Another long burst from his submachine gun silenced the enemy weapon.

He moved toward the rear of the bunker. A German officer carrying a Luger pistol exited. He pointed it at Waugh, but a blast from the tommy gun knocked the man to the ground. Two other enemy soldiers ran from the bunker. Two more bursts brought them down.

Waugh crouched behind the bunker for cover. He reloaded the Thompson with a fresh magazine and then poked his head around to see three more machine gun emplacements—two to his left, one to his right. Three more! He needed more grenades!

Looking down the hill, he spotted Strickland. Waugh pointed at him and held up a grenade.

Strickland nodded and tossed three more grenades up the hill within Waugh's reach. Waugh stuffed two of the grenades into his field jacket pocket. He pulled the pin on the third, ran to the bunker on his right, and flung the grenade into the opening. The explosion sent smoke and debris flying from the bunker's firing slit.

Waugh continued on. More Germans—more tommy gun fire. He paused, worked the magazine release on the Thompson, and the empty magazine tumbled to the ground. He inserted a fresh one and then ran toward the remaining two bunkers. His heart pounded in his chest. Sweat poured down his face. He gasped for breath.

An M-1 rifle fired directly behind him.

He turned to see a German soldier with a machine pistol fall to the ground.

Strickland waved to Waugh.

Waugh continued running. The Kraut would have shot him in the back if Strickland hadn't taken him out. He'd thank him later.

The remaining two bunkers fell to Waugh's grenades and tommy gun, clearing the intermediate ridge.

What now? Maybe they should regroup before attacking the rest of the hill?

Waugh ducked behind an embankment and waved Strickland over. "What's our status? Casualties? How many made it here?"

"Only half the platoon made it, Lieutenant. Some are wounded. And Second and Third Platoons are catching hell comin' up behind us—the Jerries from the adjacent hills are cutting 'em to pieces with their machine guns and mortars, so we can't count on reinforcements."

"Have the men spread out—use the foxholes the Germans were in, and turn the Kraut guns around if they're still usable. We're gonna get some counterattacks."

Waugh sank to the ground, exhausted. If the Krauts on the adjacent hills were firing on Second and Third Platoon, that meant the other companies had failed in their attacks. So he and his men were cut off. And God—only half his platoon made it this far? Over forty men, and now—maybe twenty? Could any of the wounded men fight? Waugh wiped sweat from his face. Couldn't worry about that now. He had work to do.

# CHAPTER SEVENTEEN

Aaron waited in his foxhole. His hands shook. A cannonball had taken up residence in his stomach. God—what if he couldn't do it? He closed his eyes and prayed. *God—help me. I'm scared.* His breathing came in gasps. His entire body trembled. *Maggie. Oh Maggie. Help me, God. I need you. Just let me see her again.* He opened his eyes. He let out a breath. No choice. He had to do this.

Why were they waiting? It must have been at least fifteen minutes since Lieutenant Waugh launched his attack with First Platoon. Why didn't they move?

Lieutenant Slade blew a long blast on his whistle. "Second Platoon—move out!"

Aaron heaved himself from his foxhole and ran forward. Hill seventy-nine loomed ahead. Machine gun fire kicked up the dirt around him. Mortar shells exploded. Flares lit the night sky, turning the darkness to daylight.

All around him men moved forward. Some yelled, some cursed, and some panted or grunted as they ran. To his right, several men fell as a mortar round exploded in their midst.

A wave of panic swept over him. How could this be happening? How could he be here?

A burst of machine gun fire raked the area, and a man in front of him went down. Aaron hesitated, but the orders were clear: *If the man in front of you goes down, do not stop to help him. The medics will do that. Keep moving.*

"Medic, medic!" he yelled, and then leapt over the fallen soldier, ran to a shell hole, and dove in head first. Worth Haynes lay clutching his helmet tightly to his head as another mortar round landed nearby.

"We gotta get out of here!" Haynes said. "They've got the whole area bracketed."

"Yeah—keep moving," Aaron said. "Come on."

The two sprinted forward. A string of machine gun rounds struck the ground in front of them. Aaron ran faster, continuing up the steep slope. Where was Worth?

Above him, a German soldier rose and aimed his rifle down the hill.

Aaron snapped the M-1 to his shoulder and fired.

The German fell backward.

*Jesus, he'd just shot a man!*

An exploding mortar round knocked him down. Unharmed, he struggled to his feet and fired blindly uphill.

The M-1 kicked out its empty clip, making the familiar *pling* sound as it flew into the night.

Aaron fumbled at his cartridge belt for a reload, stuffed the clip into the top of the M-1's receiver, and chambered a round.

The slope became steeper. He half-crawled, half-ran up it. He fired as fast as his finger could work the trigger. Maybe it would make them keep their heads down.

Something hit the ground beside him. A potato masher grenade rolled past and exploded behind him. He pressed on. The crest of the hill rose before him. Some Germans retreated, but others stood their ground and continued firing. More grenades rolled past—more explosions.

A man he recognized pointed up the hill and yelled, "We're almost to the top! Keep moving!" Machine gun fire raked the man's torso. He fell back screaming. Aaron gasped. No need to call a medic.

Another grenade landed close by. Heart hammering, he pressed himself into the hillside as it exploded.

Dirt and rocks pelted him.

He shook his head. His ear hurt. He'd survived, though—thank God. Had to keep movin'.

He tried to stand. His right leg buckled under him. Other soldiers rushed past. Blood oozed from his leg and right arm.

Again he tried to rise and failed.

Worth Haynes stood over him. "Don't move! You're hit! Medic!"

The world began to spin and darken. Aaron closed his eyes. When he opened them, Worth was gone.

A medic crouched beside him and gave him a shot of morphine. Then he ripped open the bloody pants leg and poured sulfa powder on the wound.

"You're not hit that bad, Aaron, but you can't keep going with that leg like it is. See if you can make it to the aid station. I've gotta go. Keep your head down." The medic moved quickly up the hill.

Aaron stared after him. The shot began to take effect. Who was that man? How did he know his name? Not one of the medics he'd seen before. Must be a new guy. He sure seemed calm in the midst of all the noise and shooting. And his face—it was so clean looking. Not all dirty like everyone else. Couldn't worry about that. He fumbled for his helmet. His hands didn't seem to belong to him. He found his rifle and pulled it close.

He touched his right ear. His hand came away wet. Bloody. He wiped his fingers on his pants leg, leaving red stripes.

The battle moved up the hill, but bullets still flew and mortar rounds fell all around. He had to move.

He took a deep breath and then slid, rolled, and tumbled downward. After five minutes he reached the base of the incline. He began crawling toward the American lines.

Fifteen minutes later he forced himself to stand, using his rifle as a crutch. His right knee throbbed. His head hurt, and his vision was blurred. The continuing battle seemed muffled and far away.

He hobbled on. A squad of grim-faced soldiers hurried past him in the direction of the battle, rifles and carbines at the ready. One of the men said something to him, but Aaron couldn't make out the words. He shook his head. The men moved on.

The aid station, a stone building just inside the town, came into view.

Aaron stumbled to the doorway.

A medic looked at him. "Lie down on this cot. It's gonna be a few minutes. We got more serious cases to look after first."

Aaron collapsed onto the cot. Everything went black.

Arthur Ferdinand scrambled up hill seventy-nine. Men fell all around him. How long before he got it?

The noise. Deafening. Total confusion. His head pounded. How could anyone function in this? Bullets kicked up dirt in front of him. More zinged over his head. A mortar blast obliterated several men.

Ferdinand kept moving. He held his rifle at the ready, but there was nothing to shoot at. Germans had to be ahead, but they weren't visible. Men yelled and cursed. He yelled also, not sure why or at what.

He fell into a shell hole and peeked around. Lieutenant Waugh and Sergeant Strickland were ten or twelve yards ahead. A few other men lay prone near them. Some of them fired uphill. Others didn't move at all. And never would again.

He crawled toward Waugh and Strickland. Waugh gave the order to dig in and brace for counterattacks. Art pulled his collapsible shovel from his pack and dug furiously into the hard, rocky ground. Bullets whizzed above him.

"Help! Help me!"

Ferdinand looked down the hill. He knew that voice. Kowalski. He spun in his shallow trench and made a tentative move downhill.

"You're crazy if you go down there!" Sergeant Strickland yelled.

"I know that man. He's my friend!" Ferdinand slid down the hill on his belly. Why was he doing this? Strickland was right—he was crazy. He spotted Kowalski fifteen yards away. Wounded. Bleeding. He crawled beside him.

"Where are you hit?"

"My legs! My hand! Fingers are gone—they're gone!"

Art fumbled at the tape inside his helmet for a morphine syringe. He jabbed it into Kowalski's leg. "Can you move?"

"Pull me—I can help some."

Art grabbed Kowalski's good arm. He pulled and dragged him by his shirt collar to the hole he'd dug. He rolled the wounded man onto his side and squeezed beside him. The Germans had stopped firing. So much quieter. Movement to his right. A German! Coming to finish them off.

Art fired. The German fell, sending a spray of fire from a machine pistol into the air. Two more Germans came into view. Seeing their comrade fall, they threw up their hands.

"*Kamerad! Kamerad!*"

"Here—*komenzi* here!" Art shouted.

They dropped their rifles and approached, hands locked behind their heads.

Art looked up the hill to Strickland. "Sergeant, what do I do with these prisoners?"

Strickland shrugged. "Send them down the hill. Somebody'll pick 'em up. Or shoot 'em. We can't keep them here."

Art motioned the two enemy soldiers down the hill. They looked at him wide-eyed. They appeared to be as scared as he was. With apparent reluctance, the two prisoners began half crawling and sliding down the slope. Soon they disappeared into the darkness.

Art turned his attention to Kowalski. He had passed out from the morphine shot—or was it the pain? Art dressed his wounds as best he could. Where were the medics? He'd seen one treating that Johnson kid. Maybe he'd make his way to Kowalski later.

Now all he had to worry about was a German counterattack. Maybe reinforcements from the other platoons would reach them soon. He checked his ammo. He'd only fired the one shot. But it probably wouldn't be the last.

# Chapter Eighteen

Aaron awoke slowly as if ascending from under water. His head hurt. Vision blurry. Someone in a white coat stood over him. A doctor?

"How do you feel, soldier?"

Yes—a doctor. "Groggy—sir."

"What happened to you?"

"Grenade. Went off next to me."

"We're gonna fix you up. The bleeding's stopped. Now we gotta work on this eye."

"My eye? What's wrong with it?"

A medic stepped to the doctor's side. He looked familiar. "Who's this?" the medic asked.

The doctor lifted the chain around Aaron's neck and looked at the attached dog tag. "Says here—Johnson—Aaron S." He turned to the medic. "You know him?"

The medic recoiled. "That can't be Johnson—why, half his face is blowed off!"

Aaron tried to rise from the cot.

The doctor chuckled. "Calm down, Johnson. It looks worse than it is. Your face is good and bloody, but it's not that serious. But the concussion of the blast burst your eardrums and popped your eyeball out of its socket. We're gonna put it back in. Lie still."

Aaron swallowed and tried to look around. His eye was out of its socket? How could that happen? Would he be blind? Would they send him home?

Home? Could it happen?

But what about Worth and the rest of the company? He had to get back to them.

The doctor peered into his face and pulled at his right eyelid. After a moment, he stood back.

"There—how's it feel?"

His blurred vision cleared somewhat.

"Umm—it seems to be okay, sir. Still a little blurry."

"We'll keep it bandaged a few days, but it'll be fine. We also put your kneecap back in place. It was sitting a little lopsided when you came in. Other than that and the shrapnel wounds, you're in pretty good shape. We're gonna send you to the field hospital for a few days, and then you can get back to your unit."

The unit. Company G. Where were they? Did they make it to the top? And who was that medic who helped him? Had he really called Aaron by his name? Or did he just imagine it?

Waugh fired a burst from his tommy gun at the retreating Germans. The third counterattack had finally been beaten back. He reloaded the Thompson and then turned to Sergeant Strickland. "Check on the men. See how many wounded. And get some idea of how we stand on ammo."

"Yessir."

Waugh slumped down in his foxhole and wiped the perspiration from his face. How much longer could they hold out? They needed to move, not sit still. But taking the next section of hill seventy-nine looked all but impossible.

Strickland returned. "A coupla guys were hit, but not too bad. Doc's fixin' 'em up. Ammo's runnin' low, though—we might have enough to beat back one more counterattack. Water's the biggest problem. Most of the canteens are empty. Oh, and a few guys from Second and Third Platoon made it here."

Waugh sat up. "Good. Who? And what kinda shape are they in?"

"Klutz, Claytor, Ferdinand, and the Haynes kid. Two or three others. They're a little roughed up, but okay. And they have most of their ammo—said they was crawlin' and duckin' more than shootin'."

"Phew. So only those guys out of the other two platoons made it here?"

"Yep—Second and Third Platoon got cut up bad, sir."

Waugh shook his head. There were eighty or more men in those two platoons. And only a handful made it through. How could that be?

Waugh gazed at Strickland. "That means the other companies didn't take their objectives, or the Krauts wouldn't have been able to fire at our guys. So we're stuck out here with no support—cut off. We've gotta figure out a way to move up. Can't go back, or we'll get the same thing the other guys got comin' up."

Waugh rubbed his chin. "Okay, get Claytor, Klutz, and Ferdinand situated. Have them share some of their ammo with the other guys. Send Haynes to me. I've got a job for him."

Soon Haynes had made his way over to Waugh. "You wanted to see me, Lieutenant?"

"Yeah. Look, Haynes, we've gotta find a way to get up to the top of this hill. I want you to crawl around on our flanks and see if you can see a way we can move. Let me know what you find out."

"Yessir—just lookin' at these hills, they look kinda like where I grew up. If there's a path or a way up, I'll find it, Lieutenant."

Two hours later, Waugh and Haynes lay in a depression and gazed toward the top of hill seventy-nine.

"Yep, you found it," Waugh whispered. "If we can get past that first pillbox, I think we can get all the way up. Tell Sergeant Strickland to leave six guys to hold our position and have everyone else crawl over here and wait for me. I'm gonna see if this area is mined. I'll meet you back here."

Waugh crawled forward in the darkness, probing the ground in front of him with a bayonet. A partial moon and starlight gave just enough light to make out the terrain in front of him. In the next half hour, he used his bayonet to probe the ground and locate and disarm a dozen or so mines along the route to the first pillbox. He was crawling backward a few feet on his way to the rendezvous point when the sound of a muffled cough reached his ears. It came from dead ahead. Sweat popped out on Waugh's brow, and he struggled to control his breathing. Not now, please not now. We're so close. Please.

Another sound. A footstep. Peering into the darkness, he could see the outline of a German helmet about ten yards away. Had he been spotted? For thirty seconds he lay without moving. The enemy soldier finally moved out of sight. Hearing no other sounds, Waugh waited two full minutes and then crawled backward to the spot where he and Haynes parted.

"Crash," came a whispered challenge.

"Dive," Waugh answered.

"Good to see you, Lieutenant," Haynes said. "Sergeant Strickland and the others are here, sir."

"Good." Waugh motioned to Strickland. "Sergeant, tell the men to be ready to attack at first light."

# CHAPTER NINETEEN

A mortar round exploded twenty yards from Jack Claytor and Harry Klutz's foxhole.

"Here they come, Harry!" Jack pulled his rifle to his shoulder and aimed it downhill.

Harry copied Jack's move. "You run into anything like this in North Africa?"

"Oh yeah. Just stay calm and aim a little low. Shots go high firing downhill like this. Get ready! Come on, just a little closer, you Krauthead."

He squeezed off two quick shots.

"Got 'im!" Jack said.

"More of 'em comin'!" Harry said. He fired his own M-1 at several advancing gray-clad Germans.

A potato masher grenade flew through the air and landed behind their foxhole. Jack grabbed it and flung it back down the hill.

It exploded. A loud scream, then silence.

"Take that, damn you!" Jack fired twice more in rapid succession.

Bullets kicked up dirt around them as the Germans continued up the hill. Mauser rounds zinged just over their heads.

A soldier on their right opened up with one of the captured German machine guns.

"It's about time those MGs got in on this," Jack yelled.

From down the hill, a German shouted.

"You speak German, Harry. What's he saying?"

"He's saying, 'Stop shooting at us—we're Deutschlanders.' They think that machine gun is one of their own guys shootin' at 'em."

"Answer him! Tell that Kraut to hold their fire 'til we can make sure who they are."

As Harry shouted out the response, Jack pulled the pin on a grenade and waited.

The German fire ceased. More yelling.

"Now I see where he is," Jack said. He flung the grenade downhill and ducked back into the foxhole.

"That'll give 'em something to think about," Harry said as he picked up his rifle.

Almost immediately the German fire resumed, heavier than before. Small arms fire erupted from other G Company men as the German assault continued. Fifteen minutes later the enemy troops retreated, dragging their wounded with them.

Harry slumped into the foxhole and pushed his helmet back. "They sure want this territory back," he said. He took his canteen from his belt and tried to drink, but his hand shook so violently he spilled more than he drank.

Jack managed to get his Zippo lighter going and lit a cigarette.

"How long we been here?" Harry asked.

Jack inhaled deeply on the Chesterfield. "Seems like forever. Let's see, we got here last night. I still don't know how we made it."

"Not many of us Second or Third Platoon guys did. Strickland seemed happy to see us, though. Geez, I've been in this outfit one week, and here I am shot at from every direction," Harry said.

"Yeah, well, it ain't over yet, either. Jerry don't give up that easy. I sure hope Waugh's got some plan for gettin' us out of here."

# Chapter Twenty

"Captain Macardo, sir, wake up. Waugh's attacking!"

"What?" Macardo shook himself awake and glanced hurriedly around the bunker. Spotting his binoculars, he snatched them from their case.

Macardo's executive officer, Lieutenant Graves, already had his own glasses trained on the hillside several hundred yards away. "Sir, I thought you'd wanna see this."

The sound of small arms fire and exploding grenades reached their ears.

Macardo sucked in a breath. "Damn, look at him! Waugh just took out the first pillbox, and he's headed for the next one. How in the hell did he get into that position? He's hittin' 'em from their blind side. I'll bet the bastards never figured on that!"

Graves rubbed his unshaved face and grinned. "His men are keeping the Jerries pinned down so Waugh can get to the boxes. Swell!"

Macardo spun to his radio man. "Furlong, get battalion! Tell 'em to get Fox Company movin' on the double. If Waugh pulls this off, we could have a breakthrough any minute! And tell 'em to get some artillery onto hill sixty-six—we can't let the Jerries there fire at Waugh's platoon."

Furlong bent to the radio. Moments later an artillery round screamed overhead and landed on hill sixty-six.

"You're on target—fire for effect!" Furlong shouted into the handset.

More rounds streaked overhead and fell onto the hills to the right and left of hill seventy-nine.

"He's taken out two more bunkers," Macardo said. "By God, when this is over, I'll write a recommendation that'll make their heads spin at headquarters!"

"He's sure got that tommy gun working," Graves said.

Furlong stood and pointed. "Look, sirs. Fox Company is moving toward seventy-nine at a run. Battalion must have lit a fire under 'em to get 'em movin' that quick! The Lord is surely with us today."

Macardo jammed a cigar between his teeth. "Yeah, Furlong, and Lieutenant Waugh's his avenging angel."

"It's a good thing we moved the company CP up here last night, or we woulda missed this," Graves said.

Macardo continued scanning hill seventy-nine. "Can't see anything but smoke. Furlong, see if you can raise Waugh's radio man. We need a status report."

"Roger, sir."

Furlong clamped the earpiece tightly to his ear and spoke into the mouthpiece.

"Sir, Corporal Pearson says they've cleared all the pillboxes and bunkers. They're diggin' in—expecting counterattacks. Says they need water, ammo, food—all we can get up there, pronto."

"Tell him Fox Company's on the way and we'll get more supplies up there ASAP. Where's Bradley?"

"Right here, Cap'n."

Macardo continued peering through the binoculars. "Get your mules loaded up with all you can carry, and get up there to Waugh and his men."

"They're already loaded, sir—we'll be under way in two minutes."

"Make it *one* minute, dammit! Those boys need all we can give 'em."

Furlong again pressed his ear to the radio handset. "Sir, its battalion. Spotters from division say the Jerries are pullin' back from hills sixty-six and sixty-nine! We did it! Waugh did it! He routed 'em!"

"He sure as hell did," Macardo said. "With seventy-nine taken, the Krauts couldn't hold the line—we'd flank 'em and roll 'em up like a piecrust on a rollin' pin. If they're pullin' back here, there's a good likelihood they're gonna have to give up Monte Cassino, too. Hot damn! Come on, Graves, we gotta get up there and survey the area. Furlong— bring that radio."

Furlong hoisted the radio onto his back. "Yes sir. Congratulations, sir. The Lord has shown his favor on you and G Company today, sir."

Macardo paused and then gave Furlong a sidelong glance. "When you say your prayers tonight, Furlong, ask the Lord why so many good men had to die here to make that happen. Come on, Graves. Let's move it."

# CHAPTER TWENTY-ONE

His rifle! Where was it? He had to find it and get up the hill. So dark. Where were the others? His heart raced. Cold sweat covered his body. Where was that damned rifle! He scanned the area around him. Machine gun bullets whizzed overhead. There—six feet away! He reached for the M-1 as another artillery shell exploded. He screamed—

"Whoa there, soldier. The battle's over for you."

He opened his eyes. A white-coated doctor stood by the bed. Aaron strained to sit up but fell back against the pillow. Tired. So tired.

"Where am I?"

"Field hospital—they brought you in last night with the other wounded. You're gonna be okay in a few days."

"You said the battle's over. What happened? Did we...?"

"Yep—we broke through. The Germans are retreating all along the front."

"Thank God," Aaron said. He raised a hand to his bandaged right eye. "What about...?"

"You're gonna be fine. The bandage will come off in a few days. After your knee and the shrapnel wounds heal, you can go back to your outfit."

Aaron looked past the doctor. A dark-haired young woman in a nurse's uniform stood behind him. Pretty. A shy smile.

The doctor scribbled on papers attached to a clipboard. "And who's this Maggie you kept talking about all night? That your girl?"

Aaron blushed. "Yeah—my wife, actually. What did I say?"

"Oh, you just kept calling her name—telling her you were sorry. For what, I don't know."

"For getting wounded, probably. I promised her I'd be careful." Aaron fingered the wet gauze on his arm.

The doctor laughed. "It's kinda hard to be careful on a battle-field—too many ways to get hurt. You were lucky, though. Some of the guys weren't."

"Did we lose a lot of men?"

"Too many. But we broke through."

"What's your name, Doc? I mean, sir."

"Williams. This is Maria. She's an Italian nurse, helping out in the hospital. She'll keep a check on you and the others in the ward. I'll be around later. Now get some rest."

Williams disappeared through the door and into a hallway. Aaron looked at Maria.

She smiled.

"Do you speak English?" Aaron asked.

"Yes—I have relatives in New York City. I lived there with them before the war."

"Oh good. 'Cause I sure can't speak Italian."

She smiled. "You Americans—we make so many allowances for you."

"Maybe I'll learn Italian if I stay here long enough."

"Let's hope you get home to your Maggie before that happens."

"Yeah—that would sure make me happy."

"Now—you rest. I'll check on you later. Then you can tell me more about Maggie."

She spun and walked away. Aaron watched her go. The nurse's uniform fit her well. No. He couldn't look at other women that way. Maggie—did she know he was wounded? Probably not. He'd have to write—let her know and tell her he was okay.

He looked around the open-bay ward. Twenty or so bandaged men lay throughout the room. Some stared at the ceiling. Others read or sat up and smoked. Aaron's stomach sank. He took in a quick breath. Several had empty sleeves. One man two beds over had an empty space where a leg should have been. At the far end of the room, a heavily ban-daged man moaned softly. Aaron touched his bandaged arm. He *was* lucky—the doc wasn't just saying that. His leg hurt, but at least he still had it. And he'd be walking in a day or so. Some of those guys would be going home on crutches or in wheelchairs. He'd like to go home—but not like that.

# CHAPTER TWENTY-TWO

"Dad, will you get the door?" Maggie shouted. "I'm in the middle of changing Barry." She finished pinning her son's diaper and then walked to the front room to see who had arrived. Her father stood holding a telegram. She froze. "Daddy? What—is it Aaron?"

Lloyd looked at her. "He's been wounded—it doesn't sound too bad. He's in the hospital."

Maggie handed the baby to her father and took the telegram. Her hands shook. She tried to hold the flimsy paper still so she could read the cryptic words.

REGRET TO INFORM YOU YOUR HUSBAND PRIVATE AARON S JOHNSON WAS ON TWELVE MAY SLIGHTLY WOUNDED IN ACTION IN ITALY (STOP) FURTHER REPORT STATES CONVALESCING FIFTEEN MAY (STOP) YOU WILL BE ADVISED AS REPORTS OF CONDITION ARE RECEIVED (STOP)

DUNLOP (ACTING) THE ADJUTANT GENERAL

The room spun. She sank onto the sofa. Thank God Aaron wasn't dead. But how bad was it? What did "slightly wounded" mean?

Lloyd looked at her. "I'm sure we'll be hearing from him soon. Try not to worry too much. I bet he's just fine."

Tears rolled down her cheeks. She read the telegram again.

Barry began to fuss and cry as if sensing her anguish.

"Give him to me," she said.

She rocked him in her arms and spoke softly to soothe him. Soon he fell asleep.

"Well—we'll just have to wait and see how he is. That's what's so awful. Waiting. Always waiting." She stifled a sob. She had to be strong. He was alive. That's what mattered.

Lloyd took the sleeping baby from her. "I'll put him to bed. You rest for a bit."

Rest? How could she rest? Her mother was two months dead. Her dad was still mourning. With her mom gone, she had to run the household—cook, clean, pay the bills. Barry demanded constant attention. She never knew caring for a baby would be so trying. She hadn't counted on doing it alone, either. And then never knowing where or how Aaron was. How could she bear this?

Tears rose again within her. Stop it! Her head snapped up. She stood. There was no choice. No time for crying.

Three days later, a letter arrived from Aaron. She tore it open. Her fingers shook again as she unfolded the pages.

> Dear Maggie,
>
> I guess you've heard by now that I was wounded. I'm okay. I'm in the hospital in Naples. Don't worry, honey. Just a few scratches. I'll be out of here in a few days. I guess the censors don't want me to say much about where we were or what happened, but I'll tell you all about it someday. How is Barry? I sure would like to see you both. How's Lloyd holding up? It's good that you can be there for him. I'm sure he needs you and appreciates you being there. Well, the nurse is bringing me some pills, so I'll close for now. I love you, and I miss you more than I can say in words. Take care and stay pretty for me. Kiss Barry and tell him his daddy loves him. Thinking of you always.
>
> Love,
> Aaron

Maggie let out a breath. He really was okay. Her shoulders relaxed. She sat for a moment to collect her thoughts. He probably had more than "a few scratches"—why else would he be in the hospital? It must not be too bad, though, if he was getting out soon. Then he'd go back into battle. She couldn't think about that. He was okay for now. Now was all that mattered.

A knock sounded at the door. Before she could answer, a short, stocky man entered. Maggie winced inwardly. Oh no. Not him, not now.

Howard Starnes, her dad's supervisor at the mill, stood holding his hat and smiling at her. "Hello, Miss Maggie. And how's the prettiest woman in town today?"

She sighed. He probably wasn't such a bad man, but he was much too friendly. Her skin crawled when he looked at her.

"I wouldn't know, Howard. Why don't you go see if you can find her and ask her yourself?"

He smirked. "Aw, c'mon. You know I'm talking about you. I've watched you grow up. There's not a better lookin' woman in all these parts. How's that husband of yours doing? It's gotta be tough for you—all alone with a new baby and all."

"I'm doing just fine. And so is Aaron. It's nice of you to ask. Daddy's out back if you want to see him. I've got to check on the baby." She walked to the bedroom. Had to get away from Howard.

Barry lay sleeping peacefully. She bent over and tucked a blanket around him.

She turned.

Howard stood close behind her.

She gasped. "What are you doing in here?"

He stepped back as if he'd been slapped. "C'mon, Maggie. I just wanted to see the little fella. I didn't mean nothin'."

She sighed. "Howard, please. I'm just a little edgy. I know you didn't mean any harm. I just don't want to wake him."

Howard retreated into the hallway. Maggie followed, closing the bedroom door behind her.

"Sure, sure. I understand. I'll go," Howard said. "Besides, I just came by to…"

"To what?" Lloyd said from behind him.

"Oh, Lloyd. Maggie and I were just talking. I stopped by to remind you we gotta start the shift early tomorrow."

Lloyd stepped closer to Howard. "I know that. I'll be there on time. Is that all?"

"Yeah, that's all." Howard shuffled as if uncomfortable. He fingered the brim of the hat he held in his hands. "Uh, well, I guess I'd better be gettin' home. Supper will be waiting." He looked at Maggie. "It's always nice seeing you, Maggie. Lloyd, I'll see you tomorrow."

After Howard left, Maggie sat by Lloyd at the kitchen table. "What was going on with Howard?" her father said.

"I—I don't know. He just—makes me nervous sometimes."

"So I noticed. Look, girl. If he ever tries anything, you let me know. I can handle him."

"Thanks, Dad. But I don't think he means any harm. And I can take up for myself. Don't worry."

Maggie stood and opened the icebox. She took out the items left over from the previous day's dinner—a beef roast, a bowl of green beans, and cornbread. She took some potatoes from the pantry and peeled them at the sink. She sighed as the paring knife stripped away the peelings. She couldn't let her dad get involved in anything with Howard. She had to handle it. Howard could get Lloyd fired. One more thing for her to have to worry about.

Tears welled up in her eyes. "Oh Lord," she prayed, "please, please help me. And please, Lord—please keep Aaron safe and bring him home to me—to us."

# Chapter Twenty-three

He woke from another dream, bathed in sweat. Someone was near. Through blurred vision he could just see her—dark hair, trim figure—Maggie!

"And how are we this morning, Private Johnson?"

Maria—not Maggie.

"Oh—I was dreaming. I thought…"

"Yes, I know. You were calling to her again. Here, it's time for your pills."

He swallowed the pills she handed him and then fell back onto the pillow. Still so weak.

"How's your eye? Can you see okay?"

He turned his head to look directly at Maria. "Yes—it's really cleared up the last few days. Doc says I can get out of here in a day or two—get back to my company."

"Company…?"

"G Company—339th. I've only been with them for a few weeks. It's funny—I'd give almost anything to go home, but…"

"What?"

"I want to get back to my company."

Maria smiled. "You rest. Doctor Williams will be around later. Maybe he'll release you soon." She turned to go.

"Maria?"

"Yes?"

"Do you have someone? Are you—married—engaged…?"

"I did have someone. But he's dead now. Fighting in North Africa. With the Germans." She looked at Aaron. "He hated the Germans. But our men had no choice. Once Mussolini sided with Hitler—well—that's just how it was."

"I'm sorry. I'm sure there'll be someone else. You're too pretty and too nice to be alone—there's someone out there for you."

"Oh, I know. It's just that—right now, I'm not ready. You know?"

"Yeah—I can understand that. Maria—thanks for helping look after me. I even know a few Italian words now—thanks to you."

She smiled. "You be careful when you get back to the front. You have to get through this so you can get home to Maggie." Another smile and she was gone.

# CHAPTER TWENTY-FOUR

"Careful there, fella. Don't cut your throat."

Worth Haynes looked up from his foxhole, razor in hand. "Aaron! You're back."

"Yup," Aaron said.

"You okay?"

"Still got shrapnel in my arm and leg. The doc said it'll work its way out in time. Eye's back to normal."

"Good. I didn't know how bad you were hit. Thought you might have bought a ticket home."

Aaron shook his head. "It really wasn't that bad. What about you guys? What happened after I got hit?"

Worth brought him up to date on the attack and the actions of Lieutenant Waugh. "That guy's something else, Aaron. And with Captain Macardo pulled up to battalion, Waugh's the acting company commander now. Everybody's happy with that."

"Is Slade still in charge of Second Platoon?"

"No—he got shot up in both legs. Didn't stop him, though. Crawled the rest of the way up that hill. He and some of the other wounded men held our position while the rest of us followed Waugh up the left side of the hill. We outflanked 'em. Surprised the hell out of those Jerries. Lieutenant Shingleton's got Second Platoon now."

"Shingleton—the guy from West Virginia?"

"Yeah." Worth wiped his razor clean and put it away. "He was an enlisted man—got a battlefield commission. Seems to know his stuff."

"So, what now?" Aaron asked.

"We're pushing the Krauts toward Rome. We'll link up with the guys from the Anzio beachhead soon. But first, we've gotta take a little town called Itri. Word is we'll be attacking it in the next day or so. You might wanna draw some extra ammo and rations. Comes in handy."

"Glad you're okay. What about Harry? And Art? The rest of the squad?"

"They're okay. Harry and Jack put up a hell of a fight when we were gettin' counterattacks. They were right in the middle, takin' heat all the way."

"Neither one of 'em hurt?"

"Nope, not a scratch. Not that the Jerries didn't try."

Aaron nodded. "Good. You and me gotta look after this crew—this outfit would be in bad shape without us Carolina boys. Well, I'm gonna go check in at the company CP. And draw some ammo and food. I can't tell you how much I've been missing those C-rations."

Worth laughed. "Yeah, I'll bet. After that hospital food you've been gobbling down, you'll think C-rations are dog food."

"Fitting food for us dogface soldiers, I guess."

"Get outta here. And now that you're back, you're digging the next slit trench."

The next morning, Worth nudged Aaron. "Wake up, Aaron."

Aaron grabbed his rifle. "What?"

"Waugh's dead. We just got the word."

"What! Ah, shit! What happened?"

"He and three other guys. They went to check out a report about German tanks movin' up from Itri. A mortar round caught 'em—killed 'em all."

Aaron shook his head. "Damn." He pounded the butt of his rifle into the ground. "Damn."

Worth looked straight ahead. "This war just got a lot more personal."

"Yeah," Aaron said. "The sooner we hit Itri, the better."

Worth sighed. "Oh, Furlong came by. The chaplain's having a prayer session in a few minutes. I'm going. You?"

Aaron paused. "Yeah, I guess so. I don't know how it's gonna help, but it can't hurt. Damn. I only met the guy once, but I really liked Waugh."

"Everybody did. Except the Germans."

Private Francis Furlong and a chaplain waited under a tree just outside the company area. Aaron and Worth joined a dozen or so other men already assembled there.

Furlong cleared his throat. "Men, I thought we should have the chaplain say a few words for Lieutenant Waugh and his men—and ask the Lord to be with us in our upcoming attack."

"Thank you, Francis. For those of you who don't know me, I'm Chaplain Powell. Let's open with a prayer." Powell bowed his head. "Dear Lord, we ask your blessings on those assembled here and ask that you be with the families of those who have lost loved ones..."

Twenty minutes later, Aaron and Worth walked back to their foxhole.

Worth shook his head as if to clear his thoughts. "I'm like you. I still can't believe he's gone. If you coulda seen him during the attack, it was like he was charmed. Not a scratch through the whole thing. Then one lousy mortar round gets him."

Aaron stared into the distance. "My mother says death is no respecter of persons. I never thought about that much 'til now. Anybody could be next."

Later, as Aaron and Worth cleaned their rifles, Aaron's stomach tightened. He'd returned just in time for another attack. Would he be wounded again? Or worse? Couldn't let himself think about it. They'd be fighting in a town. That meant house to house and building to building. Snipers could be a real problem. He'd have to keep his eyes open. He needed to think about something else.

He turned to Worth. "Say, about Furlong. What's with him and all this religious talk, anyway? He's startin' to sound like a chaplain."

Worth nodded. "He's an Episcopalian I think, and he's—well, he's serious about it. Almost like a preacher. He's a good guy. Just tryin' to live right, I guess."

"It's just, I get a little suspicious of folks who come on so strong with the church stuff," Aaron said as he ran a cleaning rod down his rifle barrel. "Our church back home has some people like that."

"Did you go regular?"

"Oh yeah. Every Sunday. And Sunday evening. And Wednesday night, too. Momma saw to it we never missed. But it never really took hold with me. All that shouting the preacher did. And folks yelling out,

*'Amen!'* Then sometimes a deacon or some other self-righteous so and so would come out in the congregation and try to drag some lost soul up front to be *'saved.'* It didn't seem right to me."

Worth looked up from the bayonet he was sharpening. "Sounds like you're a Baptist. Me too. I know what you mean. I'm not so sure about some of the methods, maybe, but I do believe. In God and all, I mean."

Aaron rammed the cleaning rod down the barrel again, pushing an oil-soaked patch down its length. "Yeah, I do too—I guess. Out here, though, I have to wonder where God is sometimes. Why does He let all this happen?"

"Can't answer that one, buddy. Just gotta keep the faith." Worth smiled.

"Right now, I'm putting my faith in this M-1. If the Lord's payin' attention, I sure hope He'll look after us." He inserted a clip into the rifle, let the bolt slam shut to chamber a round, and flicked on the safety. "I've got a feelin' we're gonna need it."

# CHAPTER TWENTY-FIVE

Maggie pushed the baby buggy down the street. The afternoon sun warmed her face and arms, and a slight breeze rustled her print summer dress. A new pair of shoes would be nice, some easier to walk in, but that would have to wait. Besides, it was only a half mile to the store. Except for the shoes that didn't quite match her dress, she would probably consider it a perfect day. Perfect if she wasn't so worried about everything.

She waved to Betty Chapman, who sat in a rocker on her front porch. Her husband Paul worked with Lloyd at the local cotton mill.

"How's little Barry?" Betty asked. She busily broke snap beans into a dishpan that sat on her lap.

"He's been a little colicky lately, but he seems better today," Maggie said.

"Well, a baby's gonna have that." She reached into the pail beside her for another handful of beans. "What do you hear from Aaron?"

"I got a letter day before yesterday. He's out of the hospital and going back to his squad or company or whatever they call it." Maggie shivered despite the heat of the June day. Please God, keep him safe.

"You goin' to the store?"

"Yes—it's too pretty to sit inside all day. Gotta get some things for Daddy's supper anyway."

Daddy. He'd started drinking again since Momma died. Just a little at first, but now it was every night. Momma would have a fit if she were still alive. Now it was up to her to look after Daddy. But it was so hard, especially with the baby. No wonder Momma looked tired all the time. Too much to do, too much to take care of. Poor Momma.

Barry stirred briefly in his sleep. How nice to be that much at peace. What she'd give for a restful sleep like that. Not likely to happen, though.

She passed the red brick mill on her right, crossed the railroad tracks, turned left, and stopped outside the company store on the main road next to the factory. She lifted the still sleeping baby, climbed the two plank steps to the wooden porch, and opened the screen door. A metal sign attached to it heralded the wonderful, refreshing flavor of RC Cola. Another sign just inside boasted to the rich, satisfying taste of Mail Pouch chewing tobacco. A ceiling fan suspended from a long shaft spun slowly overhead. The smell of fresh produce mingled with the aroma of soaps, leather goods, fruits and vegetables, and various other items in the little combination market and general store.

She inhaled the familiar aroma and smiled inwardly.

"Hello, Miss Maggie." Conrad Miller sat on a stool behind the checkout counter to the left of the entry door, newspaper in hand. Conrad's slight frame, balding head, and warm smile caused her to smile back at him. He'd managed the store for as long as she could remember.

"It still seems odd to me, seeing you all grown up with a baby and all," he said. "I still think of you as the little girl who used to come in here and buy candy from me every Saturday."

"Well, it's true. I'm not a little girl anymore," she said as she turned toward the first aisle.

Conrad put down the newspaper. "Anything I can get for you?" he asked.

She glanced at him over her shoulder as she selected one of the small shopping baskets. "No thanks. I've just gotta pick up a few things. Dad'll be home from work in a couple of hours. He'll be grumpy if I don't have something ready to eat."

Maggie shifted the baby to her left hip and collected the few items she needed. A bag of flour for biscuits—she liked Red Band. Some beans, a few potatoes, a bag of coffee. Even a cantaloupe—they looked ripe. She placed them in the basket. Now, sugar. Oh heavens, did she bring the ration stamps? Yes, thank goodness.

Carrying Barry and holding the basket was awkward, but she'd learned to manage the feat over the last several months. She continued around the store accumulating a few more items and then headed up the last aisle in the direction of the checkout register. Her eyes roamed the shelf containing cornmeal. Was Conrad out of the Linney's Mill brand?

"Well, hello there," someone said from behind her.

She turned. Howard Starnes. His wrinkled khaki work clothes appeared too tight for his bulging belly. A weathered felt hat sat back on his head.

"Oh hello, Mr. Starnes. How's your wife?"

The smile disappeared from his face.

"Jennie's fine, thanks."

Maggie reached for a small bag of cornmeal and placed it in the basket and continued moving toward the front of the store. Howard continued after her.

"I'm surprised to see you here, Mr. Starnes. Is the first shift over already?"

Howard shifted his weight from one foot to the other as if he might be nervous talking to her. "No, I had to go pick up a part for one of the looms that came in on the bus in town. Besides, your daddy and the other shift hands can manage for a few minutes without me."

Howard looked down at his scuffed work shoes then raised his head. "Say, how's that soldier-boy husband of yours?"

"I get letters every day," she lied. "He's doing well."

Howard chuckled. "Oh, I'll bet he is. Where is he? Italy? I hear there's a lot of hot-blooded women in that country. You better hope he doesn't latch on to one of 'em." Howard snickered.

Maggie stared at him.

Howard smiled. "I'm just kiddin', honey."

Howard looked around absently as if searching for something on an upper shelf. "Yep, it'd be a real shame if he decided to take up with some little floozy and leave you and this little fella to fend for yourselves."

Her face went hot. She spun toward him. "Don't say that, Howard! Aaron would never dream of doing something like that."

Howard took a step back with a look of surprise on his face. "I didn't mean nothing—I said I was kiddin'."

She turned away and hurried toward the checkout counter. Dadburn him! She had enough to worry about just praying Aaron wouldn't be killed. And what would she do if Aaron did find someone else? Tears formed in her eyes. She kept her face forward. Couldn't let him see how much his words had hurt.

Howard's footsteps sounded behind her. "I'm sorry, Maggie. I didn't mean to make you mad—really."

She ignored him and brushed her arm across her cheek as she reached the counter. "It's warm in here today, Mr. Miller. Maybe that fan needs to be running a little faster." She gave a quick glance behind her.

Howard wore what appeared to be a concerned look. Some nerve—him acting like he cared.

She set the basket next to the cash register. Conrad removed the items, entering the cost of each into the machine before cranking the handle on its side. It made the same *chink-chink, ka-chunk* sound she remembered from the days when she used to buy candy. Days that now seemed so long ago.

Howard stepped beside her and placed a box of cigars on the counter.

"A dollar and thirty-seven cents, Maggie," Conrad said. He placed the items in a paper bag but did not look at her. He nodded at Howard.

"Put these stogies on my tab, Conrad," Howard said.

Conrad flicked his eyes in Howard's direction. "Umm, sure, just as soon as I finish up with Mrs. Johnson here."

Maggie handed two one-dollar bills to Conrad along with the required ration stamps. He pushed the SALE button on the register. The cash drawer flew open with the familiar loud jingle. Conrad slid coins from the appropriate sections in the drawer's tray to make change. Each coin made a *schwick-schwick* sound as it rubbed against the metal drawer. Was he deliberately taking his time? To defy Howard?

Maggie took the offered change and placed it into the pocket at the side of her dress.

Doggone that Howard. She had half a notion to go tell his wife. But what good would that do? Jennie was a beaten-down, tired-looking woman who probably welcomed every minute Howard was away from home. Besides, what could she tell her? That Howard asked about Aaron? Or that she didn't like the way Howard made her feel when he looked at her?

Couldn't say anything to Daddy, either. He worked for Howard. But that wouldn't stop Lloyd from confronting or maybe even fighting him. She couldn't let that happen. She'd just have to avoid Howard somehow.

Maggie shifted Barry to her left hip, picked up the grocery bag with her other arm, and rushed outside. She had just finished putting Barry and her purchases into the buggy when Howard stepped onto the porch. He came down the steps and stood beside her.

"I'm sorry, Maggie. I know I came on a little strong in there. I just happen to like you, that's all. Say, I've got my truck here," he said, motioning to a dirty Model A pickup. "How 'bout I give you a ride to your house? There's no need for you to walk that far by yourself."

"I'm not by myself, Mr. Starnes," she said, forcing a smile. "I have Barry with me. We'll be fine, but thanks anyway."

Howard shook his head. "Suit yourself then. You know, things don't have to be so tough on you. There's folks that'd be willing to help you out if you'd let 'em."

Maggie's hands gripped the handle of the carriage. She took a long breath and then looked at him.

"I'm just fine, Mr. Starnes—really. I like to walk. Besides, don't you need to get back inside the mill before the quittin' time whistle blows? I'd feel bad if you got in trouble because of me."

Howard chuckled. "I'm not worried about that. I'm out on company business. But say, you look out for yourself and your daddy. He's not gettin' any younger, you know."

Was that a threat? Maggie did not reply. She nodded to Howard, then maneuvered the buggy around the building and retraced her route across the railroad tracks. The bumping motion as she crossed the tracks caused the baby to stir. His little face contorted.

"Oh Barry, don't cry, sweetheart!" She lifted him from the carriage. "It's okay, honey, its okay. Everything's gonna be okay. We'll be home in just a minute. Every thing'll be fine, I promise." She patted his back and caressed the back of his head. A tear dropped from her face onto the baby's fine blond hair.

She looked upward into the blue summer sky. A bank of dark clouds covered the sky to the west. She sighed. Would things ever really be okay again?

## CHAPTER TWENTY-SIX

Lieutenant Hoy Shingleton stood before the men of Second Platoon. An ever-present smell filled the air—a combination of acrid smoke mingled with the scent of earth and dead things. Mostly farm animals—horses, cows, sheep, mules—unlucky enough to get caught in machine gun or artillery fire. Probably dead soldiers, too.

Shingleton's eyes scanned the group. "We're spearheadin' the battalion's attack on the town of Itri. Jump-off is at oh-six hundred tomorrow."

The sun beat down on Aaron's back. The weight of his helmet seemed to be pushing his neck down into his shoulders. If only he could take it off—once the steel heated up, it was like an oven.

"Intelligence indicates the town is only moderately defended, whatever that means. Our artillery has blasted the hell out of the place for days, so who knows what we'll find. Whatever it is, it's up to us to take it. We'll attack straight down the road leading into the place. Third Platoon will attack from the southeast shortly after we make the initial assault. First Platoon will guard our left flank and be in reserve if we need 'em. Don't short yourselves on ammo."

Shingleton placed his hands on his hips. "Check over your gear, write letters home, whatever. Then get some sleep—tomorrow's gonna be a long day."

A bead of sweat ran down Aaron's back. This was it. His first action since returning from the hospital. How would he do? The other guys were more seasoned now—more accustomed to battle. Could he take it? No choice. He had to push the fear down—he *had* to take it.


Just before sunrise, Lieutenant Shingleton waved his men forward. They double-timed in two columns down the road, rifles at the ready. Aaron and Worth followed close behind Shingleton and his radio man, Corporal Pearson.

Shingleton half turned, speaking over his shoulder. "Let's go! Let's go! Move, move! Don't stop."

As the town came into sight, German machine guns opened fire. Some GIs dove into the ditches that ran parallel to the road.

"Keep moving!" Shingleton yelled. "Get up! You can't stay here!"

Most rose from the ditch and ran to catch up. Others refused to budge at first, but they eventually followed.

Bullets zinged over Aaron's head. Another burst ricocheted off the road in front of him. He zigged to the right. Bullets flew by his left ear. Good thing he didn't zig left. Still close. Too close.

His breath came in gasps. His legs ached. They'd all be killed if they didn't find cover fast.

Worth ran beside him. They reached the first row of small, two-story shops along with Shingleton and Pearson. Others made their way to adjacent structures and whatever other cover they could find.

"We've gotta get a fix on those machine guns and take 'em out," Shingleton yelled above the noise.

"I'm pretty sure I saw flashes from the second-story window just ahead, sir," Aaron said.

"Same here," Worth said, pointing. "And from the ground-floor window to the left of it."

"Pearson," Shingleton ordered, "signal the machine gunners. Have our thirty-calibers give us covering fire on those two locations."

From behind them machine gun rounds poured into the walls and windows of the buildings ahead. Dust and mortar chips flew. Glass shattered.

At Shingleton's signal, he, Aaron, and Worth ducked into the street. Pearson followed with the radio. Bullets smacked into the walls around them. Aaron's chest tightened. He couldn't breathe. Beads of perspiration ran down his face and stung his eyes.

Racing to an open doorway just ahead, Aaron followed Shingleton inside. Worth and Pearson tumbled in behind him just as a burst of automatic fire tore into the outside wall. Seconds later, Corporal Wagner, with his BAR, crashed into the room and fell to his knees, panting.

"You all right, boy?" Shingleton said.

"Y-yes." Wagner's chest heaved. "Sir."

"Good, 'cause we're gonna need that BAR."

Aaron peeked out the window. There—the flash of a machine gun. "Lieutenant, if Wagner can direct some fire onto the gun in the upstairs window, and you and Pearson cover me I'll see if I can get close enough to put some grenades into that ground-floor opening where the other gun is."

"Done," Wagner said as he fed a fresh magazine into the Browning.

"Go!" Shingleton said.

Wagner pushed the automatic rifle through the window and fired a long burst. Aaron sprinted out the door and made for another doorway ten yards ahead. Ducking into it, he pulled the pin on a grenade, took a deep breath, stepped partway into the street, and hurled it toward the window. Seemingly from nowhere, Worth appeared and flung another grenade at the same window, then squeezed into the door frame behind Aaron.

Wagner and the others continued the covering fire. Aaron turned to Worth. "You ready?"

"Let's go!" Worth yelled.

They ran to the window, firing as they went. Aaron reached the side of the building and pressed his back into the rough-textured wall to the left of the opening. Worth did the same on the other side. Smoke from their grenades poured from within.

Sweat ran down Aaron's face. His hands were clammy. Now what? He needed to reload his M-1, for one thing.

The muzzle of a Mauser rifle poked out through the billowing smoke. Its operator fired a round down the street.

Aaron looked at Worth and pulled the pin on another grenade. He wheeled to his left and tossed it inside.

A muffled cry echoed within.

Fumbling noises. Hurried movement.

The smoking grenade popped back out the window.

Aaron ducked back. Worth scooped it up, pushed it through the window, and spun away from the window just as it exploded.

Aaron looked at Worth, eyes wide, and blew out a long breath that puffed his cheeks. "You idiot."

Worth grinned and stuffed a fresh clip into his M-1. Aaron followed suit.

"Let's see if we can get into the other building and get that second gun," Aaron said.

"I think Harry's beat us to it," Worth said. "He and Jack Claytor just went in."

Moments later the upstairs window of the second machine gun position exploded outward.

"They got it!" Worth shouted.

As Aaron whooped a victory yell, it caught in his throat. A German soldier popped out from behind a stone wall ahead and aimed his rifle at them from forty yards away.

"Down!" Aaron yelled as he ducked. A bullet smashed into the wall just above his head.

Worth raised his M-1 and fired. The German toppled to the ground. His coal scuttle helmet rolled onto the stone pavement.

"We gotta get off this street and find cover!" Aaron said. Worth was already moving toward another doorway. Aaron dove into it behind Worth just as a sniper round impacted the pavement where he'd been standing. Seconds later the sound of fire from an automatic rifle filled the air. Smiling, Wagner stuck his head inside the doorway. "Come on, you guys. I blasted that SOB! Let's go get some more of 'em!"

For the remainder of the morning, G Company men cleared the town. Three more machine guns were taken and several snipers killed or wounded. A number of prisoners were herded toward the rear, their hands behind their heads. The main body of the enemy force appeared to have pulled out, heading north.

At the far end of town, Aaron and Worth joined Harry Klutz outside yet another stone building. White smoke billowed from the chimney. Harry placed his finger to his ear and nodded toward the doorway.

Aaron returned the nod and motioned for Harry to kick in the door.

Harry kicked hard. The door fell off its hinges. Aaron and Worth rushed in.

A German soldier stood to Aaron's left, hoisting an MP-40 submachine gun. Aaron fired two rounds from the hip and the German fell. To the right, another German fed papers into the fireplace. He spun toward them, a P-38 pistol in his hand. Worth fired, catching the

Werhmacht trooper in the shoulder, spinning him around. The handgun clattered to the floor. "*Kamerad! Kamerad!*" he shouted, holding up his one good arm.

"Get a medic in here," Aaron said.

Harry kept his rifle on the officer while Aaron cleared the adjoining room. When he returned, he passed the wounded man. A field telephone and a thick folder sat on a small table.

"Well, look what I found." Aaron leafed through the papers.

"What is it?" Harry asked.

"Hard to tell," Aaron said. "Maps. Some other papers. I can't tell exactly. We gotta get these to Lieutenant Shingleton, ASAP."

"They're nothing," the German said in heavily accented English.

"Oh yeah?" Harry said. "Then why were you burning them?"

"Why're you still here, anyway?" Aaron asked. "Why didn't you clear out like the rest of your troops?"

"Orders—I had my orders." The German stiffened. "In my army, we follow orders. Not like you Americans who fight like gangsters."

"You better save your strength," Aaron said, pointing at the blood seeping through the wounded man's tunic. "You're gonna need it. I'd guess you're gonna get questioned pretty good after our docs patch you up."

# Chapter Twenty-seven

Aaron, panting, ran to Shingleton and saluted. He drew a quick breath. "Lieutenant, we thought you should see this stuff."

"Calm down, Johnson. What is it?"

"Some maps and papers we took from a German we captured."

"Who's 'we'?"

"Me, Haynes, and Harry Klutz, sir."

Shingleton took the documents Aaron extended toward him. He rubbed his chin as he quickly thumbed through them. "Hmm—can't say what to make of this, but we'd better get these to battalion right away. Johnson, take this stuff and go with Corporal Pearson to the battalion CP. Make sure Lieutenant Colonel English gets these things."

Aaron located Pearson. "Do you know where the battalion CP's set up?"

"No, but we'll find it. Can't be that far behind us—we'll ask somebody. Move it. I've gotta get a part for one of the radios or the old man's gonna have my ass."

They moved fast, passing through the captured streets of Itri and down the road leading out of town. There they flagged down a jeep that was headed toward them.

The jeep rolled to a stop as they saluted the major who sat in the passenger seat.

"Sir, can you tell us where the battalion CP is?" Pearson said.

"In an old farmhouse about a mile back. You'll see some trucks and jeeps parked outside—you can't miss it. Be careful, a sniper took a shot at us as we came up the road. Just as we approached an abandoned Kraut tank. The fire came from our left." The major motioned to the driver, and they sped away.

Around a bend and two hundred yards farther on, they cautiously approached the burned-out tank. Pearson peeked his head around it.

A shot rang out. The round ricocheted off the side of the tank inches from his face.

"Where'd that come from?" Pearson said.

Aaron motioned with his chin. "From those trees on the far side of this field."

Pearson appeared to be pondering their options. "Whaddya think we should do?"

"See if you can get a bead on him while I make a break for that pile of rocks at the edge of the field," Aaron said.

"No—all I've got is this little carbine—it don't have the range. You've got the M-1. I'll go. Just cover my ass."

Aaron swallowed hard. "Roger."

"One, two, three," Pearson said, and then broke for the rock pile. A shot came from the trees, kicking up dirt just behind him.

Aaron braced his rifle on the tank and fired three quick shots into the trees. A minute later he cautiously inched his head above the tank. Another shot rang out. The bullet whizzed over him. Aaron's chest tightened. That was too close, dammit.

Aaron looked at Pearson, now crouched behind the rocks. What now?

Pearson held two fingers up to his eyes and then gestured toward the trees. Aaron nodded. He found a spot between the tank's turret and its chassis where he could safely view the tree line.

Pearson removed his helmet and stuck it on the barrel of his carbine. Slowly, he lifted it above the pile of rocks.

Aaron grimaced. That old movie cowboy trick? Did Pearson really think the German would fall for that?

A shot. The helmet flew ten feet away from the rock pile.

Aaron fired three shots where he'd seen the flash of the sniper's rifle.

A guttural sound echoed from the trees. The German stumbled into the open and fell, the Mauser tumbling to the ground beside him.

Pearson looked at Aaron and smiled. "Good shootin'. You always that accurate?"

"Uhh—yeah," Aaron said. He let out a long breath. Except when he wasn't.

Pearson retrieved his helmet. He turned it over and stuck his finger through the round bullet hole.

He shook his head. "I'm gonna go make sure he's dead. Cover me."

Pearson moved toward the downed enemy rifleman. Aaron stood behind the tank, M-1 at the ready. When Pearson reached the gray-clad form, he poked at him with the carbine. Stepping back, he fired three quick rounds into the prostrate figure.

Aaron blinked. What the hell?

Pearson rejoined him.

"Why'd you shoot him again?"

Pearson stared at Aaron. "I wasn't taking any chances. Besides, that bastard put a hole in my helmet."

Ten minutes later, the two arrived at battalion headquarters. Pearson set off to find the part he needed while Aaron asked where he could find Lieutenant Colonel English.

"The G-2 guys will want to see these," English said. "Tell Shingleton I said thanks. Good work. What's your name, Private?"

"Johnson, sir."

"How was it up there?"

"They put up a bit of a fight, sir, but we pushed 'em out."

"Casualties?"

"I heard we lost several men, sir. A good number wounded."

"I'll get the official reports in the morning. Thanks again, Private. You'd better get back to your company—it'll be dark soon. It's probably not a good idea to be roaming around after dark. The Jerries likely left some snipers behind."

"Yessir—we took out a sniper on the way here, sir."

"There could be more. Not to mention the possibility of gettin' shot by one of our own sentries," English said.

# CHAPTER TWENTY-EIGHT

"Damn, Pearson, it's already dusk. We ain't gonna make it back to the company before dark," Aaron said.

"Yeah, you're right. We shoulda started out earlier. Major Collins held me up, askin' a bunch of questions about the attack. Why didn't he come up and find out for himself if he wanted to know so bad?"

Aaron gazed at the sky. The sun sat low on the western horizon. Gray clouds covered the sky. No break in the heat even with the approaching sunset. A smoky haze hung in the air. Above, a flight of B-25 Mitchell bombers headed south.

"They must be returning from a bombing run up north," Aaron said, motioning to the planes.

"Yeah, flyboys," Pearson said. "They'll be sleeping in nice warm beds tonight. A hot meal waiting for 'em when they land. But not us— not the infantry. We sleep in a muddy hole in the ground and eat cold rations."

"I tried to enlist in the Air Corps," Aaron said, shielding his eyes as he continued looking skyward. "They wouldn't take me."

Pearson smirked. "Yeah, well, look what your willingness to join up got ya. Drafted. Infantry. Don't you feel lucky?"

"Well, lucky or not," Aaron said, "we better hole up somewhere 'til morning. I doubt either of us has slept in over forty-eight hours—I'm dog tired."

"I'm past tired," Pearson said. "Besides, I don't want to risk getting shot going into the company tonight. The sentries are gonna be jumpy as hell after today's battle. Or worse, we get lost and stumble into some uncleared minefield…"

Aaron tapped Pearson's sleeve. "Look, a house up ahead. Maybe we won't have to sleep outside after all."

Pearson grinned. "Let's check it out."

As they drew close to the dilapidated structure, Pearson let out a low whistle. "Man—this place has been shot up bad. Holes in the roof, windows shattered, shutters barely hangin' on."

A partially open door hung at a crazy angle. Aaron pushed it fully open and entered. He trained his M-1 around the left side of the room. Pearson swept his carbine to the right. Except for a rough-hewn wooden table and chair and a stone fireplace in the corner, the room was deserted. Paper and shattered glass littered the dusty floor. A closed doorway on the far side of the room presumably led to a bedroom.

"Looks like whoever lived here cleared out in a hurry," Pearson said.

Aaron started toward the closed doorway.

"Forget it," Pearson said. "Ain't gonna be any Jerries this far behind the line."

Aaron nodded. "Okay, let's eat and get some shut-eye. I'm bushed."

They opened C-rations and, after gulping down the contents, curled up in separate corners of the room and immediately fell asleep.

Aaron awoke the next morning as sunlight streamed through a broken window. He stretched and yawned. "Wake up, Pearson. We gotta get outta here."

Pearson stirred, rose to a sitting position, and rubbed his eyes. "Oh, keep your shirt on, Johnson, you worry too much. I've got a can of Spam in my pack, and I'm not going anywhere 'til I eat. If you're in such a hurry to get back to the war, take off and I'll see you later."

"Uh-uh," Aaron said. "We're stickin' together. Besides, I've got some myself. Let's get a fire going."

Using wood from a smashed chair for fuel, Aaron soon had a small fire going in the fireplace.

Pearson opened the containers of meat. He cut the slabs into slices, dropped them into the metal plates from their mess kits, and placed them on the rusted metal grate in the fireplace. Soon the meat sizzled and the air was filled with the unmistakable smell of frying Spam.

Aaron cocked his head to one side. "Did you hear something?"

Pearson looked around the room. "Uh-uh. You must be a little..."

The doorway on the far side of the room burst open. Two gray-clad Germans filled the door frame.

Aaron grabbed his rifle.

*"Nein! Nein!"* The Germans waved their hands high above their heads. No visible weapons. No ammo belts. The taller of the two looked from Aaron to Pearson. *"Kamerad, kamerad."*

"Jesus, where the hell did they come from?" Pearson shouted. "Keep those hands up!" He made an upward motion with the barrel of his carbine. *"Schnell! Schnell!"*

Aaron removed his finger from the M-1's trigger and frowned at Pearson. "Pipe down, will ya? They've already got their hands up. If they wanted to hurt us, they coulda done that already. Damn. They had to be in that room beside us all night, for Chrissakes. Why didn't we check it out? Jesus!"

Aaron followed the gaze of the Germans as they eyed the Spam. "They musta smelled that food heatin' up and decided to give up. What do we do now?" Aaron said.

"I'll tell you what we do." Pearson raised the carbine from hip level to his shoulder.

A look of pure fear leapt into the Germans' eyes. *"Nein, nein,"* they pleaded, waving their hands to emphasize they had no weapons.

Aaron licked his lips. What to do? Maybe Pearson was right. Besides, who'd ever know the difference? Two Jerries stormed the house and got themselves killed. But could he live with that? What would Maggie think? Or his mother?

Momma. He could almost hear her voice: *Do unto others...*

Aaron shook his head. "No. It's one thing to kill 'em if we was in a battle or if they'd tried to kill us, but if we shoot 'em in cold blood—no. Besides, they don't have any fight left. Look. They musta been cut off from their unit days ago—they look half starved. Probably ain't eat in days. Uniforms all ragged—no rifles. Uh-uh. All they wanna do is give up—and eat."

Pearson shifted his grip on the carbine. "I don't trust 'em. How do we know this ain't a trick? That there ain't others waitin' outside to ambush us?"

Aaron shook his head. "They wouldn'ta sent these two in here unarmed. They'da just busted in here shootin'."

Pearson narrowed his eyes.

The Germans' hands shook. Their hollow, red-rimmed eyes darted between Aaron and Pearson. *"Kamerad, kamerad, nein schutzen, nein schutzen!"*

"Pearson," Aaron said, "we're takin' 'em with us. If you try to shoot them, I'll turn my M-1 on you. I mean it."

"You think they'd let us live if things was the other way around?"

"Right now they're just scared and hungry. Put your weapon down—now."

"I outrank you, you know."

"Right now that don't matter. Put it down."

Pearson glared at Aaron. After a long moment, he sighed and lowered his carbine.

Aaron gestured for the Germans to come farther into the room. He pointed to the two mess kits. "Eat," he said, moving his hand to his mouth.

They broke for the mess kits and quickly devoured the food. Aaron then took some K-rations from his field jacket pocket and tossed them to the two as well. They nodded their thanks but cast wary eyes at Pearson as they ripped open the packages.

Pearson sat against the far wall and munched on some item he took from his pack. He did not look at Aaron.

Holding his rifle in one hand, Aaron fished into his jacket again and removed a small package of crackers. He ripped open the wrapper with his teeth and wolfed them down.

When the rations were gone, Aaron and Pearson pulled on their packs and motioned the prisoners to put their hands on their heads and move to the door. Outside, they passed the rear corner of the house. Aaron glanced to his right. The Germans' rifles and ammunition belts lay on the ground outside the window of the room they had occupied.

"See that?" Aaron said. "They coulda killed us if they'd wanted to. We wouldn't have had a chance."

Pearson made no comment.

The trip to the company line was uneventful, the two Germans obediently walking ahead of the GIs. On arriving at their platoon, they approached Worth Haynes, who sat in a foxhole cleaning his rifle.

"Worth, have you seen Lieutenant Shingleton?" Aaron asked.

Worth stared up at the prisoners. "He's right over there," he said, motioning to his left.

Aaron turned. Shingleton and a uniformed man he did not recognize stood twenty yards away. The unidentified man held a notepad and pencil in his hand.

Aaron and Pearson marched their prisoners toward them.

"Well, well. Lookie what we got here. Where'd you find these two guys?" Shingleton said.

Aaron briefly explained.

Shingleton turned to the man with the notepad. "Well, you wanted a story. Can you use this?"

"I sure can." He turned to Aaron and Pearson. "I'm Matheson, a reporter with *Stars and Stripes*. Tell me what happened."

The two described the event as the reporter took notes. He then asked each of them where he was from and wrote that information down as well.

"This is a great story, men. Two GIs spend the night in the same house with a coupla Germans—neither knowing the other is there. My editor's gonna love this. You're gonna be written up in our next issue. I'll make sure your hometown newspapers get the story too. Now, let me get a few more details. Tell me again—exactly what did you do when they walked in on you?"

"Well…" Aaron said.

Pearson stepped in front of Aaron. "Johnson here grabbed his rifle soon as they came through the door, but I saw right away they was unarmed. So I says to him, 'Don't shoot, they're trying to surrender…'"

Aaron opened his mouth then shut it. Why bother?

# Chapter Twenty-nine

Maggie bent down on one knee before Barry. "Hold still, honey. Let me comb your hair."

Juanita, Maggie's younger sister, stood in the doorway, holding a brown leather purse. A trim brunette like her two sisters, Juanita had extremely dark eyes, so much so her nickname had been "Black-Eye" for as long as Maggie could remember.

"Come on, Magdalene," Juanita said. "Ella's waiting. And I need to get to town—gotta find some things to wear to my graduation next week."

Maggie smiled. Only her sisters called her by her full name. "I'm comin'—just give me a sec to get Barry settled." She gave the tow-headed boy a kiss on the forehead. "Now you be good for Daddy Lloyd, and I'll bring you some candy from town."

The toddler giggled. He looked so cute in his little overalls and the matching shirt she'd bought him.

"Don't worry," Lloyd said, "we're gonna have a good time. I might make him into a bird hunter while you're gone. Or maybe we'll go fishin'."

"Oh Daddy, you know he's too little for that. I've gotta go or I'm gonna get left." She hugged Barry one last time and headed for the door. Too bad she couldn't take him, but he just wasn't old enough yet. Besides, she needed some time with her sisters. This was the first time they'd been out together since their mother died.

Ella—Uzella, officially—sat behind the wheel of Buck's pickup. Another brunette, but with naturally curly hair, she looked the most like their mother and laughed as easily as their mother had. Three years older than Maggie, she'd married Buck as soon as she finished school. A year later she had her first child—a boy. Poor Ronald took sick and died before he was two—some kind of blood disease, the doctor said. Now Ella had another boy, Kelly—only a few months older than Barry.

Juanita and Maggie crowded onto the dusty vehicle's bench seat.

"How'd you manage to get the truck?" Juanita said.

Ella shifted into third gear and glanced at her. "I told Buck I had to get Kelly some clothes. I dropped him by the mill—we'll be back before his shift is over. He just don't want me using all the gas, what with the rationing and all."

"You won't," Maggie said. "It's only five miles to town—that can't take all that much gas."

"Oh, he's not really worried. We always have stamps—we never go anywhere hardly."

"Oh, Magdalene. Look at these shoes. Aren't they pretty?" Juanita held them up for her to see.

Maggie smiled. "They'll look nice with your graduation dress, too. You should get 'em."

Juanita spun around. "I'm gonna show them to Ella. Where is she, anyway?"

"I think she's trying to find Kelly some jeans—over in the boys' department," Maggie said.

"And I finally found some," Ella said as she approached them. "That boy's already outgrown all his clothes. Barry will be getting some hand-me-downs soon, Magdalene."

"There's the saleslady," Juanita said. "I'm gonna see if they have these in my size." She hurried away, carrying the display shoes.

Ella laughed. "Juanita's really excited about graduating, isn't she?"

"Yes," Maggie said as she picked up a cotton blouse. "She doesn't know how good she's got it. I'd sure like to be back in school. The way things were before the war. Now all the guys in my class are drafted and overseas, like Aaron. And the girls—we're either working in the mill or raising babies. I don't know the last time I saw Mary Lilly. Hmm—this top might go with that blue skirt of mine. What do you think?"

Ella wrinkled her nose and cocked her head to one side as she eyed the blouse. "Maybe—how much is it?"

Maggie looked at the price tag. "Oooh—more than I can pay. Too bad."

Juanita returned carrying a bag marked with the store's logo. "I got 'em. Where to now?"

"Buck said to look for some work shirts for him. The men's stuff is over there," Ella said, motioning to her left.

"I'll come with you," Juanita said. "I saw a nice-looking guy working in that department last time I was here."

"He's probably been drafted by now," Maggie said. "You two go ahead—I'm going next door. I'll find you in a bit."

Maggie entered the open door of the hardware store, pausing inside to let her eyes adjust to the dim light. The smells so familiar to all hardware stores reached her—a dusty, musty, oily sort of fragrance mixed with a metallic and leathery scent. Her eyes roamed the store—nails, garden tools, men's boots, fishing rods, and a rack of rifles and shotguns. A black and white dog lay in the aisle in front of her. He raised his head and thumped his tail on the wooden floor as she walked past.

"Help you find something, ma'am?" The clerk, a short, heavyset man wearing a short-sleeved shirt and khaki pants, came toward her. He smiled. "Hot, ain't it?"

"Yes," Maggie said.

The man's smile broadened. "Is that 'yes, I can help you' or 'yes, it's hot'?"

"Both," Maggie said, returning his smile. "I'm looking for a hunting knife for my husband."

"Well, we've got 'em. He's a big hunter, is he?"

"Not really—he's in the Army. In Italy. He wrote me—asked me to send him one."

"Knives are right over here. How long a blade are you—or he—looking for?"

"I—I don't have any idea. Aren't all hunting knife blades the same?"

He chuckled. "Oh no, ma'am. There's lots of different blade lengths—from five or six inches to ten or twelve. I doubt he'd want one more than seven or eight, though, if that."

Maggie frowned. "Can I just look at some? Maybe that'll give me some idea."

"Sure, just look these over," he said, pointing to a glass-fronted case.

Peering in, Maggie's eyes scanned the dozen or so knives arrayed on the two shelves. She stooped and looked closely at the different examples.

"Let me see that one," she said, pointing. "The third one from the left—with the whitish looking handle."

"Excellent choice," the man said. "That's a genuine bone-handled grip—really sets it off nice, don't it? And the good thing about it is, even if it gets wet, that type of bone never gets slippery in your hand." He reached into the counter and removed the item along with its leather sheath. "I think that length blade would be about right, too."

Maggie wrapped her fingers around the hilt. "I like it. Is this a good brand?"

"Oh yes," the clerk said. "One of the best we carry."

Maggie's brow wrinkled. "How much is it?"

"It's—let me find the box." He stooped behind the counter and rose with a long, narrow cardboard box. "It's four dollars and ninety-five cents—but since it's going to a soldier overseas and all, I can take ten percent off that."

Maggie dug into her purse. "I'll take it."

Back at her father's home, with Barry sleeping in the next room, Maggie took the boxed knife and set it on the table in front of her. She picked up Lloyd's fountain pen and wrote.

Dear Aaron,

> I hope you are okay. Things are going pretty well here— it's hot, but that's to be expected. I try not to worry about you, but sometimes I can't help it. I listen to the news every night, but they don't say much about Italy. I pray that means things aren't so bad there. It sounds like the guys in the Pacific are really having it rough. I went shopping in town with Ella and Juanita today. Daddy kept Barry, and I think Dad was really glad to see me when we got back. Barry wore him out. I wish you could see him. I'm sending a picture so you can see how much he's grown. And I found a hunting knife like you asked for. The man at Carson's Hardware said it is a good one. I liked the handle. Well, that's about it from here. Please write when you can. I miss you so.
> Love,
> Maggie

# Chapter Thirty

The entire division marched north along Highway 7 toward Rome. Tanks, jeeps, and supply trucks roared by, raising massive clouds of dust. GIs loaded down with rifles and field packs moved up both sides of the road. The men of G Company occupied their assigned position near the middle of the long column.

Aaron peered over his shoulder at the town of Itri. A heavy black haze floated above it. The acrid smell of charred wood and burning debris hung in the air, and even from half a mile away the smoke stung his eyes. A church steeple poked from among the smoldering ruins. Was God in that church? In that town? Sure didn't seem like He was anywhere around when the shootin' started. Why would He let a nice little town like that be the scene of such death and devastation?

"How far is it to Rome?" someone behind him asked.

Aaron shook his head. What difference did it make? Just keep quiet and march.

"The lootenant said about ninety kil-o-meters," someone else answered.

"What's a kil-o-meter?" another voice asked.

Aaron smiled. Dogfaces. Always gotta talk.

"It's a thing the Jerries use to keep score of how many of us they knock off," Jack Claytor said.

"Knock it off yourself, screwball. You'll scare the new guys," Harry Klutz said. "And it's not 'kil-o-meter,' you idiot. It's 'kuh-lom-it-er.' About five-eighths of a mile."

"Well, ain't you the math genius," Patrick Davis said. "How'd you get so smart?"

Harry grinned. "I stayed awake in school—you obviously didn't."

"Hmmpf," Davis said. "Fat lotta good it did ya. You're still in the infantry—"

A sound like someone ripping a bed sheet pierced the air.

"Take cover!"

The 105-millimeter round exploded somewhere behind Aaron. Shoulders hunched, bent at the waist, he sprinted for the roadside ditch. He dove into it just as another shell exploded a hundred yards away. The earth shook as more and more shells landed.

Vile-tasting muck from the ditch filled his open mouth. He spat and reached for his canteen. The blasts came closer. He crammed his helmet tight to his head and drew his knees up to his chest. The canteen could wait. He spat again.

Each blast sent shrapnel whining and zinging through the air. Aaron buried his face in the muck. Please, please, no airbursts.

Another massive blast rocked the ground. Dirt and debris rained down around him. He formed himself into an even tighter ball and clamped both hands over his ears. Dear God! Make it stop!

A man somewhere behind him screamed, "My leg! Oh God! My leg!"

"Medic! Medic!" someone yelled.

Frank Church, carrying his aid kit, rushed by Aaron, headed toward the wounded man. More cries for help rang out up and down the line. Stretcher-bearers hustled by, crouched low and moving fast. How did those guys do it?

The barrage lasted for ten minutes.

"On your feet," someone from ahead shouted. "Double-time!"

"Double-time, my ass," Davis said. "I'm too tired for single-time."

Aaron stumbled to his feet. He couldn't agree more.

"Shut up and move," Shingleton said. "We gotta get outta here."

Aaron joined the rest of his platoon. How long could he keep going? He glanced behind him. Church and the other medics and stretcher-bearers tended to several wounded men. A lone combat boot sat upright in the road. A torn, bloody pants leg extended from it. Aaron's mouth fell open. Was that part of a leg in the boot? Nausea gripped him.

Another medic, Jacobs, gave a morphine shot to a man lying on a stretcher. His face was chalk-white. His right arm was missing. Farther down the road, a number of bodies had already been covered with blankets. They were beyond help.

Aaron quickened his pace. Maybe he wasn't too tired to move after all. He looked at the sky. God—why?

At noon on the third day of marching, crawling, cowering, and fighting, Hoy Shingleton halted the platoon. "Fall out. Ten minutes. Smoke 'em if you got 'em."

Aaron plopped by the roadside. He'd never been so tired. Or so scared. From their positions on the hills ahead, the Germans could shell them at any time. And if a 105 or an 88 had your name on it—oh well. He lit a Lucky Strike and took a deep drag. A Pall Mall would have been better, but he didn't have any. Maybe there'd be some in the next ration package. His buddies sat or lay on the ground nearby. Some slept, falling asleep as soon as they collapsed to the ground. Others, like Aaron, smoked and eyed the terrain ahead.

"Damn!" Art Ferdinand said. "Look at those hills!"

Jack Claytor nodded. "Steep—worse than hill seventy-nine even. They're gonna be dug in there tight as ticks. The brass expects us to take that ground?"

Shingleton gave the two a long look. "And we will. Everybody listen up. Orders are to drop your packs, take only the essentials. Supplies and whatever else we can't carry will be brought up by truck or mule train. First Battalion's in the lead, then us.

"There's a little town ahead of us in those hills called Sonnino. It's heavily defended. First Battalion will attack head-on. We're gonna push our way to some higher ground overlooking the town. Our job will be to pin the Krauts down while the First goes in. Any questions?"

Aaron looked at the men around him. For once they'd been dealt a good card—better than First Battalion, anyway.

Two miles farther on, First Battalion swung to the left. Aaron and the rest of Second Battalion veered right and spread out, swarming up a steep hillside covered in scrub brush and olive trees. Aaron crouched low, moved fast. The earth had a damp, earthy scent much like his father's apple orchard after a fall rain. It would be time to pick those apples soon. Come on, Johnson—stay alert. Or you won't be around to pick any more of anything.

Sporadic rifle fire sounded from the crest of the hill above. A lone machine gun chimed in. Aaron ducked lower, moved faster.

"Don't stop!" Shingleton shouted. "They'll box us in with mortars! Keep moving!"

It took thirty minutes to reach the top. Several machine guns were destroyed and a number of prisoners taken. The Germans appeared dazed and confused, maybe even surprised to have been overrun in such a short time.

"Dig in—find cover," Shingleton said. "Be ready to fire when I give the word."

Aaron stared at the mountain town below. Situated in a valley ringed by steep hills on either side, it was neither large nor small. A typical town square sat in the center, with a fountain surrounded by a number of stone and stucco-looking buildings. No movement. No sign of Germans or civilians.

He shifted his gaze. First Battalion men moved forward. As they neared the outskirts of town, they began firing. The Germans returned the fire, and white smoke from their weapons puffed from the windows and drifted away in the breeze. The sounds of M-1s, carbines, and Thompsons mingled with those of the Mausers and burp guns. The GIs' .30-caliber Brownings opened up. German MG-42s responded.

"Pour it on!" Shingleton yelled. Every weapon in Second Battalion opened up, sweeping the buildings below with devastating covering fire. Aaron's ears rang from the deafening cacophony. The smell of burned powder permeated the air.

Concentrating his M-1's fire on the windows of several buildings, Aaron emptied several clips. Was he helping at all? Who could tell? At least the Germans weren't shooting back at him.

Men of First Battalion scrambled forward in groups of two or three. Aaron bit his lip. Come on, guys. Get in there quick. German fire felled two men as they scrambled toward a house. More men moved up and threw grenades into the window. After the grenades exploded, a man with a tommy gun kicked in the door and let go a long burst. Soldiers poured into Sonnino, continuing to fire and move.

"Cease fire! Cease fire!" Shingleton waved his arms. "First Battalion's in the town! Hold your fire."

Intermittent small arms fire echoed up the hill for another hour as the GIs cleared the buildings.

Then stillness.

As dusk fell, Aaron joined Worth and a group of others from the platoon sprawled on the ground among an outcropping of rocks. Aaron scanned the group. Every man looked haggard, exhausted. Dark circles under their eyes hinted at premature old age.

Harry Klutz removed his combat boots and massaged his feet. "Did you hear what the Jerry commander told Captain Carroll from B Company? Told him they were totally surprised. Said they never thought we could get to 'em over these mountains."

"I'll tell you one thing," Charles Bradley said, "if they was surprised, I sure hate to think how much harder they woulda fought if they'da known we was comin'." He frowned as he spooned something brown from a small ration tin. "It's still a long way to Rome, boys. Say, Worth, whaddya think this is?" he said, extending the spoon toward him.

"Beats me," Worth said, recoiling. "A chunk of beef? Horse, maybe? Dog?"

Charles raised his eyebrows, shrugged, and stuck the spoon in his mouth.

"How long we been at this? What day is it, anyway?" Art Ferdinand asked.

"Well, we first went on line April tenth," Aaron said. "Today's May twenty-fifth—what's that, forty-five days straight?"

"Not for all of us," Charles said, waving his now empty spoon in Aaron's direction. "As I recall, somebody here spent ten or more of those days in the hospital flirtin' with the nurses."

Aaron's eyes narrowed. "Yeah, and I was damn glad to be there, too. But I figured I had to get back up here and help you guys win the war or we'd never get home."

"Forty-five days? Feels like forty-five weeks—or months, even," Worth said. "I thought we was supposed to be relieved by now."

"Yeah, my achin' feet need a rest," Harry said. He looked around the group. "Hey, any of you fellas got a pair of dry socks you could spare?"

"You're funny," Charles said. "The only people with dry socks in this outfit are sittin' in division headquarters with General Coulter."

Furlong motioned to Charles. "You think you can bring some more coffee up on your next run, Charles? I'm almost out."

"Dadgum it, Francis. I've got the whole company to supply, and you sit there and expect me to bring you extra coffee?" Charles grinned. "Okay, okay, I'll bring some tomorrow night. You pray I make it up here again. A damn German machine gun 'bout cooked my goose this trip. I thought you guys cleaned out all those pockets."

"We thought so too. One musta hid out 'til we passed. D'you want some of us to go down the trail with you when you leave and take it out?" Aaron asked.

"Nah," Charles said. "I got him. I knew the joker had to reload sometime. When he did, I tossed a grenade his way—while he was still duckin' that little pineapple, I got close enough to let him have it. He won't bother me again." He shrugged. "But who knows what else the Jerries have waitin'?"

Furlong nodded. "I'll pray you make it okay, Charles."

"Shoot," Charles said, "you'll only be doing it so the Lord will see you get your precious coffee." He turned away from Furlong and winked at the rest of the group.

Furlong blinked and opened his mouth, then closed it without speaking.

"Ah, I'm only pickin' at ya," Charles said. "I'll be okay. But pray for me if you want to."

Shingleton approached the group. "Good news, men. The units at Anzio have broken out and will be coming up on our left flank soon."

"Hey, hey! They can help chase the Jerries," Harry said.

"There's more. When the link-up is complete, we're coming off the line for a rest. Should be soon. Sit tight and be ready to pull back when the word comes down."


Two days later, the men marched into a rest area near the seacoast resort area of Sabaudia. The sparkling blue-green ocean and bright sun highlighted the scenic coastline—a dramatic change from the battlefield they'd left behind. Aaron stared at the landscape before him. Maybe in a day or so it would seem real. For now a shower and clean clothes—and sleep—would do.

After lunch, a real meal of concentrated beef stew, potatoes, and hot coffee from the field kitchen, Aaron got his turn at the large tent serving as a makeshift shower. He stood on a wooden pallet as the tepid water streamed over his aching body and onto the muddy ground beneath the slats of the pallet.

God, the water felt good.

"Hurry up—you can't take all day in there," came a cry from outside.

Aaron sighed. Leave it to the Army—bad things went on non-stop—good things, only a short while.

After exiting the tent, he joined dozens of other GIs fishing through piles of laundered uniforms. He grabbed a clean set of fatigues and dressed. From there, he and Worth found a spot to set up the pup tent they'd been issued. It would be nice to have a roof over his head, even if the roof was only GI canvas.

While Worth napped, Aaron sat outside the tent and dug in his pack for a pencil and paper. Time to write Maggie. But what could he say? He couldn't tell her about the fighting they'd been through—all the bloodshed he'd seen. The censors would probably chop it up anyway. He'd try to keep it as light as possible. He rubbed his forehead for a moment and then put pencil to paper.

Hello sweetheart,

I got your letters today. The mail finally caught up with us. It was great hearing from you. I'm writing to let you know I'm well. We've been moved to a rest area. I can't tell you where it is or where we've been, but I can say that being here sure beats where we were. How is Barry? I bet he is growing a lot. Try to send me some pictures of the two of you if you can. How's your dad? Is the mill team still playing baseball? I sure wish I was there to play with them. I can't begin to tell you how much I miss you.

Have you talked to Graydon lately? He wrote me he might quit school. Try to talk him out of it if you can. He'll get drafted for sure if he quits now. And I wouldn't wish this Army life on anybody. If you can't talk him out of it, try to get him to join the Navy. Those guys have it made. They sleep in a nice warm bunk, and they always eat good.

I don't know how long we'll be here, but I'm hoping it will be several days at least. I'll write again tomorrow. Take care of you and Barry—and your dad. I love you.

Aaron

Two hours after Aaron finished his letter, Lieutenant Shingleton called the platoon together. "Listen up, men. General Clark has issued new orders. We're going back to the front."

Aaron cursed under his breath. That couldn't be right! There had to be a mistake!

Groans and curses filled the air.

Patrick Davis flung the bayonet he'd been sharpening to the ground, burying half its blade in the hard-packed earth. "Goddamn Army! We just got here!"

"Pipe down," Shingleton said, hands on his hips. "I know it's tough and not fair and all the rest of yer bellyaching. Can it. General Clark says we're going to Rome. He wants all units pushing hard. Check your gear and be ready to move out in an hour."

"Can you believe this?" Aaron said to Worth. "Some rest. One day—damn."

"We shoulda known it was too good to be true," Worth said. "Typical Army."

Not long afterward, Aaron and Worth hopped aboard one of the olive drab deuce-and-a-half trucks along with others of their squad. No one smiled or joked. When all the trucks were loaded, the convoy roared down the dirt road leading from the rest area.

"Hey, look at all the civilians," someone shouted.

Italians—men, women, and children—lined both sides of the highway, cheering, waving handkerchiefs, and holding up their fingers in the V for victory sign.

"They sure seem glad to see us, don't they?" Worth said.

"Well, I sure ain't gonna be glad to see the Germans," Aaron said.

# CHAPTER THIRTY-ONE

Three days later, Aaron kicked at a rock on the roadway before him. "Hell, I'm starting the think there's no such place as Rome. We've been on the move for three days, took one damn hill after another, dodged machine gun and mortar fire—"

"Don't forget all the shelling—especially from those self-propelled guns," Harry said.

"Don't the doggone Germans ever quit?"

"Oh, they're good alright," Harry said, "but we're moving. It won't be much longer. The question is, will we have to take it street by street? That'd be like Itri, only a hundred times worse."

From up ahead the word came. "Fall out. Bed down. We'll continue in the morning."

Men fell to the side of the road. Aaron pulled his rifle next to him and immediately slept.

"Get up, men! Grab your rifles and your gear. Breakfast is at the field kitchen today. Be ready to move out in one hour."

Aaron stretched and yawned. "Damn, it seems like I barely got my eyes closed. You mean the field kitchen caught up with us finally? And I was so looking forward to more cold C-rations."

"You and your C-rations," Worth said. "Let's get down to the kitchen before everything gets eaten up."

When they reached the kitchen area, Aaron and Worth stopped and stared.

"Is that pancakes?" Worth said.

"Yeah, and lots of 'em. What's goin' on?" Aaron asked.

A cook set a tray of fresh hotcakes on the extended chow table. "Eat up, you dogfaces. We're going to Rome today. There won't be any more chow 'til we get there, so you better load up now."

Each filled their mess kits with cakes and ladled on syrup in great quantities. Francis Furlong walked past with a stack of cakes and his canteen mug filled with hot coffee.

"How's this for a treat, Francis?" Aaron said.

Furlong smiled. "Good, real good. And fresh coffee to go with it. What a blessing."

"You can say that again," Worth said.

They sat on the ground and dug into the cakes. "Hmm…these ain't as good as Momma makes, but they taste pretty darn good," Aaron said. He raised his metal canteen cup to sip more coffee. "How much farther you reckon it is to Rome?"

Worth swallowed and then shook his head. "I got no idea. But if we're going there today, it can't be all that far. I'm just wonderin' what the Germans will have in store for us. It probably won't be much fun."

Aaron nodded. "I'd guess not. Maybe G Company won't be in front this time. Seems like we're always at the head of these marches."

"Not today, men," First Sergeant Gibbs said. "And to answer your question, we're only three miles from Rome."

Aaron and Worth turned to face him.

"We'll be in reserve for a change. But don't you worry none. Ole Jerry will have enough fight to go 'round for all of us, especially before they give up Rome. So don't get too relaxed today. Anything could happen."

After eating, the men gathered their belongings and fell in with the rest of the company. Captain Atwell gave the order to march. All morning they marched as the hot June sun beat down on them. Soldiers, trucks, and a few tanks filled the road and the fields to the left and right as they pushed forward. In the distance the sound of small arms and mortar fire could be heard.

"I'da thought we'd be shelled by now," Aaron said. "I wonder what the guys up ahead are runnin' into?"

Worth tugged at the rifle sling on his left shoulder. "Yeah, it's a little strange. Makes me nervous. The Germans have never been stingy with their artillery before. We haven't taken a single 88 or 105 round. What d'you think they're up to?"

"We'll probably find out sooner'n we'd like," Aaron countered.

Fifteen minutes later the order was shouted out. "Double-time—let's go!" They passed other units lining the side of the road. Twenty minutes later Captain Atwell ordered the company to halt. Platoon leaders were called forward for a briefing.

Ten minutes later Shingleton addressed the platoon. "Reports from civilians indicate the Germans are pulling out of Rome and heading north. We're going in shortly. But stay alert. We still don't know what to expect."

Worth and Aaron exchanged glances. "Does this mean we can just waltz into Rome?" Worth asked.

"Let's hope so. I don't know what's goin' on, but I sure like the idea of not having to fight door to door," Aaron said.

An hour later the company passed through the outskirts of Rome. Italian civilians lined both sides of the highway, waving and yelling and holding out flowers and wine bottles to the advancing troops. As they entered the heart of the city, the crowds were greater and the noise became louder as the citizens of Rome welcomed them, crowds of civilians so thick the advancing troops could hardly walk. Jeeps and trucks slowed to a crawl.

As they marched farther into the city, a soldier near Aaron commented, "Look at that tumble-down building. Our artillery must have really been effective. It looks like it's ready to fall over."

Art Ferdinand laughed. "That's the Colosseum, you dope. Its two thousand years old or something. It's looked like that for centuries. Artillery, my ass."

"Look at this," Aaron said. "They're everywhere. Every window and every balcony is filled with civilians waving and shoutin' at us."

"Yeah, I can hardly hear myself think," Worth said.

"What'd you say," Aaron shouted. "I can't hear you for all these screaming people!"

Up ahead, some of the men broke ranks and stopped to drink from the offered bottles of wine. Women surrounded them and showered them with flowers, hugs, and kisses.

Officers yelled and attempted to keep the units in order, with little success.

"This is crazy," Aaron said.

The crowd surrounded them. Where the heck did Worth get to?

A dark-haired woman in a floral dress grabbed his left arm and spun him around. She moved to hug him but spied the identification bracelet on his wrist. She grasped his left hand and looked at his gold wedding band. She threw his arm down, waved a hand at him as if pushing him away, and disappeared. Aaron smiled. Oh well.

Worth reappeared at his side. "Look, Aaron. What're they doin' to those women?"

Aaron followed Worth's gaze. A group of civilians had surrounded three women. A man shoved one of the women to her knees while a second man produced a set of hair clippers and began cutting her hair, clear down to her scalp. The woman cried and begged, but to no avail. When the man finished, she was completely bald. The second woman experienced the same fate. As the third woman was pushed to her knees, Worth said, "We've gotta stop them. Why are they doing that?"

"You men stay right where you are," Lieutenant Shingleton said from behind them. "Those women slept with Germans—the locals are marking them so everyone will know."

"That's a little harsh, isn't it?" Aaron said.

Shingleton shrugged. "Not our problem. Our orders are we don't interfere."

A few streets farther on, a disheveled looking Italian man ran past Aaron and Worth. The man gasped for air and appeared to be panic-stricken. Four or five men pursued him. They apprehended him just as he tried to duck inside a doorway. One of the men drew a pistol and shot the man in the head. His body fell to the pavement. His blood poured onto the sidewalk and into the gutter. The men moved on as if nothing had happened.

"Whew!" Worth said. "I guess he must've been a German sympathizer too. Maybe those women got off light, huh?"

"Yeah," Aaron said. "The lieutenant said to stay alert. That's a good reminder, but it's kinda hard to do with the streets filled with all these people." His eyes surveyed the upper stories of the buildings ahead. Shutters on a third-floor window flew open. The unmistakable outline of a German helmet appeared.

"Take cover!" Aaron shouted.

Machine gun fire spewed from the window, and bullets ricocheted off the pavement and the walls of the buildings. Screams echoed in the street. Soldiers and civilians ran for cover. Several people lay motionless. Others, wounded, crawled and hobbled away.

More bursts followed.

Aaron ducked into a doorway, his back pressed hard against the door. The street was now empty. But a hundred and fifty yards away in both directions the revelry continued as if nothing had happened.

Another burst of fire from the window. Across the street, a GI with a rifle grenade on his M-1 leaned out of a doorway and fired it toward the window. The grenade smacked against the wall next to the window and exploded harmlessly. The gun continued firing. Two other soldiers followed suit, sending more rifle grenades toward the building. Behind Aaron, from another doorway, a Thompson submachine gun appeared. Only the soldier's hands were visible as he poured automatic fire toward the upper floors of the building.

Aaron blinked—do something. He snapped the M-1 to his shoulder and fired in the general direction of the enemy gun. Eight quick rounds, then the familiar *pling* as the rifle ejected its empty clip. He clawed at his ammo belt for a reload.

Across the street, three soldiers ran to the building and kicked in the door. Shots rang out. Minutes later, grenades exploded on the third floor.

Aaron sighed and wiped sweat from his brow. Too close. Way too close.

Worth and Harry ran up beside Aaron. "You okay?" Harry asked, breathing hard. "We couldn't see you from where we were— thought you might've caught a round."

Aaron's breath came in shallow gasps. His hands shook. "Yeah, I'm okay. Guess the war definitely isn't over, even if we have taken Rome."

Hours later, officers and MPs finally succeeded in separating the soldiers from the civilians. Units were reassembled and orders given for bivouac arrangements and guard details. Aaron, Worth, and Harry slept in a small room next to a bakery shop.

"This is the first time I've had a roof over my head since I left the hospital," Aaron said.

"Well, you should feel good. It's the first time for me since we first went on line." Harry said. "Maybe we can stay here for a while. I could get used to this."

# CHAPTER THIRTY-TWO

The next day G Company, along with the rest of the 339th Battalion, moved quickly across the Tiber River just north of Rome. Soon the entire division pursued the retreating Germans up Highway 2 toward Viterbo.

"The Krauts are headed toward the Arno River," Lieutenant Shingleton told the men of Second Platoon. "We're gonna stay on 'em and try to keep 'em from setting up defenses around Florence. So move fast, stay alert. When we encounter resistance, if we can't push through it, we'll go around it. Other units will mop up. So drop your cocks and grab your socks. Let's march."

The men hoisted their rifles and moved at double time. Twenty minutes later, Aaron let out a low whistle. "Look at all this. Both sides of the road—abandoned guns, trucks, burned-out tanks. I'll say they're retreatin'."

Worth nodded. "The lieutenant said the Jerries are using any vehicle that moves—buses, civilian cars and trucks, even bicycles to try and outrun us."

Harry joined in. "If I know them, they'll set up some delaying actions. We better not get too sure of ourselves."

As if in response to his comment, machine gun fire swept the road ahead of them. Men rushed to cover in the ditches and fields beside the highway. Ten minutes later First Platoon silenced the gun, but not before two more men suffered wounds.

"This country's more like it—not them steep mountains we fought our way up coming into Rome," Aaron said. "These rolling hills are a lot easier to get around in. Our tanks can even give us support here."

"Hmmpff," Harry said. "It's about time they helped us. They ain't been able to do much so far. I'll be glad to let them get kissed."

Four days later the entire Eighty-fifth Division was relieved by the French Third Algerian Infantry Division.

"Give 'em hell, Frenchy," Art Ferdinand yelled to the Algerian troops as they moved past the men of G Company.

"If you need us, we'll call you," Charles Bradley chimed in.

The French soldiers waved but made no comments.

"Where d'ya think we'll go from here?" Aaron asked.

"Somewhere where we can get some rest and have some decent coffee, I hope," Furlong said.

"Yeah, I counted it up last night," Worth said. "Since we first went on line—that was April tenth—we've been in action sixty days out of the last sixty-two."

"You ain't the only one keeping score," Harry said. "Since we jumped off May eleventh, we've come about a hundred and thirty-five miles—that's almost five miles a day—while we was bein' shot at, no less. We've pushed the Jerries for forty-six miles just since Rome. We're all dog tired. The least they can do is give us at least a month off the line."

A day later the men jumped from trucks at a rest area ten miles west of Rome. The entire battalion assembled for an address from Colonel Brady.

"At ease men," the colonel began. "I have a copy of a message sent to General Clark from the Army Chief of Staff, General Marshall. General Clark wanted it read to everyone in the division. Listen up."

General Clark:

I wish to extend my personal congratulations to you and to the commanders and men of all Fifth Army units. Your exemplary leadership and their splendid performance and fortitude in liberating the Italian capital of Rome have awakened great enthusiasm here at home and will have a depressing effect on the German high command.

Brady looked up. "Needless to say, General Coulter, our division commander, is very pleased with all that you have done. He also sends along this personal message to you."

Officers and men of the Eighty-Fifth Division. Congratulations on your notable successes in this hard-fought campaign to liberate Rome, the Eternal City. Through your valiant efforts, you have accomplished something that has never been done before— something that will go down as one of the truly great feats of military history. In all the battles that have been fought in and around the city of Rome, it has never been taken from the south. Until now. In fact, until you did it, most believed such a feat to be impossible given the rugged mountainous terrain in the southern approach to Rome. Through your intrepid actions you have freed the first of the three Axis capitals occupied by the Germans. I salute you and wish you God's blessings in the days to come.

John B. Coulter
Major General, U.S. Army
Commander, Eighty-fifth Infantry Division

Colonel Brady folded the messages and put them away. "Now, men, I'd like to add a few words of my own. You may or may not know that there was much concern on the part of our high command prior to your entry into combat. This division and your sister unit, the Eighty-eighth, are the first two infantry divisions comprised almost entirely of draftees to see combat in this war. Many of the brass feared you wouldn't give a good account of yourselves once the bullets started flying. I'm proud to say that you have proven them wrong. But the war is not over. Many difficult days lie ahead. I urge you to train with vigor and determination while you are here. And when called back to the front line, to pursue the enemy with the same gusto and fervor you have shown in the last two months. Your officers and noncoms have been briefed on your training schedule, which will get under way immediately. Again, thanks to each of you. Good day."

Colonel Brady turned to leave.

"Ten-shun!"

The men snapped to attention as Brady climbed into his jeep. The driver shifted into gear and immediately drove away.

"Training?" someone behind Aaron said. "I thought we were here to rest!"

"Yeah," another voice chimed in. "What's that shit? We're trained already. What's goin' on here?"

*Aaron Johnson, my Dad*

*Maggie Johnson, my Mom*

*Worth Haynes*

*Dad and Art Ferdinand*

*Charles Bradley*

*Francis Furlong*

*Harry Klutz*

*Jack Claytor and Coco*

*First Sergeant Gibbs*

*Hoy Shingleton*

# CHAPTER THIRTY-THREE

Aaron rushed the bunker which was dug into the side of a hill and fortified with logs across its top. A deadly MG-43 poked through the firing port. The rest of the squad laid down covering fire. He panted hard as he pressed against the side of the earthen structure, pulled the pin on a grenade, and signaled to the others—cease firing. He spun and tossed the pineapple through the firing slit. He ducked back, waited for the muffled explosion, and then whirled, poked his rifle through the slit, and emptied a full clip into the now smoking interior.

A whistle sounded.

Sergeant Palmer stood with hands on hips, the whistle dangling from a chain around his neck. "Okay all you new guys, that's one way to take out a reinforced bunker. Now, fall in and double-time back to the main rest area."

Aaron fell in beside Worth as the men moved out. "Some rest. We've been doing this kinda stuff eight hours a day, six days a week. I'm almost as tired as I was when we were on the line. And this heat don't make it any better."

"Yeah—all this to bring the replacements up to speed," Worth said.

"Well, I sure hope it does. We're gonna need all the help we can get when we go against the Jerries again. They'll be waitin'—just like before." The July sun beat down on them. Aaron wiped his brow. The Jerries. He frowned.

"At least we get a day off tomorrow—and Rome is just a few miles away. I hear it's not so bad now that all the snipers have been cleared out."

"We'll find out tonight and tomorrow," Aaron said.

The truck lumbered toward Rome. Aaron and Worth sat in back with others from the platoon. Everyone wore a fresh uniform and spit-shined boots. No helmets—only overseas caps were authorized for men on leave.

"What you got in that sack?" Worth asked, pointing to a cloth bag between Aaron's feet.

"Oh, a few things I've been savin' up. Mostly cigarettes, some chocolate, that kinda stuff."

Worth frowned. "You know black market activity is verboten," he said.

"Yeah, so I hear."

"Just don't get caught."

An hour before dusk, the truck rolled to a stop in Rome. The men jumped to the pavement and looked around.

"I'll be back here tomorrow at sixteen hundred," the driver said. "If you're late, too bad. You can walk back." The truck roared away.

"Well, what say we find us a place to bed down, and then we'll get a look at this city. Maybe it'll look better than it did when we were gettin' shot at," Aaron said.

Half an hour later, Aaron stepped onto the city street from the hotel they'd selected. Worth and Harry had already left to find an eating establishment they'd heard about. Aaron agreed to meet them there later.

He walked with an easy gait, carrying the sack he'd brought. His head turned from side to side as he surveyed the buildings and the streets. Civilians and GIs seemed to be everywhere. He passed the entrance to a café. Laughter and music reached his ears. He continued down the street.

"Psst! Hey, Joe! What you got in the sack?"

Aaron turned. A young Italian boy, probably about twelve years old, stood near the entrance to an alley. He swept a mop of black hair away from his face and motioned Aaron over.

"Cigarettes," Aaron said.

"Come."

Without waiting for a reply, the lad hurried down the alley. Aaron paused momentarily, took a breath, and followed.

The alley twisted and turned as the boy led him on. Five minutes later they stepped down a short flight of steps leading to a basement doorway. The boy knocked in what appeared to be a prearranged code.

The door swung slowly open. The boy motioned for Aaron to follow.

They entered a dimly lit room; a candle set in a wine bottle sat on a crude wooden table providing the only light. There were no windows.

Several Italian men sat around the room eyeing him. They wore hats and civilian clothing. The hair on Aaron's neck stood up. Had he made a mistake?

A man in a black leather jacket emerged from the shadows and stood at the table.

"What you got, GI?" he said.

Aaron told him.

"How much?"

Aaron stated an amount per carton.

The man waved his hands and shook his head. "No. No. Too much, too much."

Finally, after Aaron had turned twice to leave before being called back, a price was agreed to.

Aaron hoisted the sack to the table and began counting out packs of cigarettes. Each time he laid out a carton, the Italian placed a stack of lira on the table. Aaron left the basement with a wad of bills stuffed in every pocket.

The boy led him back to the square where they had met, and Aaron tipped him handsomely.

The boy smiled. "Thanks, Joe. Wanna meet my sister? She's a virgin."

Aaron shook his head. "I gotta go find my buddies. How'd you learn to speak such good English?"

The boy shrugged. "American cousins. And I learn fast. I listen to you GIs. It's not hard."

Aaron smiled. "What's your name?"

"Guisseppe."

"Well, here, Guisseppe. Take this too." He extended a chocolate bar. Guisseppe snatched it, smiled, and ran down the alley.

Aaron stared after him. If it weren't for the children—poor and ragged as they were—he feared he and maybe all soldiers would turn into pure savages.

At the packed restaurant where he'd agreed to meet Worth and Harry, he scanned the room. They were nowhere to be seen. Pushing his way to the bar in back, he encountered Patrick Davis. "Have you seen Haynes and Klutz?"

"Saw 'em earlier—I think they left with some Italian girls. Come have a drink with me."

"I can't." Aaron glanced at his watch. "I gotta find them."

"Aw, c'mon," Davis said. "I'm buyin'."

"Patrick, I'm really not much of a drinker."

"C'mon, dammit. Just one drink." Davis grabbed Aaron's arm.

"Okay, okay," Aaron said. "Just one."


Aaron staggered into the room he'd booked with Worth. "Carolina Moon, keep shining…"

Worth sat up in his bed and turned on the bedside lamp. "What the heck…? Daggone—Aaron, you're plastered." He looked at his watch. "It's four a.m. Where the heck have you been?"

"…shining on the one that waits for meeee." Aaron smiled and plopped onto his bed. "I ran into Patrick Davis. We had a few drinks."

"I'd say so," Worth said. "Well, you better bed down and get some sleep. We're gonna sightsee Rome tomorrow. Early."

"Oh, don't worry. I'll be up," Aaron said. He unbuttoned his shirt, pulled off his boots, and stretched out on the bed.


"Wake up." Worth shook Aaron's shoulder. "Get up—now—Harry's waitin'."

Aaron opened one eye. "What? Where am I? Oh, my head! Damn! Go away."

"C'mon, we're goin' sightseein', remember?"

"I'm not goin' anywhere. I think I'm gonna be sick."

"Oh no you're not. Get up. There's water in that pitcher on the nightstand. Wash your face. The latrine's down the hall. We're meetin' Harry in ten minutes."

Aaron pulled a pillow over his head. "Maybe you are. I'm stayin' right here."

"No you're not—we had a plan, and we're stickin' to it. Get outta that sack or I'll pull you out."

Twenty minutes later Worth and a groggy Aaron met Harry on the street outside.

Harry looked at Aaron, then at Worth. "What happened to him?"

"He got mixed up with Patrick Davis and a bottle of cognac," Worth said.

"Knock it off." Aaron held a hand to his forehead. "And don't talk so loud, you guys. My head's killing me."

Harry chuckled. "Serves you right. I thought everybody in the platoon knew better than to drink with Davis. That guy can put it down."

"I'll say," Aaron said. "He wasn't even tipsy when we split up."

"Did you find a buyer for your cigarettes?" Worth asked.

"Oh yeah," Aaron said. "I sold 'em to a scary-lookin' Italian guy—got enough to pay for all our drinks. And sometime or other me and Davis ate—and I paid for that too. Then I tipped the waiter, and…" He placed his hands in his pants pockets. "I've still got—I'm sure I've got…" he pulled a few bills from his pocket. "Uh, oh—this is all that's left. Think this is enough to get some breakfast?"

Worth looked at Harry. "Let's hope so. I think we better get some food in you. I hope we can find some coffee, at least."

After they had breakfast at an outdoor café, the three set out on foot through the streets of Rome. Throughout the day they toured the city's famous sites—the Roman Walls, the Catacombs, the Roman Baths, the Colosseum, the Roman Theatre, the Pantheon, Pompeii, and a host of cathedrals.

"Sure looks different now than when we captured it in June, don't it?" Harry said.

"I'll say," Worth said. "It's a lot cheerier lookin'"

"They probably like our money," Aaron said. "Everything sure costs enough."

"You're just sore 'cause Davis finagled you into paying for everything and spending all your dough," Harry said. "Keep that in mind next time you decide to crawl into a bottle."

"Oh, pipe down," Aaron said. "And stop walking so fast. Have some pity on a sick man."

"Ha," Worth said. "You ain't sick, you're hung over. You did that to yourself."

At the end of the day, they boarded waiting trucks for the return trip to the rest area. Aaron slumped onto the bench seat and looked at Worth. "Don't ever let me do that again. I feel awful."

"Don't worry. Things'll be better tomorrow when we're doing PT in the nice hot sun." Worth patted him on the leg and smiled.

Aaron put his head in his hands and moaned.

The next day's training schedule began at sunup. Calisthenics and then a two-mile run. Aaron struggled to keep up and lost his breakfast halfway through.

"I'm never touching alcohol again," he told Harry. He eyed Patrick Davis, who ran at a steady lope near the front of the platoon, totally unfazed by the night of heavy drinking.

At the end of the day, the Second Platoon men ate by a fire. Aaron's appetite had improved, and he wolfed down the meat and potatoes prepared by the field kitchen cooks. Lieutenant Shingleton joined the group as they finished eating.

"Did you men enjoy your time in Rome?"

There were multiple grins with a few "yes sirs" thrown in.

"I'm not so sure about some of the guys," Harry said, nodding toward Aaron. "I think a few came back with some 105-millimeter-size headaches."

Shingleton smiled. "Get into the wine and cognac a bit, did you?"

Aaron shook his head. "Too much."

"You better watch that—Furlong here will be getting on your back. Right, Francis?"

Furlong took a sip of coffee from his canteen cup. He looked directly into the fire. "Well, the Bible does say we shouldn't be given to strong drink."

Aaron dropped his head. He knew that verse.

Some of the men snickered.

"Leave it to Saint Francis," Davis said. "Might know he'd go all Holy Joe on us."

"Come on, Furlong," Shingleton said. "You can't mean we shouldn't unwind a little now and then. I think we've earned it."

"I'm just telling you what the good book says, Lieutenant." Furlong drank more coffee.

Shingleton shook his head. "Dadburn it, Furlong. I don't see any difference in me having a few drinks and you havin' all that coffee. As I see it, your coffee drinkin' is just as big a sin as me putting down some alcohol now and then."

Furlong stared into the fire for a long moment. No one spoke.

Aaron hung his head lower, careful not to make eye contact with anyone. Why did they have to talk about this?

"Alright," Furlong said. "I won't drink any more coffee." He emptied his cup onto the ground.

Shingleton drew back. "Aw, Francis, you know that's not what I meant," he said. "Don't stop drinkin' coffee on my account. I sure don't plan on curtailing my alcohol consumption."

"No, Lieutenant. You've got a point. I hadn't thought about it that way. You men are my brothers, and I don't want to offend any of you. There's a verse in the Bible about that too."

Furlong rose and walked away.

Shingleton sighed. "Damn."

"Ah, let him go, Lieutenant," Davis said. "He's been pushing that religion stuff on us ever since Camp Shelby. It's about time somebody put him in his place."

Shingleton whirled around. His eyes narrowed. "Don't let me hear you say that again. Furlong's a good man. A damn sight better'n all of us put together. I may not see things the same way he does, but I admire the man. And now look what I've done."

Aaron clamped his lips together and gazed into his own coffee cup. He may not stop drinking coffee, but he'd sure think twice before getting drunk again.

After almost a month of arduous training, G Company's men awoke expecting yet another day of training in small unit tactics. Immediately following the morning PT, Captain Atwell called all platoon leaders to his tent for a briefing.

"What d'ya think's up?" Worth asked Aaron.

"I dunno—we've been here a long time. Maybe our vacation's over."

An hour later Lieutenant Shingleton returned and called the platoon together. They sat on the ground before him.

"Alright, men, we've got orders. We're going back on the line. Get your gear and be ready to pull out at noon."

Groans and cries of, "Oh no," filled the air.

"I was just gettin' used to this place, Lieutenant," Claytor said.

"Quiet, quit your bitching," Shingleton snapped. "And another thing. We ain't Company G of the 339th Infantry Battalion anymore. Somebody in the head shed figured out that we'd be better off if we had a direct line to artillery, armor, and medical support, rather than filter each request through division HQ. So now those elements are under our direct control. We have officially been renamed the 339th Regimental Combat Team. The 337th and 338th got the same deal.

"The rest of the good news is we get to ride trucks to the front this time. Form up down by the highway. The trucks will be there in half an hour."

# CHAPTER THIRTY-FOUR

Sergeant Palmer raised his right hand. The patrol froze. Aaron stared into the darkness. What was that shape? Definitely a person. Moving toward them. Had they been spotted?

The moon emerged from behind a cloud. The clear outline of a German helmet came into view. Continued to move directly at them. Cautious. But deliberate.

Palmer crouched. Waited. Aaron placed his finger on the safety of the M-1. Beside him Patrick Davis held his trench knife at the ready.

When the German came abreast of him, Palmer rose and knocked him to the ground with the butt of his rifle. The downed man moved as if to struggle, but the barrel of Palmer's rifle in his face made him stop.

"*Kamerad, kamerad,*" the German whispered, eyes wide.


"Johnson, take the prisoner down to the company CP. I gotta go to the latrine," Palmer said. "Tell Captain Atwell I'll be there shortly. The rest of you men go get some chow and grab some shut-eye."

Aaron motioned the prisoner to move along.

The Jerry walked with his hands behind his head, staring straight ahead. Even though his uniform was dirty and he looked as if he hadn't eaten in days, he walked erect with his back straight. Aaron shook his head. Good soldiers. But this one didn't look so tough now, especially with that damn helmet off.

Aaron's eyes burned. He took one hand from his rifle to rub them. Damn. He doubted that he looked any better than his captive. How long had it been since he'd had more than a couple of hours sleep at night?

He shook his head to fight off the fatigue. Every day the same. Move until a Kraut machine gun or mortar opened up. Take cover. It was usually just one or two Germans left behind to slow the American advance. If they couldn't flank them, they'd wait for the Jerries to run out of ammo. Most of them surrendered when they ran empty. But they weren't always treated kindly when they came out with their hands up, yelling, *"Kamerad, kamerad."*

Then patrols every night. Next day, more fighting, more movement. Each step wondering when another Kraut machine gun was gonna open up. Or worse, a mortar with its shells set to go off at treetop level. His stomach tightened. The mortars scared him. Not that there wasn't a time when he wasn't scared. It was just a matter of how scared at any given moment.

They approached the company CP. Aaron marched the prisoner into the tent.

Captain Atwell, First Sergeant Gibbs, and Corporal Pearson huddled around a field telephone unit.

"Damn it, Pearson. I asked about this two days ago. What's the holdup?" Atwell lit a cigarette and blew out a stream of smoke. He glanced at the German and then turned to Aaron. He raised an eyebrow.

"Excuse me, sir," Aaron said. "We captured this Kraut on our way back from patrol. Sergeant Palmer said he'd be down in a couple minutes to brief you."

Atwell nodded and then turned his attention back to Pearson.

Gibbs stood and motioned toward a sandy-haired private. "Schwalek, you speak some German—see if you can get anything useful out of this Jerry, and then get him to battalion."

Schwalek took the prisoner in tow. Gibbs returned to his seat beside the captain and Pearson.

"Why can't we do it?" Captain Atwell said to Pearson.

An open field manual rested on Pearson's lap. "Sir, I can't hook up any more sets to this configuration. The manual shows no way to add any more."

Atwell frowned. "Damn it, I want to be able to communicate with our mortar squads and the medics. Sending messengers back and forth isn't working. Isn't there some way to jury-rig it?"

Pearson shook his head. "I have extra handsets, sir, but I can't see how to do it. Maybe somebody from battalion can figure it out."

"That might take days," Gibbs said. "We need this done now."

Atwell's frown deepened. "Explain it to me one more time. Why can't we do it?"

Pearson went through a lengthy explanation.

Aaron cleared his throat. "Excuse me, sir?"

Atwell looked up and stared at Aaron. "You still here? Well, what is it, Private? I'm kinda busy."

"Sir, I think I might be able to help. What we need to do is run an auxiliary line to the other locations and then ground the sets."

"Huh?" Atwell said. "What the hell are you talking about?"

"Sir, I think it's all about completing the circuit—if we can come up with enough wire to add onto the main set here, we can—"

"If you can do something, stop jabberin' and do it."

Aaron stepped to the telephone equipment, found a spool of wire, and cut off a six-foot section. He attached one end of the wire to a terminal on the set and then turned to Pearson.

"Do you have another field set handy?"

Pearson stared at him and then fumbled through some communications gear. He handed Aaron a handset.

After splicing the wire from the main set into the auxiliary unit, he attached a shorter section of wire into the handset and wrapped the other end of that wire around his bayonet.

"Now, I think when I ground this," he said to Pearson, pushing his bayonet into the ground, "that this set will tie right into the main set." He raised the handset to his ear. "See if you can hear me."

Pearson turned to the main set and placed headphones on his head.

Aaron spoke into his handset.

"Well, damn," Pearson said, "it works."

Aaron smiled.

Atwell looked at Aaron and then turned to Pearson.

"So, can you rig this up tonight?"

Pearson's face reddened. "Uhh—yessir, I can now, sir." He glared at Aaron.

"Get on it then," Atwell said.

"Yessir."

Pearson rummaged around the CP for additional equipment. He brushed past Aaron on his way out, bumping him hard. Under his breath he said, "Watch your back, smart-ass. I won't forget you showin' me up like this."

Aaron grimaced. "I wasn't trying to..."

Pearson was already gone.

Sergeant Palmer entered the tent and saluted the captain. "Sir, I can brief you about last night's patrol whenever you like."

"Sure, Sergeant. Stick around. I'll be right with you." He turned to Aaron. "Thanks, Private. What's your name?"

"Johnson, sir."

"What'd you do before the Army?"

"Mechanic, sir."

"So how did you know how to fix this telephone setup?"

"Sir, it's just like with the electrical system on a car. It has to be grounded or it won't run—lights won't burn, gauges won't work—it's all got to do with completing the electrical circuit."

"Okay. Well, you better get back to your squad."

Aaron saluted and left the tent.


Sergeant Palmer briefed Atwell and left the tent. The captain turned to Gibbs.

"First Sergeant, I want you to cut me a promotion recommendation and get it to battalion today."

"Sure, Captain. Who for?"

"I want to promote that Johnson kid—make him the company communications sergeant."

Gibbs looked at Atwell. "Sir?"

"Today."

"Uhh, sir, Johnson's not trained as a communications operator. And Corporal Pearson's been actin' in the job since Donohue got wounded. I think he's expecting—"

"I don't care about that. I want somebody who can do the job. Any man who can figure out what Johnson did just from listenin' to us talk can learn whatever he needs to know in short order. Besides, did you see how blond that kid is? We've gotta get him out of that rifle squad—the Germans can see us comin' in the middle of the night with him out there. If he's back here at the company CP, maybe we can hide him."

Gibbs laughed. "Okay, Captain. I'll cut the orders for you to sign, and we'll get 'em to battalion before we pull out today."

# CHAPTER THIRTY-FIVE

Aaron and Worth sat at opposite ends of their foxhole. Worth popped a chunk of a chocolate bar into his mouth. After he'd chewed and swallowed, he looked at Aaron. "This new CO is really shakin' things up, buddy."

Aaron glanced up for a moment and then continued sewing sergeant stripes onto the sleeve of his khaki shirt. He shook his head. "I'll say—one minute I'm tryin' to help the cap'n out with the telephone setup, and the next thing I know, I'm the company communications sergeant. Damn."

Worth eyed him.

"What?" Aaron said.

"You're sewing with your left hand. I've noticed you do a lot of things left-handed."

"Yeah, well, until I started school, I was left-handed. Ole man Harrington said he wasn't havin' any southpaws in his class. He tied my left arm down to my side. Kept it that way all year. Now I'm a righty— for most things."

"So that's what passes for education in your neck of the woods, huh? Now—about this promotion…look on the bright side," Worth said as he rummaged through another ration box. "You'll be hangin' around the company CP all the time—you'll get all the scuttlebutt firsthand. And now that you're a noncom, you can send Maggie a picture of you with those stripes on your sleeve—she'll be real proud. Your folks will be too."

Aaron sighed as he pulled the needle through for the last stitch. He broke the thread with his teeth and then turned toward Worth.

"The problem is, you Carolina hillbilly, I don't know shit from shinola about all this communications stuff." He frowned. "How'm I gonna learn all that?"

Worth busied himself opening a small package of crackers. "Relax. You said Gibbs told you they'd send you to the battalion communications guys for training. You're a smart guy. You'll catch on in no time. If, that is, those Yankee boys at battalion can understand a slow-talkin' mountain boy like you."

Aaron put on the shirt. "Oh, shut up. If they can understand you when you carry messages to 'em, they won't have any trouble with me." He finished buttoning and looked down at the stripes on each sleeve.

Worth chuckled. "Don't be so prissy. They look fine. As for me being the company messenger, there's another plus. We'll still get to see each other when the CO has me running errands back and forth to battalion. I'll be able to keep up with how soft you've got it, all snuggled in tight with Atwell and Gibbs."

"I'm not sure I'm Gibbs's favorite person. That might be a problem."

"Nah, just do your job. It's clear Atwell wanted you for communications sergeant. Gibbs is too smart to bother you as long as Atwell's backing you."

"We'll see. Maybe it'll be okay. You stay low and don't be no hero—I won't be able to keep you outta trouble now."

"Now as I recall," Worth said, "you're the only one of us who's been hurt so far. Maybe Atwell gave you the job so you won't be as likely to go trippin' over another grenade."

Aaron slung his rifle over his left shoulder and picked up his field pack. He extended his hand. "You take care."

"Don't worry, I'll be okay. Shingleton won't have us doing anything stupid."

Aaron headed for the company CP. What would this new job be like? Could he do it? What if he messed up? Tightness built in his chest. Ah, heck. If he could rebuild engines and put a wiring harness in a car, he could learn to work the radios and the phone sets. He had no choice.

# CHAPTER THIRTY-SIX

Aaron crawled through the darkness to Worth Haynes's slit trench. "Worth—it's Aaron," he whispered. "You seen Davis?"

The domed outline of Worth's helmet moved from side to side. "No—why?"

"He's been missing since dusk. Burnitz went to take a crap, and when he got back Davis was gone."

"His gear?"

"The Thompson's there and his ammo belt. Pistol and knife aren't."

"Think he got captured?"

"That's what the captain wants to know. I can't believe he'd give up without raising a ruckus. Pass the word—and keep your eyes peeled. Let us know if he turns up."

Worth nodded. "Roger."

Aaron crawled away. How could Davis have disappeared so quickly? And where the hell was he?

Two nights later Patrick Davis returned, dirty and unshaven. Atwell ordered him to the company CP as soon as he heard he was back.

Davis entered the bunker. Atwell, Gibbs, Aaron, and Francis Furlong looked up.

"Just where in the hell have you been?" Captain Atwell glared at Davis.

"I decided to do a little scouting on my own, Captain. We haven't been learnin' much from our regular patrols. I thought I might be able to—"

"Get your ass shot off, that's what," Atwell said. "From now on—"

"Sir, I got some good information if you'll just hear me out."

Atwell's eyes narrowed. "Okay, wise guy. I'll hear you out. It better be good."

"I know where all the enemy outposts and machine gun nests are, as well as their mortar and artillery OPs. And that's not all…"

When Davis finished talking, Atwell rubbed his chin and frowned. "So you learned all this just by sneakin' around behind the Jerry lines? You've got balls, I'll give you that. Can you pinpoint those bunker and artillery positions on a map?"

Davis smiled and reached inside his field jacket. "Thought you might want that, sir. Got it right here."

Atwell snatched the folded map from Davis and studied it. Gibbs moved beside him and looked over his shoulder.

"Furlong," Atwell said, "get Haynes—I want him to take this to battalion. I'm sure they can use it."

Furlong left the CP, Davis's map in hand.

Atwell stared at Davis. "How'd you get close enough to get a firm fix on these emplacements?"

"Well, sir, they had guards posted and all, but I took 'em out with my knife." He patted the sheathed trench knife on his belt.

"You think you're the Shadow or some super commando, Davis? You got some good dope, but you took unnecessary risks gettin' it. Don't let it happen again. Now get outta here."

"Yessir." Davis saluted and left.

The captain turned to Gibbs and Aaron. "That guy's nuts!"

"He may be, Captain, but it looks like he hit pay dirt," Gibbs said.

"What do you think, Johnson?" Atwell asked.

"Sir, I don't know. Davis is—a little odd, but he's made of some pretty tough stuff."

Atwell frowned. "Hmm—he'd better not push his luck. I'm sure the Jerries didn't like finding their guards knifed."

The next night, based largely on the information Davis provided, Lieutenant Shingleton's platoon launched an attack and took out a strong pocket of German resistance. Afterward, Shingleton reported to Captain Atwell. "Davis was right about everything, sir. I put him on point—he showed us where and how to flank the Jerry outposts, and then we took out the emplacements. They never knew what hit 'em."

Davis disappeared twice more during the next week. Each time he returned with excellent information about the German positions. Atwell no longer chewed him out. "He's crazy—but the intel he's gettin' is golden. I should probably stop him—"

Gibbs snorted. "Do you really think you can stop him, sir? Short of pullin' him off the line and placing him in a straightjacket?"

"You're right," Atwell sighed. "Davis travels to the beat of his own drum."

The following night Davis disappeared once again and didn't return for three days.

Harry Klutz looked up as Davis neared him. His mouth fell open. "What the hell happened to you?"

Aaron and Worth stared at Davis. No helmet. No pistol. Knife sheath empty.

"Gimme some water," Davis gasped, sinking to the ground.

Harry handed him his canteen.

Davis gulped the water.

"You okay?" Harry asked.

Davis fixed them with a stare. "Hell no."

Aaron leaned toward Davis. "What happened, Patrick?"

"Cigarette," Davis said.

He took the Camel Aaron offered and bent low, cupping his hands around the match Worth extended toward him. He took a long drag, exhaled, and then ran his fingers through his hair.

"Damn German nearly killed my ass. I found this Kraut command center set up in a big house, see. Looked like a lot going on— thought I'd try to get close, maybe find out something useful. Came up on this big Jerry walkin' guard around the place."

He took another drag on the cigarette. "So I sneak up behind him—gonna take him out with my knife. I grabbed him from behind, but before I could gig him, the bastard grabbed my arm and threw me over his shoulder. Lost the knife when I hit the ground—then he was on me like stink on shit. Damn."

Davis shook his head as if trying to clear his thoughts. "So I pull my pistol. He kicked it outta my hand before I could get the safety off."

"How the hell'd you get away?" Aaron asked.

Davis rubbed his forehead. "I've been in a lot of scrapes and a lot of fights growing up on the streets in Philly." He shook his head.

"Nothing like this guy. I kicked. I punched. I bit him 'til my mouth was full of blood. Managed to get free for a second and ran like mad. Lucky for me he wasn't fast enough to catch me. I heard him yellin' as I ran— I'm sure they sent patrols out lookin' for me, but they never got close. Not the way I was movin'."

He took another drag on the cigarette and lowered his head. "I'm never goin' out like that again. No sir. Not me."

Aaron looked at Worth and Harry.

Harry seemed to be stifling a grin. He nudged Davis on the shoulder. "Well, Patrick, you gotta admit it's kinda funny in a way. I mean, you're the one who started it and all. The Kraut was just doin' what he'd been trained to do."

Worth snickered.

Aaron placed a hand over his mouth and turned away.

Davis threw the cigarette to the ground. "You bastards," he said. "I almost got killed by that storm trooper, and you birds think it's funny!"

Harry laughed. "Patrick, can't help it. It is funny. And I'm glad you got away, too. If that Jerry'd killed you, we wouldn't have heard this great story, and we'd never have known what happened to you."

# Chapter Thirty-seven

Aaron sat before the communications set. "Cello One to Maestro. Come in, Maestro."

"This is Maestro, go ahead, Cel—"

"Maestro, come in. Do you read, Maestro?"

Silence.

"Damn!" Aaron slammed his fist onto the wooden table. "Line's out again. Must be a break between here and battalion."

He turned to Gibbs. "Sarge, I've gotta fix the wire."

Gibbs nodded. "With all the incoming artillery and mortar fire we been getting, one of the rounds prob'ly blew it up again. Watch yourself out there."

The small house serving as the company command post was lit by only a few candles stuck into wine bottles. Blankets covered the windows. A damp, musty smell permeated the entire building. The flickering light gave an eerie glow to the occupants. With Captain Atwell attending a company commanders' meeting, Sergeant Gibbs, Aaron, and Francis Furlong were the only ones on hand.

Aaron crammed on his helmet, grabbed his carbine, and picked up a ten-inch-diameter spool of wire by its U-shaped handle. He frowned. Pulling the reel of wire as he went would make noise, but it couldn't be helped.

"Do you want someone to go with you?" Gibbs asked. "I can't afford to lose my communications sergeant. And you know what happened at Fox Company."

Aaron nodded. Two nights before, Fox Company reported that one of their men went out to fix a broken phone line. He was found dead the next day, throat cut, presumably by a German infiltrator.

Aaron looked around. Furlong lay curled into a corner on the far side of the room, snoring away. "No, Francis is exhausted. I'll be okay, Sarge."

Aaron stepped out of the CP and looked to the north. Darkness, fog, and low clouds obscured the Apennine Mountains for the time being. In daylight he'd stared at the sharp peaks through binoculars. Rugged, tent-like in appearance, some rose to seven thousand feet. The Germans, occupying the high ground as usual, waited there. The Allies would soon move from the low hills to attack those heavily defended positions.

A misting rain fell and threatened to intensify. Aaron shivered. He turned up the collar of his field jacket. Maybe he could get back before the deluge set in.

Leaning down, he reached for the phone line coming out of the bunker and curled his hand loosely around it. Using it as a guide, he set off in the direction of battalion headquarters. He crouched low for a few yards and then began to crawl along the line. The carbine was slung over his right shoulder. He dragged the squeaking spool behind him.

A breeze from the west sent a chill through him. No moon out. Overcast sky. Pitch black. Rain fell faster and ran off the back of his helmet onto his jacket. Some trickled inside his collar and down his back. Water dripped from the helmet's front as well. Damn, he could barely see anything.

He tugged lightly on the wire. No tension. Definitely broken somewhere ahead. This was the worst part of the job. Fixing these breaks. He paused. The Fox Company incident had been two nights ago. No way would a Kraut infiltrator still be hanging around behind American lines now.

After crawling ten more yards, Aaron paused and listened. Small arms fire rattled in the distance. He sighed. The farther away the better. Had to stay low, though. Ricochets could tag you anywhere, anytime. He shuddered, the dampness of his clothes mingling with the chilling awareness of his precarious mortality. Couldn't think about what might lie ahead. Fix the line. Do the job. Get back to the CP.

Another ten yards.

Something rustled to his left.

He froze in mid-crawl and ever so slightly cocked an ear in that direction. Was someone there? Hard as hell to hear anything while wearing the damned helmet, especially in the blustery wind.

A minute passed.

Aaron's ears rang from the strain. Only the low whistle of wind and the ever-present pop of small arms in the distance reached him.

He crawled on.

Would the storm sounds cover his movements as he approached the break? Probably not. If a German waited, he'd hear him dragging the squeaking spool.

He needed to move faster—get this over with.

The carbine was slowing him down—damn. He stopped. Staying as prone as possible, he slowly unslung the weapon and placed it on the ground.

After fumbling open the buttons of his field jacket, Aaron pulled the .45 automatic from its holster. He retracted the slide and then eased it forward, chambering a round as quietly as possible. He winced. It still made a lot of noise. Why hadn't he done that before he left the CP? If a Kraut heard it, his goose was cooked.

He moved the gun toward its holster. Wait! He snicked on the safety. Now—cocked and locked. Gibbs said it was the only safe way to handle a .45. Aaron looked into the darkened sky. Please, God, help me get through this.

Wire in hand again, Aaron crawled several feet. He glanced over his shoulder. A flare far to his left lit up the sky. There, too far away to be of use now, lay the carbine. It was a shame to leave it. But it was too awkward. He'd pick it up on his return trip.

If there was one.

A sudden shudder ran down Aaron's spine, raising the hairs on his arms and neck. He had to stop thinking that way.

Despite the cold and the rain, sweat slicked his forehead as he continued moving through the mud. His heart pounded so hard it felt as if it might explode from his chest. What in God's name was he doing out here all alone? He stopped. It was as if he could hear his mother speaking.

*Yea, though I walk through the valley of the shadow of death, I will fear no evil.*

She'd recited these words often as he was growing up. The gooey mud sucked hard against his elbows and mud-covered combat boots. Even worse, rocks stabbed against his chest, elbows, and knees. Minor inconveniences considering what was at stake, though he'd no doubt be covered in bruises tomorrow.

Tomorrow. "God, please give me a tomorrow," he said under his breath.

Cold, wet, dirty, and sweaty. Maggie wouldn't touch him if she could see him now. A vision of her sweet face filled his mind. Aaron shook his head. Couldn't think about her. Had to keep his mind on the job if he ever wanted to see her again.

His eyes had adjusted to the inky blackness, but the precipitation played hell with his depth perception. Aaron blinked hard, squeezing the rain from his eyes. He could barely see five feet ahead. In basic training he'd hated night maneuvers. Now, the darker the better. Unless someone was waiting in that darkness with a razor-sharp knife. He took a long, slow breath. He had to get hold of himself. This was just a line break. He'd fixed dozens of them. Why was he getting so worked up now? He just needed to find it, fix it, and get back to—

He stopped short.

Surely he'd heard something this time. Another minute of waiting. He barely breathed. No sounds except for the double-time cadence of his beating heart. Hell, anyone lying in ambush could hear it, probably before they heard the spool of wire he dragged.

He had to stop thinking so much. It was just the wind. He rubbed his chin and then released his grip on the spool's handle. After he found the break, he'd come back and get it.

Two minutes later he found the severed wire. His finger brushed over the end of it.

Damn. It had been cut—not blown apart.

He stared into the misty darkness. Should he run? No. He'd be an easy target. What now? He crawled backward a few feet and eased the .45 from its holster.

He listened.

A thump like a footstep to his left.

He rose to one knee and fired twice, the big pistol bucking in his hand as a two-foot flame spat from the barrel, lighting the darkness. Aaron's ears rang.

A crashing blow hit him from the rear, knocking the pistol and his helmet into the darkness. A huge meaty hand slapped onto Aaron's forehead, reaching to pull his head back and expose his throat. But the wet hand slipped off his sweaty brow, making his attacker tilt backward.

Aaron ducked his chin and rolled onto his side. The German rocked forward, pinning him down. He could smell the Kraut's fetid, hot breath.

A break in the clouds allowed moonlight to reflect off the German's oncoming blade. Aaron pushed up with all his might. The man lost his balance and rolled to the side. Aaron grabbed the knife-wielding wrist with both hands and held on tight. Inching downward, the blade looked like a gleaming icicle in the pale light. Aaron's arms shook. The German, bigger, stronger, continued pushing the steel toward him.

Please, God! Help! Aaron gasped for air.

Bending his right knee, he kicked hard. His boot landed a glancing blow somewhere on the man's torso. The Kraut shifted his weight. Aaron jerked from under him, rolled several feet, and then made it to his knees, his back to the larger man. Lunging, the German grabbed him by the collar of his field jacket and yanked it. The jacket came away in his attacker's hands. Thank God he hadn't re-buttoned it after drawing the pistol. The pistol! Where was it? Aaron groped frantically in the muddy ground, searching desperately.

The German snarled, tossed the jacket aside, dropped into a crouch, and rushed toward him. Feet spread wide, Aaron also crouched low, his eyes fixed on the oncoming blade. The Kraut made several feints and then executed a quick thrust.

Caught flat-footed, Aaron was fully exposed to the flashing weapon. But the German stumbled and fell forward. Aaron sidestepped and grabbed his wrist. Using the enemy's own momentum to pull him forward, Aaron pivoted to his side and wrapped his left arm around the upper portion of the German's now extended limb.

With all his might, Aaron pulled up with his left arm while pushing down with his right. The Kraut's arm snapped with a loud crack. He yelped. Aaron brought a knee up, bashing the enemy's knife-wielding hand against it. As the blade fell, Aaron punched at the man's neck, but he only succeeded in hitting him in the nose.

Though the large man stumbled backward, he did not fall.

Damn. What did it take to put this guy down? Aaron retreated several steps. If he could only find the .45.

The injured man moved forward and then leaned over. Blood poured from his broken nose. He picked up the knife in his left hand.

"American gangster, huh? Think this will stop me?" He gestured toward his dangling arm. "Now I kill you with my left hand."

Oh shit. This man was not human. Aaron's gaze swept the ground. Where in the hell was the pistol?

His hand went to his belt and brushed the hilt of the knife—the one Maggie had sent. He jerked it from its sheath. When the German lunged again, Aaron shifted it to his left hand and jumped away from the slashing blade, but not before it sliced through his shirt, cutting a gash in his right side. Blood spilled from the wound, soaking his shirt.

Aaron clenched his teeth and sucked in a breath. With no gun and now bleeding, what did he have to lose? He had to end this or die.

Lunging forward, Aaron stepped into the gray-clad figure and clasped his right hand onto the German's left wrist.

The two locked together in a deadly dance. Aaron knocked the German's dangling right arm aside, thrust his blade upward into his exposed solar plexus, and pushed hard. The German grunted like an enraged bear. Aaron jerked the knife out and then drove it into the man again. Their eyes met as a strange sigh escaped the German's lips.

"I know how to use my left hand too," Aaron whispered. He stepped back and pulled hard on his blade. Blood gushed from the open wound, covering Aaron's hand and sleeve. A metallic, coppery smell hung in the air. He pushed the enemy soldier away.

A guttural sound, softer and more desolate, rushed from the German as he stumbled backward. Blood poured from his lips, mixing with the stream falling from his nose. He stared at his chest and tried to speak. Then a whimper, like a wounded animal. He looked at Aaron, a questioning look crossing his face.

With a final spasm, he sank to his knees, pitched forward, and fell face down in the mud. One leg twitched, and then he lay still.

Aaron gasped, sucking air through his nose and mouth. He staggered to the prostrate body. Holding his knife at the ready, he placed two fingers to the German's neck. No pulse.

Dropping his bloody knife, Aaron spun away and vomited. He crossed his arms across his chest and rocked back and forth. He looked up. "Oh God. Oh God!" The rain fell harder and mingled with his tears.

His sobs increased, as did the rain. The sky began to spin. The driving rain seemed to press him into the frigid mud. He moaned. Everything went black.

When he came to, the rain pelted him. His nostrils filled with the smell of blood. His own? His lungs burned as he gasped for air. Where was he? Oh yes...

Repair the line.

He rolled over and came up on his knees. His side hurt. He looked at the slit in his shirt. Blood oozed from the wound. He pulled a bandage from a pouch on his pistol belt and covered the wound. Then he probed for the phone wire. After five minutes of searching, he found the other end ten yards away. The German had not just cut the wire, but snipped out a long section. The repair would be more difficult.

After retrieving the spool, he cut a piece of wire long enough to splice the break. His hands shook so badly he could hardly work. He vomited again, dry heaves this time, but he eventually managed to finish the repair. Time to locate his gear and get back to the CP.

A search that seemed to take forever yielded his helmet. He found the .45 nearby, buried in a muddy depression. He shook his head as he rubbed the slimy goop from its dull finish. "Now I find you."

He looked toward his dead adversary, crawled over, and retrieved his knife. Maggie's knife. If he hadn't had it...if the German hadn't stumbled as he made his killing lunge...

Overhead the clouds broke. Stars twinkled. Maybe he hadn't been completely alone after all.

He wiped the bloody blade on his rain-soaked pants leg and slid it into its sheath. He could never tell Maggie how close he'd come to dying tonight or that he'd looked into a man's eyes as he'd killed him. No. He could never tell her about any of this.

# CHAPTER THIRTY-EIGHT

Rain dripped off the back of Aaron's helmet and ran down his back. He shivered, came awake, and blinked. The dream—what was it? Oh yeah. He'd been changing a water pump on a '35 Ford—or at least trying to. He couldn't seem to get the wrench on the bolt—it kept slipping off. Crazy dream.

He adjusted the shelter half above him to redirect the rain, to no avail. It continued pouring into the foxhole unabated. He sighed. Steady, heavy rain had fallen for four days straight. Knee-deep mud everywhere—a soupy mixture of water, mud, and God only knew what else. Trucks and jeeps bogged down to their axles. No matter. The war must go on.

He peeked around the edge of the canvas covering, tilting his head to gaze at the sky. A raindrop plopped into his eye. "Damn."

Thick clouds above. No sign of a letup. He ducked back, trying to find a spot where the nonstop downpour wasn't flowing in. The bottom of the foxhole was filled with brown, ugly looking water. His leather combat boots were soaked. He wiggled his toes. Soggy feet. And no dry socks. Yesterday's socks—tucked inside his shirt—were still damp. No need to think about changing them.

He used a dirty finger to brush his teeth, spitting into the muck after. He'd lost his toothbrush somewhere three days ago. Maybe the next ration pack would have one in it. If there was another ration pack anytime soon. Even the supply mules had trouble making it up the sodden hills.

He recalled mortar rounds exploding sometime during the night. Nothing new there. The Jerries had a clear view of them from the heights above. Why no counter battery fire from our side? Who knows—maybe the artillery guys gave up and went home. He chuckled at his little joke. Gonna be a long day. Just like the one before.

At least he could sneak a smoke here in his earthen shelter. He pulled a damp cigarette from his shirt pocket, lit up, and inhaled deeply. Sure would like some coffee. Have to settle for the next best thing. He pulled his canteen cup from its pouch and collected a half cup of rain water. Pulling a D-ration chocolate bar from his field jacket pocket, he shaved off several chunks, chopped it up into fine shavings, dropped them into the cup, and stirred. Not the best, but better than nothing.

What would this day bring—other than more rain? He looked at his watch. Time to check in with Captain Atwell.

"Johnson, goddammit, tell those assholes in battalion if we don't get some artillery support up here in the next twenty minutes, the Jerries will be sitting in *their* laps 'cause there won't be any of us left to hold them off."

"Roger." Aaron yelled into the headset, trying to be heard above the sound of exploding shells and small arms fire. Another day. Another ridge. More mud. The endless rock face of the mountains. More men wounded. More dead. How many replacements had arrived and how many of them were left? For some reason the newer guys seemed to get hit a lot. Aaron didn't even know the names of most of them.

"This is Maestro. Copy your message. Stand by."

Stand by. Didn't they know the company was getting shot to pieces? Couldn't they hear the sound of battle through the radio? Or did the guys at battalion just not care?

"Cello—this is Maestro. Come in."

"Cello here—what's the word?"

"We're sending a tank up to give you some fire support. It's all we've got available. Out."

Aaron groaned. Shit. A damn tank was little help—even assuming it could get up to where they were in the first place. Captain Atwell wasn't gonna like this.

"Uhh, Captain," Aaron said.

"Wha'd battalion say?" Atwell said.

An 88-millimeter shell exploded behind them. "They're sending a tank up, sir."

"Jesus Christ!" Atwell said. He shook his head. "The poor bastard. Let me know if it makes it up here."

Aaron heard the *clank, clank* of its steel treads before he saw it. A Sherman tank rounded the mountain path, somehow making its way through the ever-present mud. It stopped seventy-five yards downhill.

"Captain—"

"I hear it," Atwell said. "Go talk to him."

Aaron moved downhill fast, crouching low as he went. He reached the tank, which sat idling in the protection of a huge rock outcropping. He climbed onto the tank as the turret hatch opened and its commander stuck his head out. Aaron pointed up the mountain and told the tanker where the nearest German 88 battery was located. The tank commander nodded, ducked back inside, and closed the hatch.

Aaron shook his head. One lone tank against a German 88? With no room to maneuver—and he'd have no cover when he pulled out from behind those rocks. He jumped from the tank and rejoined Atwell.

"I told him his best bet was to try to get a few quick rounds into the area where the 88 is and then get the hell out of here. He didn't disagree."

The Sherman's engine roared, smoke belched from its exhaust, and it chugged up the steep hillside. The turret spun in the direction Aaron had pointed. The steel behemoth clanked past them and came to a stop thirty yards ahead. Several of the newer men cheered when the muddy tank pulled up. Two or three ran behind it, apparently seeking cover.

"Get the hell away from that tank!" Atwell yelled. "Where do you think that 88's gonna be shootin', you dumbasses!"

The Sherman's 75-millimeter gun fired—once, twice. The shells exploded near the site of the German 88.

"He's got a damn good loader and gunner, I'll give him that," Atwell said.

An 88 round tore through the air and exploded next to the tank. Gears ground and the Sherman shot back down the ridge in reverse. Another shell landed in the spot it had just vacated. Gaining speed, the massive hulk flew past the CP and continued down the mountain, around the rock outcropping, and out of sight, the sound of its engine fading as it went.

The Germans shelled the company continuously for another fifteen minutes. Cries of, "Medic, medic," filled the air.

Atwell touched Aaron's shoulder. "Give battalion another call. Tell 'em not to bother sending us any more help."

# CHAPTER THIRTY-NINE

Aaron lay prone twenty-five yards ahead of the company line and carefully poked his head above the mound of dirt he'd crawled behind. He scanned the terrain through a set of field glasses. The first shadows of darkness covered his movements. An olive grove sat before him, its short trees twisted and mangled. At the far end of the field, he could just make out the edge of a terraced embankment.

"See anything?" Art Ferdinand asked from beside him.

"Nothin' unusual," Aaron said. "We'll take the patrol out an hour after dark, move through that olive grove up ahead, then through the terraced fields beyond," Aaron said.

"What are we lookin' for?"

"Same as always—anything we can find out about enemy positions and strengths. Take a prisoner if we get a chance. No engaging the Jerries unless they shoot first."

"'Til then, let's get some shut-eye. Could be a long night."

Ninety minutes later Aaron, Ferdinand, and two others crept and crawled through the olive grove. A half-moon and the stars provided just enough light to allow them to make their way.

Aaron gripped his rifle and peered through the darkness. He might be the company communications sergeant now, but it didn't get him out of going on patrols. Sweat ran down his face, and the tightness in his chest made his breathing shallow. Would he ever get over these feelings? Probably not. After all, somewhere out there was an army of enemy soldiers, and they wanted to kill him.

Ten minutes out, the men made it to the base of the first terrace. Aaron pressed his body against the earthen wall as he rose and peeked over the top of the chest-high embankment. Nothing.

Aaron pulled himself onto the ground above and slowly crawled forward. Rough ground tore at his clothing and bruised his body.

The Italian farmers probably dug the large rocks from the vineyards and threw them to the sides of the field. He'd done the same on his father's farm when he'd plowed the fields behind a mule.

The others came up behind him. Would they be heard? Would a machine gun open up on them? Or a mortar? He took a breath and then inched forward. In the distance a machine gun fired a long burst. Not close.

The patrol reached the next terrace. So far, so good. Aaron repeated the crawl onto the higher levels at two more terraces. His back ached and his legs were rubbery. Perspiration covered his face and ran into his eyes, clouding his vision. The rocks seemed more numerous at each new field. If they didn't find anything soon, he would give the order to head back.

At the next terrace, Aaron again poked his head above the embankment and froze. Three yards away, the barrel of a German Mauser was pointed directly at his face.

Aaron's eyes opened wide. He stifled a yell.

The German's head rested on the rifle's stock. He was sound asleep.

Aaron fell backward, heart pounding, and fell onto the man coming up behind him. "Outta here!" Aaron hissed. As the two untangled, the others apparently sensed the danger and were already moving away fast.

A shot from the Mauser rang out. Nowhere close, thank God. Aaron crouched low, moving at full speed now. The German must've been as startled as he'd been. Probably fired straight into the air after being jolted awake. But all the Germans couldn't be sleeping, and the shot would—

A machine gun fired, tracer rounds licking out toward them. Looking like roman candle blasts, but moving ten times faster. Rifle and submachine gun fire joined in. As the men scrambled down the terraced embankment at the far end of the field, a flare ignited the night sky and more machine gun fire erupted. Bullets zinged above Aaron's head. More tracers flew wildly through the night sky.

"Stay low! Move!" Aaron said. He frowned. No need to say that—everyone was sprinting now. In a few more minutes they'd be back to their lines. His lungs burned as he sucked in air.

A half hour later Aaron stood inside the bunker that served as company headquarters. He pointed to a map, showing Captain Atwell approximately where they'd encountered the Germans.

"Did you get any idea of their strength?" Atwell asked.

"Couldn't say for sure, sir. Based on the amount of fire they put on us, I'd say at least company size."

"Anybody hurt?"

"No sir, everyone made it back okay."

Atwell nodded. Had the captain even heard his response?

"And there was no way you could capture that German? It would have been great to have a prisoner," Atwell said as he studied the map.

Aaron shook his head. "No sir, it all happened too fast. If we'd tried to snatch him, we'd never have made it back." No need to tell the captain his own startled reaction had blown any chance at making a capture.

Atwell chewed his lower lip. "Okay. Get some sleep. We'll probably be moving out tomorrow. Maybe you'll get another crack at that German then."

"Yes sir. Good night, sir. If I do find him again, I hope he's still asleep."


Two nights later a German patrol crossed the river and captured an entire squad of men from E Company.

"One of the guys got away. He said the sentry must have gone to sleep. The Germans were on 'em before they knew what was up," Worth said.

"Who was the squad leader?" Aaron asked.

"Tolliver."

"Oh shit," Aaron said.

"Yeah—he said he'd never be captured. Couldn't stand the thought of being a POW."

"I hope he's okay—didn't try anything stupid."

"Yeah, me too."

The next night when the evening patrol returned, they carried a body with them. Sergeant Tolliver.

"How'd he get it?" Aaron asked Patrick Davis.

"Bullet in the back of the head. Either he was trying to get away, or he put up such a fight the Krauts just blew his brains out on the spot."

"Poor bastard," Aaron said.

Davis spat and hefted his Thompson. "Yeah. Poor bastard."

The next day the entire division was ordered off the line.

# CHAPTER FORTY

The entire company of dirty, unshaven, mud-covered men assembled in a field well behind the front line. Standing at parade rest, they stared straight ahead. The autumn sun sank low. They had stood like this for hours. Several men had passed out and had to be carried away. Gray clouds covered the sky. Even behind the battle line, the stench of death and mayhem still filled the air.

Aaron's throat was parched. If only he could reach for his canteen. His stomach growled. How long did they have to stand there? When were they moving to the rest area?

Captain Atwell stepped before them.

"Ten-hut!" First Sergeant Gibbs barked.

The GIs snapped to attention.

Eyeing his men, hands on hips, Atwell wore the same dirty uniform as the soldiers before him. Only his clean-shaven face distinguished him from the ragtag group he commanded. "Men, you've fought hard, and you deserve the rest we're getting. Trucks will be here soon to carry us to the rear. In the meantime, remove all unit insignias. Don't let anything show that indicates your division. Don't talk to any civilians or anyone outside your individual unit."

Aaron caught Worth's eye and raised an eyebrow.

Worth shrugged.

The trucks arrived an hour later. They bore no markings—none of the usual white lettering on the cab doors, no circled stars. Even the typical markings on the canvas coverings on the beds of the trucks had been blacked out.

Aaron climbed into a truck with a group of enlisted men from the company headquarters unit. The convoy departed, traveling over the deeply rutted road in the darkness. No headlights—just the faint glow from tiny blackout lights. The going was slow, and twice the procession got lost and had to backtrack.

189

After a two-hour bone-jarring ride, the trucks stopped and the men were ordered out. Aaron jumped from the truck. It was pitch black. Who cared? They weren't at the front anymore.

He slept on the hard ground with no blanket. He awoke in the morning with no idea where they were.

Setting up tents and digging latrines occupied the entire first day. Aaron carried his communications equipment to the company headquarters tent. First Sergeant Gibbs entered just as Aaron finished setting up.

"Sergeant Gibbs, why all the secrecy?" Aaron asked. "Why'd we have to take our patches off?"

"We're gonna be making a big attack soon," Gibbs said. "The brass is afraid some Italians are still loyal to the Jerries and are keeping them apprised of troop movements. The brass don't want the Krauts to know what unit we are, where we are, or what we're doing."

"Speaking of that, do you know where we are? It's a lot cooler here—lots of trees. Poplars, pines—and olive groves. Even flowers."

"Somebody said this is mid-Tuscany," Gibbs said. "As for me, I'd say we were somewhere just this side of hell—that's what our next mission is gonna be."

The second day small unit tactics training began. Rumors of the impending major attack circulated around the camp.

"We ain't gonna make no more attacks," Charles Bradley said as the platoon took its midmorning break. "Now that we've invaded southern France, the Germans'll have to quit. Our guys have already pushed 'em dang near out of there—Paris has been liberated. Our guys will be in Berlin before you know it—the Jerries are whipped."

"I wouldn't count on it," Patrick Davis said. "They've still got a lot of fight in 'em. And they'll fight harder once they're on their home soil—wait and see."

"Anybody wanna bet on it?" Jack Claytor said. "I'll give two-to-one odds that Davis is right." He held out a cracker to his monkey Coco, perched on his shoulder. The furry animal snatched the morsel and chewed furiously.

Corporal Wagner took off his helmet and wiped his brow. "Yeah, I'll take some of that action. They can't hold out much longer."

Lieutenant Shingleton approached.

"Alright, listen up," Shingleton said. "We've got work to do. Forget about the Jerries bein' beat. Let the brass worry about the big picture."

The platoon headed out to work on the next field problem. Aaron picked up his carbine and fell in beside Harry.

"So, how do you like the little carbine?" Harry asked.

"It's fine. A lot lighter than the M-1."

"I'm surprised you have to do these training exercises," Harry said, "you being attached to company HQ now."

"Gibbs says I have to. Can't be getting rusty on him, he said."

Harry chuckled. "Sounds like him." His voice dropped to a whisper. "How's Furlong doing? Has he had any..."

"Nope," Aaron said. "Not a drop."

"That's too bad. That boy loves his coffee. It's clear the lieutenant feels bad about it. Has he talked to Francis?"

"Tried to—more'n once. Furlong just shakes his head and says it wouldn't be right if he has coffee now."

"Well, some might say Furlong's bein' hardheaded, but I have to admire him stickin' to what he believes."

"Yeah," Aaron said. "I guess so."


Throughout August the training continued. Rigorous calisthenics every day. Mountain warfare tactics again and again. Infantry-tank coordination. Each segment carried out under the warm Tuscany sun.

One afternoon after an exhausting day of training, several men of G Company listened to a battery-powered radio someone had scrounged. Aaron wrote a letter to Maggie. Harry sharpened his bayonet. Others lounged on the ground, talking quietly.

The sounds of Glenn Miller's "Moonlight Serenade" poured from the radio's speaker. Each day and night the Nazi station played American songs between episodes of propaganda and rhetoric aimed at the Allied troops. When the song ended, the silky voice of "Axis Sally" began its sultry spiel.

"This is for the boys in the Eighty-fifth Division, hiding out in the woods down in Tuscany. It's okay, fellas—you can remove your insignias and other identifying markers, but we know you're there and we know what you plan to do. Come on, fellas. Why do you keep fighting? You have no chance, you know. Why don't you put down your rifles and tell General Clark you've had enough. Then you can go home to your wives and girlfriends. I know you miss them. They probably miss you too—unless some four flusher is looking after your girl while you're over here. But if you insist on making your fruitless attack—as soon as you work up the courage, come on up to see us—we're waiting for you. Goodnight, boys."

A blur of movement caught Aaron's eye. Harry's bayonet now sat imbedded in the radio's casing, silencing it permanently.

"Bitch," Harry said.

"I still ain't sure about some of these new replacements," Gibbs said. "The platoon leaders tell me they don't seem to be getting it."

Captain Atwell sipped coffee from his canteen cup.

Aaron fiddled with the radio set and pretended not to be listening.

Atwell lowered his cup. "They'll be okay. When we attack, the training will kick in. But it ain't gonna be easy."

"What does G-2 say about what we're gonna be up against?" Gibbs said.

Atwell sat. "Well, when we took Rome, the Jerries didn't have a real defensive line to fall back to. That's why we were able to chase 'em as far as we did. And when the Brits ran them out of Florence, they had to fall back from the Arno River Line. Now they're in the Apennines. They've been workin' on defenses there for over a year—call it the Gothic Line."

"More mountains, huh?"

"Yeah, high ones—some are seven thousand feet. And steep. No roads to speak of—just goat paths, mostly. They're dug deep into the rocks. Every approach will be zeroed in with artillery, mortars, machine guns—it's gonna be rough, First Sergeant."

"And those bastards always have the high ground," Gibbs said.

Aaron's stomach tightened. More mountains. More fighting. More men dying.

"Not to mention," Atwell said, "with all the divisions they've pulled out of Italy and sent to France, we're now seriously undermanned going up against some of the best the Germans have. The book says an attacking force needs superior numbers to breach fortified positions. We won't have anywhere near that."

# CHAPTER FORTY-ONE

The second week in September, the division was ordered to the front, twenty miles northeast of Florence.

As the company communications sergeant, Aaron joined the platoon leaders and other key noncoms for a briefing outside Captain Atwell's tent. A map of the area rested on a makeshift easel.

"Here's the scoop," Atwell said, pointing to the map. "We'll be making the main thrust for the entire corps. General Clark's putting a lot of trust in our ability to break this line because of what we did at Tremensuoli. The entire battalion will be here," he said, pointing to a position on the map. "Our objective is Mount Verucca, overlooking the Il Giogo Pass. Taking Verucca will open up access to the only thing that can be called a road heading north."

Atwell's pointer moved across the map. "The 338th will be on our left. Their objective is Mount Altuzzo to our west. The 337th will be in regimental reserve, ready to fall in wherever needed." The pointer moved again. "The British First Division will be on our immediate right. Their job is to push the Jerries back and guard our flank.

"It's imperative we stay in constant radio and messenger contact with all of them throughout. If the Jerries manage to drive a wedge between us at any point, our flanks will be exposed and the entire Fifth and Eighth Army lines will have to withdraw."

Aaron grimaced. Keeping those lines open would be his job.

"Heavy artillery and aerial bombardment will precede the attack. But intelligence reports indicate the Jerries are dug in deep, so we can't count on that having a great effect." Atwell put down the pointer.

"So when do we attack, sir?" Lieutenant Shingleton asked.

"Day after tomorrow—September thirteenth, at oh-six hundred."

After meeting with Atwell and Sergeant Gibbs to lay out a plan for establishing and maintaining the necessary contact with the other units, Aaron sat outside his tent and chewed on the stub of a pencil. Couldn't let Maggie know what was coming or how scared he was. Had to let her know he missed her, though, and somehow tell her that if he didn't make it…no, he couldn't think like that. He had to make it. Somehow, some way.

Dear Maggie,
  We've been real busy lately, so I haven't had a chance to write. I hope you're not mad at me. The weather here has been great. A little hot, but not as bad as August back home. Fall is coming on now, and it's real pleasant. I wish you could see how pretty the country is here. Maybe we can come here together someday when this war is over.
  I need to tell you that you may not hear from me for a while, but don't worry. The Army has something special for us to do, but it shouldn't take too long. In the meantime, I want you and Barry to know I think of you constantly and can't wait to get home. It's getting dark, so I'd better close while I can still see to write. I love you.
  Aaron

The following day the battalion moved into its jump-off position facing Mount Verucca.

"Can you believe how high those damn mountains are? And how steep?" Art Ferdinand said.

"They're up there alright," Aaron said. "This is gonna be tough."

He raised binoculars to his eyes and surveyed the mountainside. "Geez—what a sight. They've got concertina wire strung all across the mountain. Two—no—three rows deep. Some of it even bends backward from the face of the mountain. How are we supposed to get through that? And mines everywhere—you can count on that. Damn. I hope somebody's got a good plan. I sure don't."

"I guess we'll find out tomorrow. Hey—look!" Art pointed skyward.

A German Me-109 fighter plane streaked overhead, smoke pouring from its engine. Close behind it an American P-38 fighter poured rounds into the fleeing German.

"He's got 'im—he's got 'im!" Art shouted.

The Messerschmitt trailed more black smoke, and its nose dipped downward. Seconds later it crashed into the mountainside, creating a huge fireball.

The P-38 pulled up sharply, engines straining to gain altitude.

"Wow—did you see that guy?" Aaron said. "He almost plowed into the mountain himself. Made short work of that Nazi. Did you hear those engines? Man, what I'd give to fly one of those babies."

"He's packin' some firepower, too," Art said. "I'd like to be able to cut loose like that."

The twin-tailed fighter waggled its wings as if to say, "Glad to give you a show, guys," and disappeared to the south.

"Well—I guess the show's over," Aaron said. "Back to work. Are Worth and Harry okay? Ready for the attack, I mean?"

"As much as any of us. Worth will be carrying messages back and forth from E Company on our left. Harry—well, Harry's always ready."

"I think we've done all we can as far as the communications equipment goes," Aaron said. "The com gear's been checked and double-checked. Francis is with the 337th as communications liaison. We've got plenty of wire hooking up the field phones. Generator for the main set is working okay. I can't think of anything else, can you?"

"Just one."

"What's that?"

"Did you tell Furlong to pray hard?"

"I don't think we need to tell Saint Francis that."


As planned, the artillery and air bombardments began at dawn on the thirteenth. Shells screamed overhead and landed with a loud *whump* on the mountainside ahead. Above, P-47 fighters launched bombs and rockets. P-38s zoomed in behind them, strafing suspected enemy locations.

Men in foxholes gripped their rifles and stared at the towering peaks in the distance.

At 0600, whistles blew up and down the line, signaling the men to move forward. Aaron checked his radio for the tenth time. His heart pounded and his hands were clammy. Fear gripped his stomach. Rubbery legs carried him forward. Holding the carbine tightly, he double-timed after Gibbs. He blew out a breath. Surely no one could ever get used to going into battle.

"Pull back! Pull back!" Atwell waved his arm. A hail of incoming machine gun fire punctuated his order. Mortar rounds fell all around. Men yelled and screamed. Dead and wounded GIs lay all around.

The third attack in three days had failed to take even a foot of ground. From their entrenched positions dug well into the rocks and steep mountain crevices, the Germans had no problem holding them at bay. GIs retreated en masse, scrambling, crawling, sliding, and falling down the steep, rock-strewn muddy hillside, eager to escape the deadly kill zone and seek cover behind the large boulders below. Stretcher-bearers, hunched low, carried some of the dead and wounded down the mountain trail. Soldiers who were able carried or dragged their injured buddies as they went.

Atwell turned to Aaron. "Johnson! Artillery! Now!"

Aaron nodded. He'd already called in the coordinates. He shouted into the handset. "Fire for effect! Repeat—fire for effect!"

Within seconds 105-millimeter rounds whistled overhead and exploded on the ridge above the retreating soldiers. The combined noise from Allied and German fire made spoken commands impossible. Atwell motioned to Aaron and pointed downhill. Aaron grabbed his carbine and set out after his CO, the heavy radio bouncing against his back as he ran. Maybe having General Clark's favor wasn't such a good thing after all.

# CHAPTER FORTY-TWO

For the fourth time in two days, G Company attacked a German defensive position situated around an abandoned farmhouse and a few scattered outbuildings. A steady rain fell. The sky was overcast, the terrain almost straight up. Rocks and sticky, gooey mud. Relentless German fire pinned them down.

After several hours the Germans fell back. Captain Atwell urged the men forward even as the retreating Germans turned to fire a few last rounds.

"Gibbs, tell Mike to position his machine guns pronto and have the men dig in. We'll set up the company CP in the farmhouse."

"Right, Cap'n." Gibbs moved away, barking orders to the heavy weapons squad.

Captain Atwell moved toward the house. "Johnson, bring that radio inside. I want to check in with battalion right away and let 'em know we've finally taken our objective."

Inside, Atwell removed his helmet and jerked a map from the case strapped across his chest. "I can't believe it took us all day to take this place." He blew out a long breath and spread the map onto a table.

"I'll set up the radio in here, sir." Aaron motioned toward an adjoining room.

"Let me know when you get headquarters," Atwell said.

Aaron shrugged the radio off his back and set it on a shelf which ran the length of the room's back wall. He flexed his shoulders and rubbed the back of his neck. Damn. The radio got heavier every day.

He completed the set-up procedures. Sweat rolled down his face. His heart raced. Every day for—how long now? Attack. Dig in. Attack.

Tired. Always tired. And casualties. Heavy. New replacements joined them every day.

Would it ever end? It ended for some today. He didn't want it to end that way for him. He glanced out the window. The Jerries had retreated, but to even higher ground, as usual. Was Italy uphill all the way to—to where? The damn North Pole as far as he knew.

He moved away from the window and pushed the radio set further against the wall. Germans on the ridge above could be watching him. Couldn't be too careful. He adjusted the radio frequency, made contact with battalion headquarters, and gave the coded call sign.

"Cap'n, I've got battalion," he said as he walked into the main room.

Atwell and Gibbs stood staring at a map resting on the table.

"Thanks, Priv—I mean, Sergeant." Atwell straightened and turned.

A whooshing sound tore through the house, followed by a loud explosion.

Gibbs looked up. "What the—?"

"Eighty-eights!" Atwell yelled. "Cover!"

Aaron ran to the next room, snatched the radio and code books, and followed the captain to the doorway. Exploding artillery rounds struck the area in rapid succession.

Atwell ran out the doorway. "Fall back—find cover!"

Aaron struggled with the radio. Everywhere men were running, some without helmets; some without rifles. One barefoot soldier raced by carrying a combat boot in each hand. More artillery rounds exploded among them, then mortar rounds. Shrapnel filled the air. Men yelled, screamed, and shouted in pain.

Machine guns opened up. A full burst caught one man in the back, his body jerking spasmodically as his arms flailed. An agonized cry escaped his lips. "Momma! Momma!" Bullets tore through another man, virtually cutting him in two. Dark red splotches covered the back of his field jacket as he pitched forward.

Another artillery round landed nearby. Two men on Aaron's left disappeared in the blast.

"God help us!" Aaron prayed through clenched teeth. A man ahead screamed and fell. "My leg!" he yelled. Blood poured from his thigh as he tried to regain his feet.

What was his name? Bertrand? Yes. Aaron grabbed the struggling man and half-carried, half-dragged him several yards to a low stone wall. He helped Bertrand over it and fell to the ground beside him. More artillery rounds exploded, shaking the ground, and the high-pitched, zinging sound of flying shrapnel accompanied the earsplitting explosions. Machine gun fire struck the wall where they had been only moments before. Another soldier attempted to clamber over the wall. A machine gun round tore through his head, splattering blood and brains onto Aaron. The lifeless body fell onto Bertrand, landing on his wounded leg. Bertrand screamed. Aaron rolled the body away. Couldn't help him. But Bertrand needed attention.

"Medic! Medic!" Aaron shouted.

Frank Church rushed to Bertrand, tore open his pants leg, and poured sulfa powder into the gaping wound. Blood spewed from the torn flesh. Church ripped a bandage out of its wrapping and slapped it onto the spewing leg. "We gotta get him outta here," he said. "Stretchers—over here!"

Two men with a stretcher arrived and placed the wounded soldier onto it. Bertrand turned his head to look at Aaron. His face had gone pale and his eyes were glazed. "Thanks, Johnson, I couldn't have made it if you hadn't helped me."

"Hang on, Bertrand. You'll be in a hospital bed flirting with the nurses soon," Aaron said. Aaron tore his eyes away from Bertrand. Maybe not. Bertrand's breathing was shallower. His chalk-white face contrasted the faint morphine smile on his lips.

The stretcher-bearers crawled away, pulling the stretcher behind them.

Aaron looked up. Captain Atwell hugged the ground about six feet away. The CO motioned Aaron to his side as another artillery shell shook the earth. Aaron reached him just as Gibbs shouted, "Captain, they've turned antiaircraft guns on us. Eighty-eights! They only pulled back to suck us in. They'll blow this place to kingdom come and us with it unless we get some counter battery fire on that ridge."

"Johnson, call it in," Atwell ordered. "Tell 'em we've gotta have artillery on that ridge!"

Aaron barked coordinates from his map into the telephone handset. American artillery fire soon fell on the German position, but not before enemy infantry reoccupied the area G Company had just left.

Thirty yards away an artillery shell ripped through the stone wall and tore through one man, severing both legs above the knee. The projectile traveled another twenty yards, burrowed into a mud embankment, and exploded.

The man stared, wide-eyed. "Oh God! My legs!"

Doc Church rushed to him, poured sulfa powder on the bloody stumps, and tied tourniquets around them. The man grabbed the front of Church's field jacket and pulled him close. "Don't let me die! Don't let me die, Doc!"

Church stuck a morphine shot into the man's arm, but it did little to settle him down.

Two minutes later Aaron took a radio message from headquarters. Pull back. Regroup. Atwell signaled the men. They began to move out in groups of three or four while the remaining GIs attempted to give covering fire.

Aaron stayed crouched next to the CO. Atwell motioned Church to his side. "Can we move that man?" he asked, gesturing with his head toward the now legless soldier.

Church shook his head. "If we move him, he'll bleed out before we get fifty feet. Best bet's to leave him here—maybe the Jerries will pick him up."

Atwell sighed. Rubbed his hand across his face. A burst of MG-42 fire zinged over and against the wall. "Okay—move out. We've got no choice." He motioned to Aaron. "Let's go, Johnson."

As they moved away from the wall, the wounded man cried out, "Don't leave me! Please! Please don't leave me!"

The man yelled, begged, and cursed at them until they were out of earshot.

No one spoke.

At nightfall headquarters ordered the battered GIs to dig in where they were and hold their position.

Two days later, after two more unsuccessful attacks, G Company finally succeeded in capturing the area. There was no sign of the wounded soldier. The next day, Company M moved in to relieve them.


A day later, Aaron and several others sat on the ground eating C-rations.

"It was pretty damn mean of them to turn them antiaircraft pieces on us," Jack Claytor said. "They was firing on us at point blank range, you know. They blew that house you and Captain Atwell were in into toothpicks, didn't they, Aaron?"

"Yeah—we were damn lucky to get out. I realized later the first round must've passed right through the roof and out the other side. If it'd exploded inside, we'd have been goners."

"Hey, did any of you guys notice Ralph Watts when we were runnin' away from that farmhouse?" Art Ferdinand said.

Claytor fed a treat to his monkey, Coco, and then chuckled. "Yeah, he lost his helmet and the dang fool went back and picked it up."

Art nodded. "But did you see how he went back? He was in front of me and I saw him. He didn't run straight back after it. He made a big, looping circle—must've been fifty feet across—and then reached down and picked up that helmet, crammed it on his head, and never broke stride. And with all that he still beat me to cover."

"Didja ever ask him why he did that?" Aaron asked.

"Yeah—he said he thought he needed his helmet and going back for it the way he did just seemed like the best way to do it at the time."

Charles Bradley snorted. "Shoot, our helmets are a damn joke. I had a BB gun when I was a kid that I bet would shoot right through one of 'em."

"Yeah, but I hear the Army is coming up with a way to make 'em better," Worth said.

Bradley narrowed his eyes and looked at Worth. "Yeah—how's that?"

"They're gonna collect all the used metal cans that mystery meat in our C-rations come in, flatten 'em out, and have us add 'em to the inside of our helmets. They ain't no way the Krauts' bullets can shoot through that stuff."

"Hell, they'd do better to throw the cans away and use the meat," Charles said.

"Wouldn't be a bad idea at all if it didn't smell so bad," Art chimed in.

Harry Klutz looked up from a copy of *Stars and Stripes*. "Hey guys, listen to what the brass is saying really happened to us."

*Elements of the 339th Infantry Regiment executed a tactical withdrawal to consolidate and strengthen the Allied line along the Italian front. Lieutenant General Mark Clark, Fifth Army Commander, said the move will strengthen offensive capabilities in the American sector and help prepare for later major action in the Apennine mountain range.*

Harry crumpled the paper and threw it on the ground. "Tactical withdrawal, my ass. The only thing we 'executed' was a rout."

# CHAPTER FORTY-THREE

The next day Aaron took a coded radio message from battalion HQ. They were ordered back to the front. Moving at night, they occupied the same position they had left two days before. Company M had made no progress since taking over the area. Two more days of fighting yielded no gains.

Rain fell in torrents. Nonstop deluges that turned the earth to pure muck. Sticky, gooey mud so thick in places it was impossible for trucks and jeeps to move forward. So soupy in other spots that even the mules were mired up to their bellies.

German artillery barrages rained down on them each night. A lone German bomber, soon nicknamed "Bed-check Charlie," made a bombing and strafing run each evening. Heavy patrol action yielded no useful information—just more casualties.

Aaron attempted to dig a slit trench in the pouring rain. He collapsed into the shallow, muddy hole that already held several inches of dirty brown water. He removed his helmet and wiped sweat and raindrops from his brow. That damn helmet—so heavy, always pushing his neck down into his shoulders. Tired. So tired. How many days since Rome? A hundred? Two hundred? He closed his eyes.

"Aaron! Aaron!" Maggie screamed at him. Her face—so lovely—but she looked scared. What was she trying to tell him? Her mouth moved, but he couldn't understand what she was saying. He reached for her, but she disappeared. Now his son, Barry, stood looking at him. White-blond hair. Holding a baby bottle. Smiling at him.

"Where's your mother?"

"I'm here. Behind you."

He spun around. She fell into his arms. So wonderful to hold her. The sweet aroma of lilac filled his nostrils, and he pulled her tighter. He wanted her. "I'll never let you go," he said. "Never." He lowered his head to kiss her, but she melted away.

"Maggie—come back!"

Footsteps came toward him from behind. He spun. Barry charged at him wearing a German helmet and carrying a rifle with a bayonet pointed directly at him. "Barry, stop! I'm your—"

Aaron jumped awake and stared into Furlong's face. Oh no. It was all a dream. Just a dream.

"That must've been some nightmare you were having. I could hear you from ten feet away," Furlong said. "We've lost communications with the 338th—there must be another break in the line."

"What time is it?" Aaron rubbed his eyes and looked at his watch. He'd only been asleep for fifteen minutes. First sleep he'd had in thirty-six hours. "Okay—who's available?"

"Me and Roberts."

Aaron stalled, taking extra time to gather his gear, waiting for his erection to subside. "Still raining, I see."

"We're about ready to start building the ark," Furlong said.

"Great," Aaron said. Even Furlong's humor was Bible-based. "Let's go then."

The three men crawled through inky blackness and the pouring rain, following the telephone wire. Aaron sighed. How many times had he spliced it? Five? Six? He'd repaired the line to the 337th an equal or greater number of times. Since his encounter with the infiltrator, Captain Atwell insisted that repair teams go in threes. While one man fixed the broken wire, the other two acted as guards—one ten or fifteen yards to the left of the worker, one a like distance to the right.

Locating the severed wire, Aaron whispered in Roberts's ear, "Your turn to fix the line. I'll take right guard. Furlong's already moved ahead on the other side."

"Look," Roberts hissed, "let me take the guard spot. You work faster than me. We can get outta here quicker."

Aaron shrugged. "Okay—sit tight. We'll pick you up when I'm finished. I'll give a tug on the line so you'll know we're on the way."

"Roger."

Aaron lay on his belly and busied himself with the wire. Working in the dark and in the rain was a bitch. His hands were slippery—almost numb because of the cold.

In the distance a machine gun fired. Small arms fire rattled in response. A flare brightened the darkness far to the right as it floated in the night sky.

Aaron pushed his body tighter to the ground. He finished his task and then tugged lightly on the line, first in Furlong's direction, then in Roberts's.

Furlong appeared out of the darkness moments later, crawling quietly through the mud, M-1 cradled in his arms. They moved along the wire toward Roberts's location. Fifteen yards along, Aaron could just make out the shape of a prone figure. He crawled forward and placed his hand on the man's shoulder.

"Roberts—let's go," Aaron whispered, giving him a slight nudge.

No movement.

Aaron crawled closer. Putting his face scant millimeters from Roberts, he squinted. Rain dropped off his helmet onto the pale countenance before him.

Unblinking, unseeing eyes stared back at him.

Aaron placed two fingers to Roberts's neck.

Roberts was dead.

Aaron moved his hand around the man's back. It came away wet—sticky. Not rain. Blood.

He informed Furlong.

Aaron passed his carbine to Francis, crawled past the still form, and grasped the collar of Roberts's field jacket. He tugged, finally overcoming the inertia of the dead man's body. The slick mud made pulling the body somewhat easier than it would have been otherwise.


"So what happened?" Gibbs asked.

Furlong shrugged.

"All I can figure is a stray round or ricochet just caught him. Tore right through his back," Aaron said.

"Damn," Gibbs said.

Aaron nodded. He glanced at Furlong.

"I know what you're thinking, Aaron," Furlong said. "Don't let yourself think that way."

"Can't help it, Francis. If I'd taken my turn as guard, it probably would've been me."

"It wasn't your time. The Lord decides that. Get some coffee. It'll help you warm up."

Aaron raised an eyebrow. "How 'bout you—why don't you have some coffee?"

"No thanks." Furlong said.

# CHAPTER FORTY-FOUR

Maggie put Barry in his bed and pulled a blanket over him. She sighed. His blond curls looked positively angelic, like those of cherubs in the paintings at church. He was growing so fast—trying to walk already, at only nine months. Maybe looking after him would be easier when he started walking. At least he wouldn't have to be carried everywhere.

She glanced at the bed where Ella had placed her son, Kelly, his dark hair a sharp contrast to Barry's blondness. His little chest rose and fell as he breathed.

She tiptoed into the living room. Ella and Juanita sat facing each other on the sofa.

"Are they both asleep now?" Ella asked, turning toward her.

"Yes—Barry finally gave up after he finished his bottle," Maggie said. "Kelly's really out. How do you get him to sleep so fast? He's sleeping like a rock."

Ella laughed. "He sleeps like his daddy. Nothing wakes Buck."

"Good," Maggie said. "They both needed a nap. Maybe they'll stay down awhile." She sat next to a window and pulled back the curtain. Afternoon light streamed in. "The leaves on the trees are turning colors. Fall's in the air. Heavy fog the last three mornings."

"Tell me about it," Juanita said. "Coming home from work this morning I couldn't see ten feet in front of me. And I've gotta go back tonight." She kicked off her shoes and wiggled her toes. "I don't like having to stand up all night. My feet hurt like crazy. Why didn't you two tell me that working is so much harder than school?"

"Now you know how it is," Ella said. "You were in such a hurry to graduate. You didn't know when you had it good. Wait 'til you get married and have babies to look after—then you'll really get a taste of grown-up life."

"Shoot. I'd be glad to be married and have some kids. You sure don't have it so bad. Buck's a supervisor at the mill, and you've got a nice house." She smiled. "When I'm your age, I hope I have as much. And as for work—at least this way I get paid." She spun toward Maggie as if to speak, but didn't. She frowned. "What's the matter, Maggie? Why are you so quiet?"

"Oh, I'm just tired, I guess."

Juanita cocked her head to one side. "Still no letter from Aaron?"

"No. How long is this dumb war gonna last? And things aren't getting any better here, either. Daddy's drinkin' again. I know he misses Momma."

Ella shook her head. "I don't think he'll let it get outta hand. He hasn't come home really drunk, has he?"

"No—but I can smell it on him. I don't like it. You know Momma would have a hissy fit if she was still living."

"She would that," Ella said.

"Barry seems better today," Juanita said. "Is he still running a fever?"

"No fever. But he's still cranky," Maggie said. "I hope he gets better soon. He's been sick two weeks. Doc Crouch said it would just have to run its course. I don't know when I've had a decent night's sleep."

"It's been a few weeks since your last letter from Aaron, hasn't it?" Ella said.

Maggie nodded. "Over three weeks. He said it might be a while, but he's never gone this long without writing before. He said he got the knife I sent him, too. Sounded like he was pleased with it." She stared out the window again. "I don't think he's in any heavy fighting. Sounds like all the really dangerous stuff's in France now. There's almost no mention of Italy in the paper or on the radio. One article said it's just a 'holding action' there now—that wouldn't be dangerous, would it? So why doesn't he write?"

"I read that since things have gone so well in France, the Germans might give up by Christmas," Ella said.

"Oh, I hope so," Maggie said. "Aaron needs to be home. It's been almost a year and a half."

"Has Mildred heard from J.L.?" Juanita said.

"She gets letters 'bout every day. And he's in the Pacific—there's supposedly lots of fighting there." Maggie leaned back, letting her head rest on the chair's rear cushion.

Juanita sat up straight. "Oh, I got another letter from Graydon. He's almost done with basic training. He said he's afraid the war'll be over before he gets a chance to get in on it."

Ella grinned. "Sounds like you're interested in him."

Juanita blushed. "I am not—he's just a nice guy, that's all. And he is Aaron's brother—so, I'm just writing him to be sociable. Same as I'm writing that Haynes guy in Aaron's company. He looks really cute in the pictures Aaron sent."

"Uh-huh," Ella said. "But I've seen you sneaking looks at the pictures of Graydon, too." She looked from Maggie to Juanita and back. "Wouldn't it be something if you two wound up married to brothers?"

Juanita gave her hair a quick flip. "Oh hush, Ella. That's not gonna happen."

"Trust me," Ella said. "Where men are involved, anything can happen. I sure never thought I'd marry Buck when we first dated, but I did. Sometimes I wish I hadn't married so young."

Juanita reached for the pack of cigarettes on the end table. "How old were you? I can't remember—I was too young then to think about it."

"I wondered whose cigarettes those were," Maggie said. "When did you start that?"

"I was seventeen—just out of school—when Buck convinced me to run off and get married," Ella said. "And Maggie's right—you ought to leave cigarettes alone."

Juanita struck a match and held it to the end of the Lucky Strike. "Oh, my foot. I know both of you have smoked. Everyone at the mill does. I'm old enough."

Maggie turned her head and wiped a tear away. Everyone was getting letters but her. Why didn't Aaron write? If there was no heavy fighting going on in Italy now, what would keep him from it? She grasped the apron she wore, twisting the corner. Was he in some town or city where there were civilians—women civilians?

Maybe something was wrong. Maybe he was hurt, or—no, she would have heard. Just last week a green vehicle had pulled up in front of Joyce Fincannon's house. A uniformed man had delivered a telegram. Poor Joyce had broken down right in the doorway when she heard that Tommy, her only son, was dead. Killed on an island in some place Maggie'd never heard of.

Please, God. Don't let a telegram like that come to my house. She wiped another tear away and stared out the window again. The afternoon sun cast long shadows on the yard and the street outside. A swirling breeze kicked up leaves and road dust. Aaron. Where was he?

# CHAPTER FORTY-FIVE

Pinned down. Again. All day. Anything that moved drew a hail of machine gun fire, mortar and heavy artillery fire. And no help from battalion. Repeated calls for counter battery fire got the same response. "No artillery support's available. We're rationed—all the resupply is going to France for the big push. You've used up your allotment already."

Aaron sat in the CP—a hastily dug hole roughly eight by eight carved out of a hillside and buttressed with a few logs. A thin opening in the logs provided a view slit where Captain Atwell periodically studied the higher ground above with his binoculars. Hunched over the radio set, Aaron fought to keep his eyes open. What he'd give for a few hours of shut-eye.

Atwell lowered the field glasses. "Johnson, stick close by the set. If the Jerries counterattack, I'm gonna need to be in touch with battalion ASAP."

"Yes sir," Aaron said. He glanced sidelong at Atwell. The Jerries weren't likely to attack—why should they? They had plenty of time to wait for the GIs to come to them. And cut them down. Until some artillery could be brought to bear, there was nothing the ground-pounders could do but hold their positions.

Aaron yawned, then reached into his field jacket pocket and took out a pencil and a folded sheet of paper.

Dear Maggie,

   I'd like to tell you I'm having a great time here in sunny Italy, but I'd be lying. Truth is, it's really been rough lately. We're in the mountains now, and the going is slow. I thought we had mountains back home, but these Apennines make the Brushy Mountains around town look like midgets. These mountains are even taller and steeper than the Blue Ridge chain—more than

Grandfather Mountain, even. And they are ugly. Nothing but a little scrub of growth here and there—mostly just rocks. And rain nonstop. But we still have to try to push the Germans. What I'd give to have the terrain they have to shoot at us from. They're always above us. Always dug in.

The other day we were moving by a little hillside village. It was raining. Kinda gray and cold. The village had one of those low stone walls around it. As we marched along it, the Jerries opened up on us from the hill above the town. We all flattened out behind that wall. It was a little lower where I was, and the top half of the radio on my back was sticking up above it. The Germans started putting machine gun rounds through it like crazy. Chewed it all to pieces. Burned some big red stripes across my back, too. I couldn't move, either—when I hit the ground, I realized I hadn't hooked the bottom set of straps that go around my waist to hold the radio in place. So it slapped down on my back—felt like a sledge hammer—and knocked the breath out of me. I don't know what might have happened if First Sergeant Gibbs hadn't come back, grabbed my arms, and pulled me to a better spot behind the wall.

Another day was even worse. They ran us out of a house we'd captured and then started firing 88-millimeter antiaircraft guns at the wall we were hiding behind. One on those shells came through and hit a poor guy about twenty yards behind me. It cut both his legs off above the knee. He was screaming like crazy. More guys got hit. We finally got orders to pull out immediately. We weren't able to take the guy who got his legs shot off. He yelled and screamed at us, begging us not to leave him. I hope the Germans found him before he bled to death.

I haven't been able to sleep very much since that day. I can still hear that guy crying and pleading with us not to leave him. I don't even know his name—he hadn't been with us long. But if I make it through this war and live to be a hundred, I'll never forget the sound of his voice when he yelled after us.

Well, I know this letter would never make it past the censors, Maggie. I knew that when I started writing it. But I just had to try and find some way to talk to you about things without really talking to you, if that makes any sense. I'll write another letter after while that won't have this kind of stuff in it. Take care. I love you. Kiss Barry for me.

Aaron.

He crumpled the pages of the letter into a ball and dropped it on the dirt beside him. He propped his elbow on the crate holding the radio set and rested his head on his hand.

"Wake up, Johnson."

"Yes sir." Aaron shook himself awake.

Gibbs laughed. "Don't 'sir' me, I ain't no gentleman."

"Sorry, Sergeant Gibbs. I thought you were the captain."

"He went out to check with the platoon leaders—see if they need anything. Things have been quiet for several hours. Almost too quiet."

"What can I do for you, Sarge?" Aaron said. "Why'd you wake me?"

"I just wanted somebody to talk to. You ever want somebody to talk to, Johnson?"

"Um—yeah—sometimes."

Gibbs cocked his head to the side. "I've been watching you lately. Seems to me something's botherin' you. What is it?"

"I don't know of anything in particular. I'd just like to get the war over and go home, like everybody else." Aaron turned away from Gibbs's stare.

"I've seen a lot of men come and go in this man's Army, Johnson. You do a decent job. You've caught on to the communications job real well. The cap'n said you would. But there's something—I don't know what it is. You seem to kinda hold back sometimes from speakin' up or puttin' in your two cents worth. Am I getting through to you?"

Aaron locked eyes with Gibbs. "You think I'm yellow, First Sergeant?"

Gibbs stared back. "The real question is, do you?"

Aaron took a deep breath. "I—sometimes—I don't know. I'm scared all the time, but—"

"Hell, we're all scared. There's a whole army of Germans tryin' to kill us. Only a crazy man's not scared. Take Davis, for instance. I wonder about him from time to time. He don't strike me as bein' scared enough."

"If he is, he don't show it," Aaron said.

"So what is it? What's makin' you doubt yourself, Johnson?"

Aaron squirmed. "Well—you know when we made that first attack, on hill seventy-nine?"

"I'll never forget it," Gibbs said.

"I was wounded going up the hill. A medic patched me up and told me to get to the aid station. So I did. They sent me to the hospital for two weeks."

"Yeah, so?"

"Well, I was lookin' through the after-action reports a week or so ago, and I found the list of casualties from the attack. And—well, it lists me as wounded, but it says 'LWA'—*lightly* wounded in action. I'm the only one listed that way. I—it bothers me. Does that mean I shouldn't have gone to the aid station or the hospital? I just did what the medic said."

"And you were in the hospital for two weeks?"

"Roger."

"Well, here's how I see it. You'd never been in combat. You got hit—prob'ly didn't know how bad it was. The medic said to take off, and you did. If you hadn't needed the hospital stay, believe me, they would have sent you right back to the line. Maybe someone who wrote up the report decided to take a little liberty with the coding. What the hell?"

Aaron looked at Gibbs. "I know some men crawled up that hill even if they were wounded and shot up. Lieutenant Slade for one. Hit in both legs and he still crawled up there to be with his men."

"So—you think that makes him Superman? Problem was, no medic was around to tell him to get out of there. Or maybe crawlin' up the hill from where he was made more sense than goin' down. You can't judge the situation after the fact."

Aaron sighed. "Still—"

"Look—that run-in you had with the Jerry in the rain that night. When you used your knife. You think you could have done that if you was yellow?"

"I was just tryin' to stay alive, Sergeant. I sure wasn't brave—I had no choice."

"Yes, you did. You could've given up. Let that Kraut kill you."

"I got lucky, Sergeant. That don't make me brave."

"Brave?" Gibbs spat. "You want to feel like some hero in a movie or somethin'? That it? Let me tell you, get that shit out of your head now. We're all doin' the best job we can out here. There's only been one hero in this outfit—Waugh. And he's dead. Look, it all comes down to the law of averages. Some of us will make it and some won't. Bravery don't have anything to do with it—it's all just random—it ain't up to us. When our number's up, it's up."

"So, what are you tellin' me?"

"I'm tellin' you just keep doin' your job. Do your best to be careful, but get over worryin' about dyin'. Best thing is to figure it don't matter much one way or another. Put it in someone else's hands."

"You mean like Furlong does?"

Gibbs shrugged his shoulders. "Maybe kinda like that. But for Chrissake, don't go around thinkin' you ain't good enough or that you don't have what it takes. You wouldn't have lasted this long up here if you didn't have it."

Gibbs walked away and opened a box of K-rations. "How 'bout some coffee? It'll be cold—can't light no fire to heat the water."

Aaron smiled. "Cold coffee's better'n no coffee, Sergeant. Thanks."

Gibbs smiled back at him. "Don't mention it."

Aaron sipped his coffee and then lowered the cup. "First Sergeant, there's just one last thing I wanna say about that night on hill seventy-nine. After I got hit, this medic—he comes outta nowhere. I'd never seen him before. I remember thinking how clean he looked. His clothes weren't dirty and muddy, and his face was—I can't describe it really. Just—so clean. He looked like he'd just come through an inspection. And he worked on me like—like he wasn't worried about bein' hit or anything. But the funniest thing is he called me by my name. He couldn't have known who I was. Never seen him before—never seen him since. I asked Haynes if he knew who he was, but he said there weren't any medics anywhere near us. "

Gibbs looked at Aaron over the top of his cup. "Johnson, you can drive yourself crazy dwellin' on stuff like that. Just be glad he found you. Let the rest of it go."

# CHAPTER FORTY-SIX

From a forward OP, Hoy Shingleton and Sergeant Palmer peered at the men of Easy Company's First Platoon as they moved toward their objective.

"I don't like the look of things up there," Shingleton said. "The Germans have been too quiet, if you ask me. Two days and not even the usual artillery or mortar attacks. Got a gut feeling something ain't right."

Two hundred yards away, Lieutenant Carl DiNardo led the thirty men of his platoon up a hillside so steep that in places the soldiers were on hands and knees as they scrambled over rocky outcroppings and scrub growth. The terrain was bare, no trees standing—artillery had destroyed them all. An overcast sky cast a gray pallor on the entire scene as a northerly wind blew misty rain onto the advancing GIs.

Shingleton rubbed his chin. Why attack such a difficult location in broad daylight? And with a frontal assault? Why not try to flank it? Didn't make sense. Sometimes the brass didn't get it. But then, they didn't have to watch men die.

"Are the men ready to move out?" Shingleton asked, turning to Palmer. "As soon as DiNardo and his men get to the top, we're movin' up behind them."

"Yes sir," Palmer said. "They'll be ready—if those poor sons-of-bitches make it to the top."

Shingleton nodded. "You feel as uneasy as me?"

"Yeah—whoever came up with this plan for an attack should have his head examined. Our guys are totally exposed out there. It's insane—all due respect to the battalion planners, sir."

"You don't have to sugarcoat it for me," Shingleton said. " Let's pray the intel's right and the Germans have already pulled back. Otherwise—"

Palmer pointed to the ridge. "They're almost to the top, sir. Looks like they're gonna make it. I'll go give the order to the men to—"

Machine gun fire erupted on the ridge. Several of DiNardo's men fell at the first burst.

"Goddammit!" Shingleton said. He threw his helmet to the ground and kicked the side of the earthen bunker. "They ain't got a chance in hell!"

Scathing fire from the German guns cut down more of the E Company men. Their bodies twisted and jerked as the bullets ripped through them. Some sought nonexistent cover as the unrelenting automatic fire swept in, on and around them.

"Get some suppressing—"

Even as Shingleton spoke, G Company's machine gunners poured fire onto the ridge in a fruitless attempt to provide cover to their fellow soldiers.

More troops on the ridge fell, ripped apart by the fire coming at them from the front and both flanks. It looked as if DiNardo tried to rally his few remaining men forward in a desperate attempt to scramble to the top of the ridge and escape the kill zone, but it was too late. He and the men around him fell backward as more deadly rounds knifed through them.

"Oh God," Shingleton said. "Goddammit! Shit!" He balled his right hand into a fist and pounded it into his left palm. He yelled after Palmer, "Get the medics! Have them ready to help out if anybody gets off that ridge."

An hour later Shingleton briefed Captain Atwell. "It was a slaughter. Suicide. Only five men out of the whole platoon made it back, sir. All wounded—three of them real bad. We tried to get suppressing fire up there, but the guns were dug in too well—our fire didn't slow them down a bit. The Krauts just kept raking the ridge—they must've had five, maybe six guns goin. DiNardo and his guys were massacred, pure and simple. Captain, I know my platoon's scheduled to go next, but sir, I think battalion needs to rethink this plan. It won't work. If I take my men there, it'll be the same all over again."

Atwell rubbed his eyes. "Let me call them. Colonel English isn't there—he's in the hospital with dysentery. Major Fagan's acting OIC."

Shingleton saluted and returned to his platoon. Palmer and two other squad leaders met him as he approached.

"What's the captain say?" Palmer asked. "We're not going up that ridge, are we? It's murder."

"The captain's talking to Fagan now. We'll see."

Palmer looked at him. "Fagan—this was his idea? Why did Colonel English—?"

"English isn't there. Fagan's got the ball."

Palmer rolled his eyes but remained silent. He looked past Shingleton. "Sir, Sergeant Johnson's coming. Maybe he's got news from the old man."

Aaron saluted Shingleton. "Sir, Captain Atwell wants to see you right away at the company CP."

Shingleton turned to Palmer. "Have the men sit tight."

"What's battalion say, sir?" Shingleton asked Captain Atwell.

Atwell sighed. "They won't budge. They want you to attack within the hour."

Shingleton sucked in a breath and came to attention. "Sir, I can't order my men to attack that ridge."

"We have no choice, Hoy. It's a direct order."

"Sir, with all due respect, I have to disagree. Again, I can't order my men to make the attack. The book says an officer doesn't have to carry out an unlawful order, and if I've ever seen one, this is it."

Atwell looked at Shingleton for a long moment. "Careful, Lieutenant. Don't go all barracks lawyer on me. You know what this means. You're a good officer. Don't blow this."

"Sir, yes, I know. And I don't like doing this, but—"

"So don't do this. Just make the attack. I'll double the suppressing fire. That should keep the Jerries pinned down 'til you can get close enough to put some grenades—"

"Captain, we'll never get anywhere close to grenade range, no matter how much fire we put on that ridge. Those guns are perfectly placed to cover the entire area with interlocking fire. We won't have any more chance than DiNardo did. Let me take a patrol and scout the flanks. I've looked at the maps. I think I see a way we might be able to take it without making a direct attack."

Atwell shook his head. "I already tried selling that. Battalion won't hear of it. A frontal attack it is. You know what it means if you don't attempt to carry it out."

"Very well, sir. If battalion insists on an attack, I'll go. By myself. But I can't bring myself to order my men to go. After I'm—gone—you can tell battalion the attack failed. That'll get you off the hook. I'm sorry, sir, that's the best I can do."

Atwell sighed. He stared at Shingleton for a long moment. "Are you sure you want to push this, Hoy? You're letting yourself in for a lot of heat."

Hoy stared straight ahead. "I can't let it go, Captain."

"Let me talk to Fagan again," Atwell said. "Johnson, get Major Fagan for me."

As the captain spoke to Fagan, Aaron looked at Shingleton. The lieutenant had a lot of guts to buck this order. Every man in the company knew he was right, but that might not make any difference. Shingleton could be in really hot water. Aaron wouldn't want to be in his shoes. Maybe being an officer wasn't such a good deal sometimes.

Atwell finished speaking and handed the telephone to Aaron, who replaced it in its handset.

"No dice," Atwell said, looking at Shingleton. "Fagan says if you won't take your platoon on the attack, then I have to relieve you of your command and send you back to battalion. I'm sorry, Hoy. Give me your sidearm."

Shingleton undid his pistol belt and handed it to Atwell.

"Johnson," Atwell said, "escort Lieutenant Shingleton to battalion. Don't speak to him about this—just make sure he gets there."

At battalion headquarters, Shingleton was met with threats and curses from Fagan but refused to change his position. After ranting for an hour, Fagan sent Shingleton to the regimental CO, where the process repeated itself. Then to the division executive officer and the division commander. At each meeting, Shingleton fought back anger mixed with fear and uncertainty. But he did not relent. After a night under guard by two MPs, he was ferried by jeep to Fifth Army headquarters. Mark Clark, the commanding general, insisted on speaking with him personally. Per General Clark's orders, the attack was put on hold until he decided what to do with Shingleton.

At 0900 hours, Shingleton, still dressed in his field uniform, steel helmet, and muddy combat boots, was ushered into Clark's office. He tucked the helmet under his left arm, stood at attention, and saluted.

Clark, tall and lean, sat at a large wooden desk, immaculately dressed in a perfectly fitting, pressed uniform, his dark hair neatly combed. A file folder lay open before him. He looked up at Shingleton. "At ease, Lieutenant. I've been hearing quite a lot about you."

Hoy took a deep breath and assumed a parade rest position. "I'm sorry to trouble you, sir."

"Whether you're sorry or not remains to be seen. I've looked at your personnel jacket." Clark motioned to the folder. "You've been with your outfit since its formation in the States. Battlefield commission. Three Bronze Stars for valor. A Silver Star may be pending. I made a few calls, too. Captain Atwell says you're the best platoon leader he's got. So what's up? Have you lost your moxie, Lieutenant? Too much combat? Your nerves shot?"

"Umm—I—I never really thought about it, sir. I've always tried to do my job. I've never shied away from a tough assignment. I think my record shows that."

"Hmm—so it does," Clark said. He stroked his chin then put the folder aside. "The charges against you are extremely serious. You're aware of that?"

"Yes sir."

"Yet you still won't reconsider? All you have to do is follow the order and all this goes away. Don't you want to keep your command?"

Hoy took a deep breath. "Yes, General, I do. But the command won't do me any good if every man in my platoon is dead—me included, sir. And if we try to make the same attack as the guys in E Company, we'll be cut to pieces, General, just like they were. With all due respect, I don't see how that's going to help us win the war, sir."

Clark tapped his pen on the desk blotter. His eyes narrowed as he studied Shingleton. "Okay then, Lieutenant. Why don't you tell me exactly what's going on here. Tell me about what happened with E Company. I've read the official report—but I want to hear your version."

Shingleton drew in another breath. His throat was so dry he could barely speak. He swallowed. He had to collect his thoughts. He'd only get one shot at this. Sweat popped out on his brow. What he said would determine whether he had a chance of avoiding a full-blown court-martial—maybe even a firing squad.

"Sit down, Lieutenant—take your time," Clark said.

Hoy stepped to a straight-backed chair and sat. "Thank you, sir. To start at the beginning—I had a bad feeling about that ridge from the moment I saw it."

Ten minutes later, after Hoy finished speaking, Clark leaned back in his chair and folded his hands. He stared at Hoy for a full twenty seconds. Then he picked up the phone at the side of his desk. "Have my driver get the jeep ready. Lieutenant Shingleton and I are going to the front for a look-see."

Shingleton opened his eyes wide as he rose from his chair. "Sir?"

Clark stood. "Yes, Lieutenant?"

"Sir, going to the front in broad daylight's not a good idea. The Jerries can call in artillery; there could be snipers, maybe mines on the road—"

"Just let me worry about those things, Lieutenant. I need to see this situation myself before I decide what to do with you. Let's go."

Clark came around his desk and headed for the doorway.

Shingleton followed him. This was madness.

Two hours later, Clark and Shingleton—along with Major General Coulter, the division commander; Colonel Brady, the regimental commander; Major Fagan, from battalion; and Captain Atwell—peered through the sand-bagged opening of a bunker facing the German-held ridge. The general studied the terrain through binoculars as the others waited. Clark's unannounced arrival at the front had created quite a stir. Hoy had never seen so much brass assembled in such a short time. At least the general had been convinced to observe the ridge from the company CP rather than moving to the riskier forward OP.

Clark put down the binoculars and studied a map that lay on a wooden crate. He traced the route to the ridge with his finger, looked out of the bunker again, and then back at the map.

Shingleton held his breath. His palms poured sweat and his heart pounded. He had a headache, his stomach had a knot in it the size of a cannonball, and his knees threatened to give way any second. He dared not speak.

General Clark lowered his field glasses. "I've reached a decision."

Hoy glanced at Clark. The general's face gave no indication of what he might say. Behind Clark, Sergeant Johnson sat by the communications equipment, wide-eyed, his face even paler than usual.

"Colonel Brady, see that Lieutenant Shingleton..."

Hoy closed his eyes. A court-martial for sure.

"...gets his command back immediately. Major Fagan, from now on I'll expect you to coordinate more closely with Captain Atwell and Lieutenant Shingleton in developing attack plans involving this company. Shingleton is right—a direct assault on that position is suicide. I like his idea of looking for a way around the side of the ridge. Put your heads together and work it out."

Fagan blinked, not looking at Shingleton or Atwell. "Yes, General. Right away, sir."

"Now, gentlemen, I have to get back to headquarters. Colonel Brady, let me know as soon as the ridge is in our hands. Good day, gentlemen." He turned, motioned to his driver, and left the bunker.

Shingleton exhaled and then drew in a long breath. Thank God. Or if not Him, at least General Clark.

The plan for taking the ridge was redrawn, incorporating Shingleton's idea of flanking the German positions. The ridge was taken in less than an hour with no casualties.

# CHAPTER FORTY-SEVEN

"We've been here two days," Art said to Aaron as the two hunkered together in a slit trench they'd dug into the rocky ground. "How much of a breather do you think they'll give us?"

Aaron shook his head. "One that'd last 'til this damn war's over, I wish."

"Ain't gonna happen, my Southern hillbilly friend," Art said.

"No, not likely."

"And if we keep losing guys like we have for the last month, we ain't gonna be able to mount a decent-sized patrol, let alone any more attacks."

"Bradley brought up some replacements with his mule team," Aaron said.

"Yeah—three or four kids who were cooks or clerks two days ago. They probably won't last a week here."

Aaron sighed. His body ached. If only he could see Maggie—and Barry. And home. The leaves would be turning by now. Days getting cooler. Wouldn't be long until Thanksgiving—God how he'd like to be there with them, and with his momma and poppa, too. And his brothers and sisters sitting around the table. With a turkey and ham and dressing—not to mention all the other fixings. And pie—pumpkin, apple, sweet potato—oh, what he would give—

"Johnson, the old man wants you—right away." Sergeant Palmer motioned toward the company CP.

Aaron grabbed his carbine. "Roger, Sarge."

Outside the CP, Captain Atwell talked with a shabbily dressed Italian man of medium height. Dark hair, somewhat swarthy complexion. A noticeable scar about four inches long on his right cheek. He wore a ratty, sweat-stained hat and a coat that appeared to be too big for him. No weapons in sight.

The man met Aaron's gaze and then looked away.

"Johnson, this is Giorgio. He's the head of a band of partisans operatin' around here. He says the Germans have pulled out from the mountain ahead to set up a defensive line farther on. Take a patrol and check it out—see if it's okay for us to move over there."

Aaron eyed Giorgio. You never knew about partisans—some were trustworthy, but others seemed to support whichever side had the upper hand.

Atwell turned as if to leave.

"Captain," Aaron said, nodding at Giorgio, "since he knows the area, how 'bout he goes with us—we could use a guide."

Atwell shrugged. "Okay by me." He turned to the Italian. "How 'bout it? You mind showin' my men the way?"

Giorgio raised his eyebrows and shrugged. "*Si, Capitan.* I go."

Aaron rounded up Art, Harry, and Jack Claytor, explained the mission, and told them to join him at the CP.

"Damn, Aaron, why us?" Jack said. "Why don't you take some of the newer guys? They need the experience."

Harry nodded his agreement.

"Look, guys—this is probably a cakewalk, so quit bitching. But if things go sour, I want people I can count on. So get your gear and meet me at the CP."

As he waited, Aaron inserted a loaded magazine into his carbine then removed the .45 automatic from its holster, chambered a round, and flicked on the safety. Cocked and locked. Just in case.

Attempts to engage Giorgio in conversation went nowhere. He did accept the cigarette Aaron offered. As he lit the Chesterfield with his Zippo lighter, Aaron looked into Giorgio's eyes. No expression. He tried again. "*Tu familia? Bambinos?*"

Giorgio shook his head. Aaron frowned. Most civilians he'd met wouldn't stop talking. Not this one.

The men assembled and moved down the sharp incline before them. Giorgio led the way as they headed for the deep ravine at the base of the mountain. As they passed the final outpost, Aaron paused next to the foxhole of Corporal Dan Wagner. Dan munched on a cracker, his BAR pointing menacingly downhill. A dark stubble of beard and tired, sunken eyes revealed the same fatigue that every man in the company exhibited.

"We're going over there," Aaron said, pointing to the sparsely vegetated mountainside two hundred yards away, "to see if the Jerries have pulled back like this partisan says. Keep an eye on us, okay?"

Wagner glanced at the Italian, then at Aaron. He nodded.

Ten minutes later the men stepped across a narrow stream at the base of the mountain and began the climb up the facing slope. Misty rain fell from the overcast sky. No birds sang. A slight breeze carried the scent of earth and mud.

The partisan led the way up a narrow path, walking easily, arms swinging at his sides. Aaron followed about five yards behind him, scanning the terrain. Barren landscape. No trees. No cover. Daylight patrols gave him the willies. Germans could be anywhere. Sweat trickled down his face. He drew deeper breaths as the climb grew steeper.

"Spread out," he said.

"You don't like this setup, do you?" Harry said.

Aaron shook his head. "Not even a little bit. Keep your eyes peeled. We're sittin' ducks. No more talking, guys."

Three-fourths of the way to the top, Aaron relaxed a bit. No sign of Krauts. Maybe this guy was on the level after all. The smell of damp vegetation hung in the air. Soon they would reach the crest. Gazing toward the cloudy sky, Aaron took his eyes off the Italian and the pathway ahead.

"*Achtung!*" Three gray-clad Germans appeared twenty feet up the hill, their weapons aimed directly at them.

Oh shit. Caught flat-footed. Nowhere to run. Aaron started to raise his carbine but ceased moving as the nearest German leveled an MP-40 submachine gun at his chest.

The Germans gestured—hands up. Now.

The Italian smirked and stepped over to join the enemy soldiers. Aaron's eyes narrowed. Damn him.

"Do it," Aaron said. "We got no chance." He dropped his carbine. Behind him, weapons clunked to the ground. Captured. He raised his hands. How could he have let this happen? What would they do to them? Torture? Maybe shoot them? Oh God, would he ever see home—and Maggie—again?

Should he drop the holstered .45 automatic? No—he'd let them take it when they searched him. Oh Lord, we need you now.

The Italian grinned at them. A German with a Mauser moved toward them while the other two kept their weapons directed at them.

Aaron stared at Giorgio. Gloat, you son of a bitch. He'd had a bad feeling about him from the—

Bullets from Wagner's BAR zinged past Aaron. He dove for the ground. Two of the Germans fell from the automatic fire. The third scrambled for cover, but a second burst clipped him and knocked him to the ground.

"Outta here!" Aaron yelled. Harry and the others were already moving, scrambling down the hillside.

As Aaron started to rise, dirt and rocks flew up beside him, stinging his face. Giorgio stood a few yards away. Smoke curled upward from the barrel of a small pistol he held. He pointed it at Aaron and fired again. The bullet grazed his helmet.

Aaron rolled sideways, clawing for the .45. His heart pounded. Giorgio was a blur—Aaron could only see the pistol lining up on him again. Lord—please! He yanked the automatic from the holster and came up on one knee and fired. Once, twice—again and again until the slide locked open—empty.

The pistol dropped from Giorgio's hand as he fell toward Aaron. His coat flapped open, and a small object tumbled from it.

Wagner's .30-caliber rounds still raked the area. Aaron hugged the ground. Were there more Germans? None in sight. Time to go, but— Aaron crouched and ran to the partisan. Blood oozed from Giorgio's partially open mouth. His dead eyes stared at nothing. A small camera lay next to the lifeless body, and a leather pouch extended from the coat's inside pocket.

Aaron stuffed the items inside his field jacket, scooped up his carbine, and scurried down the path. Despite their head start, he caught the others before they reached the ravine below.

Twenty minutes later Aaron, still panting, turned the camera and other items over to Captain Atwell.

Atwell opened the pouch and took out a folded map. "Look at this, Johnson," he said. "That little shit marked every one of our positions! Machine gun and mortar emplacements, the CP—everything. He was gonna give this to the Krauts, that dirty bastard. I bet this camera has important stuff on it, too." He turned. "Haynes!"

"Yessir," Worth said.

"Get this stuff to battalion G-2 right away!"

Sergeant Gibbs approached. Atwell filled him in.

"Good work, Johnson," Gibbs said. "We might make a soldier outta you yet."

Aaron blinked. Very funny. They'd almost been dead soldiers—and would have been if Wagner hadn't done such a good job.

Wagner—he had to find him.

"You saved our asses, buddy. Thanks. I owe you about a million bucks."

"No sweat, Sarge." Wagner smiled. "Just charge it to the dust and we'll let the rain settle it. All in a day's work for Uncle Sammy." He patted the BAR as if it were a pet. "I gotta tell you, though, when I fired the first burst, it looked like I was shooting right through your upraised arms." He grinned. "I'd say it's a good thing you hit the dirt when you did."

The next afternoon Atwell called for Aaron. "Battalion developed the pictures from the partisan's camera. In addition to marking our positions, he'd even taken photos so the Germans could really zero in on us. It's a good thing you picked up that stuff—otherwise the Jerries might have been able to retrieve it. They'd have blown us off this mountain."

"Yessir. Just a reaction, sir," Aaron said. "I just knew there was something about that guy I didn't trust. When I saw the camera and the pouch, I thought they might be important, so I grabbed them—I'm glad it helped out."

Atwell put his hand on Aaron's shoulder. "Listen, it did more than help out. What you did probably saved the battalion a lot of casualties. I'm putting you in for a commendation."

"Thank you, sir, but—"

"Can it. Now go get some rest."

Returning to his slit trench, Aaron stopped abruptly. Yesterday he'd been too exhausted to think about what had happened. Now—he rubbed his face with both hands and then looked up at the overcast sky. Did his prayer—poor as it was—have anything to do with them getting out of that scrape? Or was it really just Wagner doing his job? And what about the Germans—and Giorgio? Weren't they just doing their job? Did they deserve to die? Would Furlong have any answers?

A wave of nausea swept over him. He sat on the ground and drew his knees up toward him. After taking several deep breaths, he bowed his head. "Oh Lord, I want to thank you for being here. I don't understand any of this crazy war, but I know I can't make it without you. Even if I die here—" He stopped. "Please, God—please let me make it home."

# CHAPTER FORTY-EIGHT

Charles Bradley cursed under his breath as he tightened a strap securing a case of ammunition to one of his supply train mules. "Hold still, you dang cayuse. When I want you to move, I can't budge you."

The mule shifted sideways.

"I'm gonna take my forty-five to you if you don't stop that! Alfredo! Come here and calm this critter down."

The Italian mule skinner hurried forward. "*Si, si!* I take-a care. No worry. No worry."

Charles stepped aside. Gazing into the dusk, Charles let out a huff. Damn—almost dark already, and the mule train still not ready to move out. To make matters worse, he had an extra task for this night's delivery. Some bright soul had decided that a newly assigned artillery officer should accompany him to the front lines for an observation tour. Great. Not enough he had to look after the ornery animals, communicate with Alfredo, make his way up the mountain trail in total darkness, and somehow get the supplies to the company before dawn. No—he had to also babysit this rear echelon goldbrick.

Second Lieutenant Talbot, dressed in a clean, well-pressed set of fatigues and nicely shined combat boots, approached. A carbine was slung on his shoulder. "Are we about ready to move out, Sergeant?"

Bradley saluted. "Just a few more minutes, sir. If I could, sir, a word about what we'll be doing."

"Certainly—this is your show. I'm just along for the ride—well, walk."

"Yes sir. Well, you see, we'll be going up the trail single file—it's not wide enough to travel any other way. The most important thing is that we get across the ridgeline before dawn. If we don't, we'll be silhouetted against the night sky and we'll draw artillery fire. So you'll have to hang on to the mule's tail and keep up."

"Mule's tail?"

"Yes sir. In the dark, the best way to travel is to follow the mule in front of you, and the only way to really do that is to hang onto its tail. Alfredo and I will lead since we're familiar with the way up. I'd like you to be about midway in the train. That means you'll have the tail of the mule in front of you and the reins to the mule behind you. Just don't let go and you'll be fine."

Talbot frowned. "Okay—like I said, it's your show."

Bradley checked his watch. "It'll be completely dark in ten minutes. We'll move out then."

Charles led the way up the steep, rocky slope, feeling his way in the darkness. His night vision kicked in, enabling him to make out rough shapes along the way. A few stars twinkled in the overcast sky. Good. A full moon was the worst—made it too easy for the Germans to spot them.

Behind him, Alfredo matched his pace. The mules made huffing sounds, their hooves making *clop-clop* sounds as they trudged along. The straps securing the supplies emitted various creaking noises as the loads shifted on their backs.

A warm breeze did little to wick away the sweat from Charles's face. His breathing grew steadily heavier as the team progressed. The trail became steeper and rockier, snaking back and forth up the barren mountainside. He glanced behind him. No way to tell how the captain was making out in the middle of the train. Should he go back and check on him? No—too dangerous. The trail wasn't wide enough, and if he began backtracking now it might spook the mules. Surely Talbot had enough training and common sense to look after himself.

Charles and Alfredo crested the ridgeline a little before midnight. Fifteen minutes more and they'd reach G Company's position. Charles took a long breath. The worst was over.

As they neared the company area, the outline of a guard appeared out of the darkness, rifle at the ready.

He heard a hoarse whisper. "Halt! Peanuts."

"Cracker Jacks."

"Come ahead."

Charles directed Alfredo and the mules toward a clearing for unloading. He walked down the line, counting as he went. Five, six, seven—where was number eight? And Talbot? And the other seven mules? Oh shit. Nowhere—they were nowhere.

Now what?

"Alfredo, get these mules unloaded. I gotta go back—half of our train didn't make it."

Alfredo's eyes widened. "Where—?"

"Damn if I know. I'll try to find 'em and get back before first light. If I'm not back by the time you finish here, wait for me."

Charles made his way downhill, moving as fast as he dared in the darkness. He re-crossed the ridgeline and moved down the steep slope. He heard a noise to his right. A mule breaking wind. A muffled voice.

"Lieutenant Talbot! That you?"

"Bradley—yes—over here!"

Charles made his way past a large boulder. Dark shapes moved in the darkness before him. Mules. And Talbot.

"Boy am I glad to see you!" Talbot said. "I slipped—lost my grip on the mule's tail. Damn thing farted on me twice. By the time I regained my footing, you guys were gone."

"Do you have any idea where you are?"

"On the side of a mountain in Italy is all I know, Sergeant."

"That ain't the worst of it. You're in the middle of a damn mine-field. You're lucky you and all these mules haven't been blown to kingdom come. Damn—I thought any idiot could hold onto a cotton-pickin' mule's tail—sir!"

"See here, Sergeant—"

"No, you see here. These mules and these supplies are my responsibility. If they don't make it up the mountain, the guys in the company don't have any food or ammo—or anything else they need to do their jobs. So with all due respect, I don't intend for anybody or anything to keep me from doing my part. Give me the reins to that mule. When the last one passes you, you better grab its tail and this time hang on. I'm not comin' back for you again."

Charles turned and led the mule toward the trail before Talbot could reply.

# CHAPTER FORTY-NINE

Lieutenant DeYoung, CO of Second Platoon, entered the CP.

Aaron pretended to tinker with the main radio set.

DeYoung saluted Captain Atwell. "You sent for me, sir?"

"Yes. Battalion's given us our orders. We're making a raid-in-force across the river tonight to test the Kraut defenses. Capture a Jerry or two if we can. We're taking your entire platoon, plus me, Gibbs, and Johnson."

Aaron blinked. Why him?

"We'll cross at twenty-three hundred hours in the assault boats. Have your men take plenty of ammo. I've asked for an additional medic to accompany us as well."

"Sir," DeYoung said. "I appreciate you taking my platoon." He smiled. "I've been waiting to see action since arriving here from West Point. We won't let you down, sir."

"I'm sure you won't, Lieutenant," Atwell said. "Just remember this is no field exercise—we're going up against seasoned troops. They'll be hell-bent on killing us."

DeYoung's face reddened. "Sir, I didn't mean…"

"I know you didn't. You better go brief your platoon."

"Yes sir." DeYoung saluted and left.

Gibbs rolled his head to the side and closed one eye. "Why all the urgency, Captain? We've been parked here for a week. Almost nothing's gone on. What's got battalion all stirred up?"

"The fact the Jerries have hardly bothered us—battalion thinks they must be up to somethin'. They want us to try to find out what."

"Okay. But why are you going along? Shouldn't it be DeYoung's party?"

"What I'm about to say doesn't leave this CP." Atwell looked from Gibbs to Aaron. "Understood?"

"Yes sir," Aaron said.

Gibbs nodded.

"Colonel English wants me to kinda—well—watch out for DeYoung. Seems he's connected to some pretty important folks—the kind that want him to do well, if you know what I mean. Apparently they've got big plans for him while he's here and after the war, so it's gonna look good on his record if he has some combat experience. This is the way the brass decided to let him get it."

"He's been runnin' around here spoutin' off about West Point ever since he joined the company," Gibbs said. "So now we're gonna watch his back, make sure he don't screw up? That it?"

"Somethin' like that." Atwell turned to Aaron. "Remember, Johnson, not a word."

"I won't say anything, sir. But I do have one question. Exactly why are you taking me and Sergeant Gibbs?"

Atwell smiled. "Hell, that should be obvious. I want somebody out there I can trust. Make sure your radio's in top working order. Second Platoon will have theirs, but I want another set along—just in case. You two better get some shut-eye. Could be a long night."

Aaron stifled a comment. Yes—a long night all right. Or a very short one if the Jerries had their way. All to babysit an officer with connections.

Would any of them see tomorrow?

Twenty yards from the riverbank, Lieutenant DeYoung and his platoon lay in the undergrowth, along with Atwell, Gibbs, and Aaron. Four twelve-man assault boats rested in the undergrowth nearby. The river, barely seventy-five yards wide, could barely be seen in the darkness. Ripples lapped at the water's edge. The smell of wet muck hung in the air, mingling with the scent of oiled rifles and sweaty uniforms.

Aaron looked at the sky. A quarter-moon gave just enough light to maneuver. Stars peeked intermittently through wispy clouds. Maybe the Jerries wouldn't spot them. Maybe.

A cold breeze rustled the leaves on the bushes around him. The knot in his stomach tightened up all the more. It wasn't right. Risking all these men—just to make some West Point hotshot look good. Damned Army.

"I'll be in the second boat," Atwell whispered to Gibbs and Aaron. "DeYoung will lead out in his. Gibbs, you're in three, Johnson, you'll be the ranking NCO in boat four."

Five minutes before 2300, the men moved to their respective boats and hunkered down beside them. The heavy radio seemed to push Aaron into the soft earth. Sweat ran down his face. He fingered his taped dog tags. Come on. Let's go.

DeYoung, hardly visible in the low light, motioned the men forward. Each group hoisted its boat and scurried to the riverbank. Recent river-crossing training paid off. In two minutes all four boats were under way. The GIs paddled their crafts forward through the gently flowing black water. Aaron tried to focus on the far bank. Nothing visible but scrub bushes and a few trees.

Aaron set the pace from the front of the boat as the other men paddled in unison with his strokes. His shoulders ached, his breathing intensified. The radio continually shifted around, interfering with his movements.

One-quarter of the way across. Maybe. Maybe.

A flare arced into the sky from the German side, followed quickly by another, turning the darkness to daylight.

Immediately, German machine guns opened up, their tracer rounds knifing through the night sky.

"Faster, dammit!" Aaron hissed. "Keep this thing moving!"

To his left, bullets ripped into the third boat—Gibbs's boat. Men screamed as the rounds found their mark. Two men in front slumped forward. Had one of them been Gibbs?

A mortar round exploded fifteen yards away, sending a geyser of water and deadly shrapnel into the air.

"Pull! Pull!" The straps from the radio cut into Aaron's shoulders. The men behind him grunted and cursed as the boat passed the halfway point.

A burst of machine gun fire hit the water ten yards in front of the boat, kicking up a line of mini-geysers. Another mortar round exploded behind them.

Another fusillade of bullets zinged over Aaron's head, so close they sounded like a swarm of bees. He ducked, pulled the straps of the radio from his shoulders, and let them droop into the crooks of his elbows.

"Out of the boat!" he yelled. "They've got us zeroed—get out!"

Turning, he sat on the side of the boat and leaned backward. The radio's weight pulled him out of the boat and into the water. The cold took his breath away. He swallowed a mouthful of water before sinking to the bottom, his boots miring up in the mud. He wrestled free of the radio and kicked hard, clawing toward the surface.

When his head cleared the water, Aaron looked toward the boat, now shot to pieces by enemy fire. The body of one man hung over the side, a lifeless arm dangling in the water.

Other faces bobbed to the surface. More flares floated in the sky. The machine guns continued raking the water left and right.

"Come on!" Aaron said.

He swam at an angle, heading toward the darkness outside the light of the flares. Several men followed. He glanced toward the far bank. Two of the boats had made it to the other side. The third boat approached the bank. The sound of M-1s and a BAR firing full auto mixed with that of the German weapons. Grenades exploded. The Kraut machine guns went silent.

Aaron's feet struck the river bottom near the shore. Crouching low, he duck-walked forward, his .45 at the ready. He crawled onto the rocky bank and lay still. Firing continued to his left, but soon tapered off.

He motioned for the men to follow him, and then he moved forward. Five yards. Ten. No Germans. He led his group toward the sound of GI voices and soon encountered Sergeant Gibbs.

"Glad you made it, Johnson."

"You too."

"The captain's lookin' for you."

"Where is he?"

"He's over by one of the Jerry machine guns we took out." Gibbs pointed the way.

Moments later, Aaron approached Atwell.

"Sir, Sergeant Gibbs said I should see you."

"Yes, I want you to radio—where is the radio?"

"Umm—sir, it's somewhere on the bottom of the river. Our boat got shot out from under us. I couldn't carry that talk-box and swim. Sir."

"Damn—the other radio man didn't make it. You'll have to go get another one."

"Sir?"

"You heard me—take one of the boats, get another radio—on the double."

Aaron looked at the sky. "It'll be pushin' daylight by the time I return, sir."

"Then you'd better hustle, hadn't you? The medics are takin' a couple of wounded to the aid station—hitch a ride with them. They can use an extra hand on the paddles anyway. Let battalion know the Jerries pulled back from this location. Tell 'em we're gonna move farther in to try and get some prisoners."

Aaron, Frank Church, and the other medic paddled furiously as mortar rounds fell around them. Sweat ran down Aaron's face. When they finally reached the other side, Aaron took one end of a stretcher as he helped Frank carry a wounded man to the company aid station. From there, Aaron hurried to the company CP for another radio.

Near dawn, he made his way to the river again.

Frank Church and the other medic waited in the boat. "Took you long enough," Frank said. "We were about to leave without you."

"I had to check in with battalion first. Let's go—if I don't catch up with them soon, the cap'n is gonna be sore as hell."

They paddled across the river, narrowly avoiding mortar rounds once again. They reached the enemy side and headed out on foot. Ten minutes later they met Atwell and the others coming toward them at a quick pace, two prisoners in tow.

"Outta here," Atwell said. "Gotta get these prisoners across the river before they catch up to us."

Aaron shook his head. Not one minute of sleep all night. All that paddling. Just in time to turn around and do it one more time. He looked at DeYoung. The lieutenant, covered in sweat and dirt, wasn't smiling.

# CHAPTER FIFTY

Machine gun and mortar fire raked G Company. Just below the ridgeline, gray-clad German troops massed for a counterattack. The GIs hunkered low, hot lead and steel pinning them down.

Captain Atwell turned to Aaron. "Johnson—"

"Yes sir! Calling for artillery now!" Aaron spoke into the walkie-talkie, shouting out coordinates from his mud-splattered map.

"Captain, battalion says we've used our allotment. We're on our own!"

"Shit!" Atwell shouted. "Tell 'em we're gonna get pushed off this peak again if they don't give us some support!"

Aaron clasped the phone to his ear and spoke. He listened for a moment then slammed the receiver down. "No dice, sir. Said don't call again."

Atwell slapped the stock of his carbine. "Goddammit! I'd like to get hold of the bastard who decided all the ammo and supplies go to France! Don't they know we're fightin' a war here too? Patton's men are swimming in artillery support while we get our teeth kicked in. Damn! Gibbs, can you see 'em?" Atwell said, shouting above the deafening noise of gunfire and exploding mortar rounds.

"Yessir," Gibbs said from his own foxhole ten feet away and ahead of Aaron and Atwell. "Infantry's 'bout ready to hit us, I'd say."

The walkie-talkie buzzed. Aaron snatched up the handset. Had battalion changed its mind about the artillery? Aaron clasped the handset to his ear. He turned to Atwell. "Sir, Fox Company. They're in retreat! Our flank's exposed!"

"Gibbs—pass the word!" Atwell yelled. "We can't stay here! Pull back!"

Within seconds men low-crawled past Aaron and the captain, heading away from the enemy fire. Atwell tugged at Aaron's sleeve. "Let's go!"

They scrambled from the hole they'd taken only minutes before from the Germans.

Gibbs and two others scrambled downhill, ten yards ahead.

"Make for the house where we had the CP earlier," Atwell said.

On their left Mike Flannigan fired a long burst toward the enemy from his .30-caliber machine gun. He ceased firing and motioned. "Hurry, Captain! The Jerries are already on the ridge!"

"Keep 'em pinned 'til we're clear, then get outta here!" Gibbs said. Flannigan nodded as he fed another belt into the smoking gun.

A half hour later, Atwell studied a map inside the sturdy mountain house. "Thank God, we stopped 'em. They seem content to have taken the ridge again—for now. It'll be dark soon. Sure wish I knew what the Krauts are up to. Johnson, I might want you to take a patrol out later."

Aaron grimaced. Great. Bad enough he'd spent all day trying to stay alive. Now the Jerries would get another chance at him tonight.

"And I wanna find out where Fox Company is. I hope to hell they're holding somewhere on our flank. I sent Haynes to make contact with 'em. He should be here—"

Worth popped through the door. "Here, sir—bad news. Fox Company musta got pushed to the rear a long ways. They're nowhere in sight—but Krauts are. They're movin' past us on our right—battalion strength, I'd guess—probably still chasin' Fox Comp'ny. Soon as they make contact with Fox, they'll hit us so's to even up their line."

Atwell spun toward Aaron. "Get battalion!"

Aaron bent to the radio. "Nothing but static, sir."

"Keep trying."

After several minutes, Aaron looked at Atwell. "Sorry, sir. I can't get through."

Atwell stared at Aaron, then Haynes and Gibbs. "Damn—we're cut off. If we try to move back, the Krauts will hear us for sure. Can't go forward—they're dug in tight on the ridge again and probably reinforced to boot. If we stay here, its capture—or worse. Johnson!"

"Yessir?"

"Burn the codebook. Can't let the Jerries have it. Gibbs—tell the men to look for an attack from our front and our right sometime tonight. Set up an OP on our exposed flank. Have two squads dig in on that side, too. Tell Mike to reposition his guns so he can cover both approaches. We'll hold out as long as we can—then—whatever."

While Atwell talked, Aaron removed the steel section of his helmet from its inner liner and placed it on the floor. He ripped the codebook into small pieces, dropped them into the helmet, and lit the bits of paper with his Zippo. The shards curled and blackened as the small blaze obliterated the classified information. When the flames subsided, he dumped out the ashes onto the floor. He checked his carbine and pistol, and then looked out the window. It would be dark in fifteen minutes.

No one spoke for the next agonizing hour. Aaron scanned the room. Each face was set as if in stone. No one smiled or joked. A knot formed in his stomach. His throat tightened. Captured. Or killed. Which would it be? What would happen to Maggie and Barry?

"Listen up," Gibbs said. "If you men have any letters or photographs—anything that's not government issue—get rid of it. If you have any captured German weapons—or anything that might look to the Krauts like a captured weapon," he said, looking at Aaron, "ditch it. The Krauts shoot any prisoners they find with a weapon that's not standard issue. They assume you took it from one of theirs."

Aaron blinked. Why had Gibbs looked at him like that?

Maggie's knife! If the Germans took him and found it, he'd be shot. Damn. He didn't want to chuck it. Maybe he could hide it. He looked around the room. No—they'd search the place.

He took the knife and its sheath from his belt and walked to the broken rear window and threw them into the darkness.

Fifteen minutes after midnight, Atwell sat upright. "Johnson, try battalion again."

"Umm, sir, I can't—I burned the codebooks," Aaron said.

"The radio still works, though—if you can get through?" Atwell leaned forward.

"Well, yes," Aaron said. "But without the right code words, they won't know who I am—they'll think I'm some Jerry tryin' to trick 'em."

"Try anyway. If you get through, tell 'em we need help."

Aaron sighed. Officers. Why hadn't he had him keep trying before he'd ordered the damn codebook burned? Aaron picked up the handset. The static had cleared.

"L'il Abner, this is Daisy Mae. Or at least I was yesterday."

"So who are you today?" a tinny voice asked.

"I don't know—but Captain Atwell needs to speak to the ops officer."

"Look, pal. I don't know who you think you're foolin'. Call me when you've got the right codes."

"Repeat—no can do. We're surrounded and cut off. We need reinforcements."

"So, wise guy—how come you don't know the lingo?"

"We thought we were gonna be captured right away. Cap'n had me burn the codebook."

"Oh, you think I'm fallin' for that malarkey? No dice, superman. I'm signing off—"

"Don't! This is on the level, I tell ya. This is G Company. Captain Atwell's the CO. Gibbs is the first sergeant."

"You'd know that if you'd killed or captured them. Sorry, pal. I got my orders. Without the code—"

Aaron hunched his shoulders and leaned closer to the walkie-talkie. "Listen to me, you rear-echelon thumb-sucking bastard! Get your head out of your ass and listen. We're cut off, and we need help. Do you wanna be responsible for a whole company going down the crapper? Now get me the ops officer, or it's gonna be your ass!"

"Well, you sure sound like a GI, I'll give you that. Tell you what—answer me this. What's Mickey Mouse's girlfriend's name?"

"Minnie."

"And who won the '42 series?"

"Cardinals."

"And what are the words to the second verse of 'God Bless America'?"

"Goddamn if I know! But if you—"

"Ah, pipe down. I don't know either—you gotta be a GI. Stand by—I'll get him for you."

Aaron wiped his brow. "Captain, I have battalion."

Atwell stopped talking to Gibbs and jerked the phone from Aaron's hand. As he explained their situation to the battalion officer, Aaron stared at the floor. Please, God. If you're out there—please help us. He jerked his head up. Where was Furlong?

Atwell hung up the phone. "Easy Company's in reserve. They're gonna send them up here as soon as they can. They've been helping Fox Company out, but they should be able to break away within the hour."

"That's good," Gibbs said. "Now it's just a question of who gets here first—them or the Germans."

In a far corner of the room, Francis Furlong knelt, obviously praying. Head down and hands folded, he seemed oblivious to everything around him.

Aaron let out a breath. Saint Francis. No doubt Furlong carried more weight with God than any of them. But was He listening?

# CHAPTER FIFTY-ONE

The sound-powered telephone whistled, low. Aaron grabbed it. "Go ahead."

"Tango one this is tango two," Jack Claytor whispered. "We've got movement on our front. Looks like the Jerries are about to hit us."

Aaron motioned for Atwell. "Sir, Claytor says the Jerries are getting ready to attack. What are your orders?"

Atwell rubbed his face and drew in a long breath. "Tell him to get out of the OP and join the rest of the company." He looked around the room. "This is it. Let's try to hold out as long as we can. Where are those damn reinforcements?"

A flare lit the night.

"The Jerries will come as soon as it burns out," Gibbs said.

"Incoming!" Atwell yelled. A mortar round exploded nearby, followed by a half dozen more. Tracer rounds from the German machine guns arced through the darkness.

Aaron peeked through a broken window toward the ridge line above. Dark shapes crept toward them.

Outside the house, G Company's machine gunners returned fire, their own tracers racing past the enemy fire.

When the Germans closed to fifty yards, rifle fire erupted from the Americans. Soon the entire area was a cacophony of competing noises as the gunfire intensified.

Aaron flicked off the carbine's safety and then unbuttoned the .45's holster flap. This could get ugly.

More gunfire, now from the right flank.

"Captain—" Aaron shouted.

"I hear it—they're hittin' our flank, too! Damn! Get on that radio! Tell 'em our situation. We ain't gonna last long."

Aaron adjusted the radio and yelled into the handset. "We're in a hornet's nest up here! Any word from Easy Company?"

The radio crackled. "We've lost contact with 'em. They're headed your way. Hang on."

"We're down to our fingernails now! If they don't—"

Gibbs ran to the back door. "Listen! Those are M-1s firing! Easy Company's here! They made it!"

Aaron squeezed the handset and exhaled. "Easy's here! Out!" He looked to the ceiling. "Thank you, Lord. Thank you."

The added weight of the reinforcements broke the German attack.

An hour later Aaron and Furlong packed up the radio equipment. The company had been ordered to the rear for a rest. Easy Company took their place in the line.

"Francis," Aaron said. "I saw you praying last night."

Furlong shrugged.

"Look, I know some of the guys give you a hard time about it. I want you to know that when I saw you praying, I had a feeling we were gonna be okay. Thanks."

"Don't thank me. All I did was talk to God. He's the one who helped us out. And you know, you can pray too. Anytime you want."

"I did pray—I just don't know if He's gonna pay much attention to mine. I was raised in a churchgoing family. Still, I've always had doubts—"

"We all have doubts," Furlong said. "The Bible says even a faith the size—"

"I know—the size of a mustard seed. I'm just not sure about—well, lots of things."

"Do you have a Bible?"

"I do—but there's so much I don't understand."

Furlong smiled. "My preacher back home says not to worry about what we don't understand in the Bible. Just live by what we do understand."

Aaron nodded. "Thanks—again."

Furlong nodded. "Anytime."


Art Ferdinand looked up from the latest issue of *Stars and Stripes*. "Man, we're in good shape now. We've got the Jerries pushed to the Po Valley here, First and Third Armies are inside Germany, and Seventh Army's approaching the border."

"Sounds like they'll be moving inside Hitler's little sandbox any day," Worth said.

"Yep," Art said. "Says here we're bombing all major industrial centers and the Russians are advancing hard from the east. I tell you guys, this ole war's gonna be over in no time."

"I'll believe it when I see it," Patrick Davis said as he inserted a loaded magazine into his Thompson.

"You put a lot of faith in that ole tommy gun, don't you Davis?" Harry Klutz said.

"She's never let me down—unlike a lot of people I've known."

"Where is it you're from, Davis?" Aaron said.

Davis frowned. "I grew up on the streets in Philly. My old man left us before I could walk. Mom tried her best with my brother and me, but I found out quick you make your own way in this world."

Art put the paper aside. "You goin' back there when the war's over?"

"Got no reason to. Mom's gone now. I don't know where my brother is—so it don't make much difference." He looked around. "Enough of this bullshit—I'm gonna go get some of that mud the cooks call coffee. Burnitz, wanna join me?"

"Sure," Cliff Burnitz said.

Aaron stared after the two as they departed. "Burnitz is 'bout the only guy Davis pals around with, ain't he?"

"Yeah—Davis is a hell of a good soldier, he just isn't much on buddyin' up. Been that way ever since training in Mississippi."

"Sounds like he had a pretty rough time of it growin' up," Aaron said. "I guess he got used to lookin' after himself—maybe not trustin' other folks much."

Art chuckled. "I can tell you one thing he trusts—that Thompson."

"And I can tell you *two* things he loves," Charles Bradley said. "That Thompson and Jack Daniels. Do you remember that night in the bar in Mississippi? We'd just finished up our trainin' at Camp Shelby. Place was packed elbow to elbow with GIs and broads.

"Davis had a pretty good snoot full, said he was going to the bathroom. We told him if he went, he'd never find his way back to us. He said he would, too. Held up a wad of dollar bills. Started layin' them bills on the floor as he went—leavin' a trail. We told him the money would be gone before he got to the toilet. Well, dang, a few minutes later here he came, pickin' up them bills one by one, grinning like a possum. Nobody took a single one of them dollars while he was gone."

"Why didn't they take 'em?" Aaron asked.

"Who knows?" Charles said. "Everybody was prob'ly too drunk to notice he'd put 'em down."

Art Ferdinand smiled. "He's a character alright. I'll never forget him and that chicken."

"What chicken?" Harry asked.

"A few months ago, he saw a chicken outside a barn. Caught and killed it. He was gonna cook it, but about the time he got a fire goin' and stuck it in his helmet to cook, we got orders to move up. So he carries this chicken with him. We ran the Jerries out of a house, and Davis starts a fire inside to finish cookin' the thing. But the Germans counterattacked and drove us out before he was done. All day he carried that chicken—we was in that house twice and knocked out of it twice. Finally about dark he said, 'I'm eatin' this damn chicken, and I mean it.' So, sittin' there in a ditch, he ate that half-cooked chicken."

The men laughed.

"I gather he didn't offer to share any of that chicken, huh?" Charles said.

"Hey, have you guys heard? We're havin' a special dinner, it being Christmas Day and all," Harry Klutz said. Aaron, Worth, and Art stared at him.

"I'll believe that when I see it," Worth said.

"No—it's true. I just got it straight from Kotalik. The field kitchen's already set up."

Lieutenant Shingleton approached at a rapid pace. "Listen up, men. The Krauts are raisin' hell in France—we're on full alert. Intelligence says the Germans will launch a major offensive soon. Get your gear together. We're movin' out soon."

"Hey, Ferdinand," Harry yelled out. "Looks like your 'war'll be over in no time' prediction was a little premature."

"Geez, Lieutenant," Charles Bradley said, "it's Christmas Day, for Pete's sake. We're supposed to have a hot-cooked dinner today."

"What you're gonna have is a long march. Now off your asses and on your feet."

"Shit," Aaron said to Worth Haynes. "I just wrote Maggie about how peaceful it's been lately."

Shingleton scowled. "Knock it off, Johnson. All of you get this. We're headed just west of Prato. It's imperative we get there ASAP. Quit complainin' and get your gear."

Following a five-hour march, the entire battalion entered Prato, situated a few miles southeast of Pistoia. A sizable town, it contained a large, ornate cathedral. As the GIs marched past the imposing structure, huge snowflakes fell, covering the town and the surrounding Apennines in a white blanket. The cathedral's spires dwarfed everything around it.

"That's a beautiful church," Aaron said. "About a hundred times bigger than our little country church back home."

"Captain Atwell said it was built in the second century," First Sergeant Gibbs said. "Just think—only a few years after Jesus himself. Saint Paul might have passed through here, who knows?"

"I never took you for somebody who'd care about that sort of thing, Sarge," Aaron said.

"Hey, I'm Catholic—we always care."

That evening, Captain Atwell briefed the platoon leaders and ranking noncoms. Aaron sat by the radio as the CO apprised them of their situation. "We'll be the reserve division in this sector. The Ninety-second and the Indian Eighth Division are on line. If the Germans look like they're gonna break through them, we will stop them. So stay loose—find some cover. Stay as warm as you can—don't look like the snow's gonna let up anytime soon. Be ready to move fast if we get the order. Check on your men—make sure they have food and ammo. Then stand by. Dismissed."

# CHAPTER FIFTY-TWO

"Men, we have our orders," Atwell said. "The Brits are scheduled to attack on our right to push the Jerries off the hills there and stop all that fire we've been taking. Once they do that, we'll be in a position to bring up reinforcements and continue our attack." Atwell paused. "Any questions?"

"Yes sir," Shingleton said. "When do they attack?"

"In two hours. In the meantime, have your men stay in their holes—no moving around. The Jerries can see every move we make."

"Tell me about it—sir," Shingleton said.

Aaron sat hunched over the radio in the company CP—a large bunker buttressed with sandbags. He turned to Atwell. "Sir, Major Spelling at battalion wants you."

Snatching the phone from Aaron, Atwell stuck it to his ear. "Go ahead, Major. What's the status of the British attack?"

Atwell listened for a moment and then snapped, "They're *what!* Jesus Christ! We're gettin' mauled up here and they stop to make *fucking tea!* Can't somebody—yes sir. Understand. Out."

Atwell rubbed his hand across his face and took in a deep breath. "The damn Brits are making tea. Stopped their attack. General Clark's livid. The 337th's moving up from reserve to join with the Brits and push the attack. They'll keep us posted."

Two miles away, Art Ferdinand, assigned as communications liaison with B Company, 337th Battalion, nodded to his counterpart, Sergeant Bane. "Got it, Sarge. I'll call it in to our guys right away." He grabbed a field telephone and spun the handle on its side.

"Johnson, get this—the Brits just intercepted a Kraut radio message and called us. German reinforcements are moving up in your sector tonight to relieve the Jerries to your front. Get this info to battalion right away."

"Roger. Out."

Aaron turned toward the captain. "Captain Atwell, word from Art at the 337th. Our battalion guys need to know this ASAP."

The following morning Atwell stood in the CP with the radio handset to his ear. "Yes sir. Copy. I will, sir. Thank you." He handed the phone to Aaron. "Tell Art we owe the Brits one after all. Colonel Brady ordered Third Battalion to intercept the Jerries as they moved up. Caught 'em totally by surprise. Bowled them over and took hills 724 and 732 to boot. We're ordered to move out right away—the way's clear for us to hit the hills on our left front."

The battalion captured four more hills that day. More progress than they'd made in a week.

"Johnson—you got headquarters?" Atwell barked.

Aaron handed the receiver to Atwell, who spoke immediately into it. "Sir, we've secured all four objectives. Waiting for orders. Yes sir. Out here."

He handed the phone to Aaron and smiled. "First and Third Battalions have taken Verruca. We're holding here. The enemy's in retreat. We've broken the Gothic Line in our sector."

Aaron tugged at the straps holding the radio. He turned to Harry. "Take this damn radio off my back, will ya? It weighs a ton."

Harry removed the radio. Aaron's head spun. He sank to his knees and fell face forward onto the muddy ground.

Atwell laughed. "Pick that poor bastard up and get him to the aid station. He's kept our communication lines open during this entire attack—night and day. He's earned some rest."

# CHAPTER FIFTY-THREE

Aaron sat in the fortified bunker serving as company CP and gazed through the view slit at the snow-covered terrain before him. The heavy winter snows had brought the fighting in the Northern Apennines to a standstill. Storms had covered everything in sight with over a foot of snow, with drifts of three and four feet in many places. The cold temperatures—it never got above freezing and hovered around zero or below during the night—coupled with the wind, made it impossible to mount coordinated infantry attacks. Operations were limited to artillery exchanges and nightly patrols.

"See anything out there to write home about?" Gibbs asked.

"No—just more snow and more mountains. How long you think we'll be here, Sarge?"

"Big push will come in the spring when things dry out. We'll be hittin' 'em with all we got."

"Think that'll be enough?"

"You never know about ole Jerry." Gibbs laughed. "He don't give up easy."

Aaron nodded. No—quitting didn't seem to be in the Jerries' vocabulary. Stepping to the makeshift table where the radio equipment sat, Aaron seated himself and began writing a letter.

Dear Maggie,

I hope this finds you and Barry well and in good spirits. I sure wish I could have been there for Christmas. Did Barry like his presents? If you took any pictures, please send them. How is Lloyd? Is he still going out with Mary Sue's mother? It seems strange to me to think of a forty-five-year-old man dating, but if it makes him happy that's okay with me. Both their spouses are dead, so if they enjoy each other's company, why not?

I got a letter from Graydon. He's out of basic training. My guess is he will wind up in France somewhere. Sure wish he'd joined the Navy.

I can't tell you where I am, but I can tell you it's cold and snowy. The scenery is beautiful. I'd really like to bring you and Barry over here sometime if this doggone war ever ends. I think you'd enjoy seeing it.

I've been eating well lately and have put on some weight. You may not recognize me when I get home. That will be the happiest day of my life.

One last thing before I go. There's a guy in my company named Furlong. I kind of stayed away from him at first. He was always coming across like some kind of Holy Joe. But now that I've gotten to know him, I think he's a really great fellow. He's got me thinking all the stuff I learned in church growing up really is on the level. I know you tried to get me more interested in going to church after we were married, but I just didn't see the point. I'm starting to think maybe I do now.

Well, that's about it. I've got to go clean up my equipment and check on a few things. I will write as soon as I can.

Love,

Aaron

"Johnson—got a phone line out. Captain wants it fixed on the double," Gibbs said.

Aaron collected his wiring tools and donned his driest pair of socks before lacing his boots up tight. When he left the CP, a heavy fog rolled down the mountain and enveloped the entire slope. He smiled. Two more hours until daylight and a good covering fog to work in. Wouldn't have to worry about getting spotted by a German artillery observer or sniper. He wouldn't even have to wear the white capes they'd been issued. They were nothing but an aggravation anyway.

He found the wire and crawled along the snow-covered ground, cupping the line in his hand as he went. The wind whipped around him, chilling his body from head to foot. Somewhere along the American line, a .30 caliber machine gun opened fire—*rat-tat-a-tat-tat*. Mike, no doubt, firing to keep the gun from freezing up. Sounding out the all-familiar "shave and a haircut." Then *tat-tat*—"two bits."

A German gun opened up in response. *Rat-tat-a...* Aaron smiled. You'll never match it, Jerry. Sure enough, the Kraut gun ran away with the shooter. *Taaaaaaaaaaaa.* His smile broadened. Your guns fire so damn fast you can't control the trigger. That's okay—shoot up all the ammo you can. That'll mean a few less for us to take when we come after you later.

Two hundred yards out, he found the break. Looked as if an artillery round had blown it in two. With his fingers numbed by the cold, it took longer than usual to fix the line. He finally completed the splice and then tapped into it with the auxiliary handset to make sure it worked. Nothing.

"Damn," he said aloud. "Must be another break somewhere farther out."

He continued crawling through the fog, one hand on the phone line to guide him. Sure enough, fifty yards more and he found a second break. It took him five minutes to find both ends of the break. Luckily, the fog still covered his actions. It was so thick he could even sit up and work on the line rather than lying prone.

The test of the line after the second repair proved successful. He gathered up his tools. What was odd? He looked around.

Oh crap! While he was working, the fog had completely lifted and dawn had broken! He was a sitting duck.

A bullet struck the snow beside him before he heard the sound of the sniper's rifle that fired it.

His heart in his throat, he rolled toward an outcropping of rocks ten feet away. Another Mauser round zinged by, barely missing his head. A third struck the rocks and ricocheted away just as he scrambled behind the granite boulders. Thank God the rocks were close by. Otherwise...

He lay panting. No more shots fired. But he couldn't leave the safety of the rocks to try to get back to the company. The sniper would be watching. He wouldn't make it ten yards—especially in the snow. Couldn't call in, either. The auxiliary phone lay where he'd left it next to the repaired line. He'd wait until dark. It was going to be a long, cold day. At least he didn't have to worry about the sniper keeping him pinned down while another Jerry came to finish him off. They'd be crazy to show themselves in daylight. Still, he took the .45 from its holster and made sure there was a round in the chamber.

He closed his eyes, nestled among the rocks, and tried to sleep.

Well after dark that night, Aaron entered the CP and sank to the ground.

"We wondered what happened to you," Gibbs said. "Want some coffee?"

"Yeah—anything warm. Damn sniper kept me out there all day."

"Hmm—we thought about comin' to look for ya, but the phone worked and nobody else wanted to go out in the cold." Gibbs smiled.

Aaron stared at him. "Well if I'd been lyin' out there dyin', I'd have gone out happy knowing I'd at least fixed your damn phone line."

Gibbs laughed again. "Have some more coffee."

# CHAPTER FIFTY-FOUR

Lloyd pushed through the front doorway carrying a bag of groceries and a newspaper. Tall, dark-haired with just a touch of gray, he was lean and fit from hours spent walking the fields in pursuit of quail, doves, and rabbits. His agile movements gave him the appearance of a man younger than his forty-five years. And he could still hit, run, and throw a baseball better than many men half his age. If he regretted not signing the professional contract he was once offered, he never let on.

"I'm home," he called out.

Maggie stepped to the doorway leading to the kitchen. "Shh." She put her finger to her lips. "Barry's sleeping."

"Sorry," Lloyd whispered. "I picked up the groceries you ordered and got the mail. I think there's a letter here from Aaron."

"Oh good," Maggie said. She wiped her hands on the towel she carried and hurried to Lloyd's side.

"Hang on a minute," he said. "Let me at least put this bag down." He set the bag on the floor and reached into his jacket pocket for the letter.

Maggie snatched it from his hands and carried it to the sofa, ripping the envelope open as she went. "It's dated two weeks ago. Why does it take so long for the letters to get here?" Her eyes scanned the page and then returned to the beginning, reading more slowly.

"He says he's okay," she said.

"Can you read it out loud?" Lloyd asked. "Or is it too mushy for that?"

"Oh, Daddy, he doesn't write mushy stuff. Besides, the censors blocked out a lot. Listen."

Dear Maggie,

I hope this finds you and xxxxx well and in good spirits. I sure wish I could have been there for Christmas. Did xxxxx like his presents? If you took any pictures, please send them.

How is xxxxx? Is he still going out with Mary Sue's mother? It seems strange to me to think of a forty-five-year-old man dating, but if it makes him happy that's okay with me. Both their spouses are dead, so if they enjoy each other's company, why not?

I got a letter from xxxxxxx. He's xxxxxxxxxxxxxxx. My guess is he will xxxxxxxxxxxxxxxxxxxxxxxxxxxx. Sure wish he'd xxxxxx the xxxx.

I can't tell you where I am, but I can tell you it's xxxxxxxxxxxxxx. The scenery is xxxxxxxxx. I'd really like to bring you and xxxxx over here sometime if this doggone war ever ends. I think you'd enjoy seeing it.

I've been eating well lately and have put on some weight. You may not recognize me when I get home. That will be xxx xxxxxxxx xxx xx xx xxxx.

One last thing before I go. There's a guy in my company named xxxxxxx. I kind of stayed away from him at first. He was always coming across like some kind of Holy Joe. But now that I've gotten to know him, I think he's a really great fellow. He's got me thinking all the stuff I learned in church growing up really is on the level. I know you tried to get me more interested in that stuff after we were married, but I just didn't see the point. I'm starting to think maybe I do now.

Well, that's about it. I've got to go clean up my equipment and check on a few things. I will write as soon as I can.

Love,
Aaron


"Doggone those censors!" Maggie said. "How am I supposed to make any sense out of his letters with them marking out every other word? I know he's telling me about Graydon—I can figure that out. But I want to know where he is."

"That's the Army for you," Lloyd said. "They are good at messing things up."

"I'm glad he's giving more thought to church and all. He needs it—we all do. I just hope he writes again soon."

"Well, he may be a little busy. The war isn't over, you know."

Maggie frowned. "Guess not. But I wait so long to hear, and then—just one little page?"

"He'll probably write again soon. The papers are saying the Germans can't hold out much longer."

"I hope they're right." She looked up. "Hard day at the mill?"

"No—about the same as every day for the last twenty-nine years." He plopped down in his favorite upholstered chair. "Where did the time go?"

"Oh, Daddy. You're not old."

"Yeah—well, Aaron's got a point. What's a man my age doing going out with a widow woman when I could be using the time to fish and hunt more?"

"Come on, Dad. You like Bessie. It's good for the two of you to get out. Besides, Mary Sue and I think it would be neat if we ended up half sisters."

"Hey, stop that kind of talk. There was only one woman for me—your mother. Boy, I miss her."

"Dad, it's nice that you treasure your memories of Mom. But you need to move on. Juanita and I won't always be here to take care of you, you know. You'd be awfully lonely by yourself."

"You're right. But I'm in no hurry to tie the knot again. Not anytime soon, anyway. Seeing Bessie is just—well, she's good company."

Maggie smiled. "Based on what I hear from Mary Sue, her Mom thinks it's a lot more than that."

Lloyd shook his head. "Women. I had a wife and three daughters. Not one son I could take huntin' and teach how to fish. Maybe when Barry's older—"

"Let's don't rush it—he's too little to carry your shotgun, let alone shoot it."

"Well, he'll be ready for that before you know it. And I intend to make him a good'un in the field."

"There'll be plenty of time for that later. Let's talk about something else. Supper's almost ready. I cooked up those rabbits you brought home. Good thing for us you're a good hunter."

"What's left to do? I can help you with supper."

"You sit still. You just did a twelve-hour shift. I'll call you when everything's ready."

Maggie entered the kitchen and checked on the stew simmering on the stove top. She placed the biscuits she'd made into the oven. Aaron's letter. He was really thinking about church. Maybe he'd even go with her—maybe even join, when he got home. She bowed her head. Lord, please keep him safe.

# CHAPTER FIFTY-FIVE

Spring. Winter snows melted. Warm sunshine bathed the Italian countryside and its mountain peaks. The men of G Company along with the rest of the Eighty-fifth Division had spent the previous two months preparing for action. Once again, all unit insignias and markings were removed from uniforms, helmets, and vehicles. Ordered off the front line, they had spread out in the forests and farmlands around Lucca.

"Rumors are flyin'," Art said. "We'll be pushing ahead soon."

Aaron nodded. "Jerry ain't done yet. We'll have to chase 'em all the way to Berlin probably."

"It won't be easy. Why d'ya think we've had to do all this hush-hush stuff?"

"Oh, I'm sure our friend Mark Clark has some nice juicy role for us to play in the big offensive. Maybe we should stop doing such a good job."

Art laughed. "Maybe you got something there. Oh well, whatever it is, we'll find out soon enough."

Captain Atwell called the company together. Curious GIs stood at parade rest.

"Men, I have a copy of a letter here addressed to General Coulter from the Fifteenth Army Group Commander, General Mark Clark. General Coulter has ordered it be read to all personnel. So listen up."

Dear General Coulter:

Today the Eighty-fifth Infantry Division completes a year of action in Italy. I could not let such an outstanding occasion pass without noting the magnificent contribution made by the officers and men of the Eighty-fifth as part of Fifth Army in the success of the Fifteenth Army Group.

The past year has been a truly glorious one for your division. The participation in the capture of Rome and the cracking of the Gothic Line are two of its many achievements, contributing greatly to the defeat of the enemy in Italy. The capture of Monte Altuzzo by the Eighty-fifth Division after a violent five-day battle loosened the German grip on the entire Gothic Line, a well fortified position defended by the enemy's best troops.

Having been in intimate contact with the division's regiments and battalions during my days at Fifth Army, I am well aware of the quality of its work under your superior leadership. From its initial action at Minturno through the Gothic Line to its present position, its men have shown the utmost aggressiveness in materially aiding in the destruction of the German armies in Italy.

Now the time is at hand for us to deliver the final and decisive blow, and I am confident that the Eighty-fifth Division is ready to do its part in inflicting crushing defeat upon the enemy. Sincerely,

Mark W. Clark

Atwell folded the letter and put it away. "Men, the spring offensive will be under way soon. I know you'll do the same fine job you've always done. As of this moment, be prepared to move on short notice. That's all."

The next day the entire division was placed on a six-hour alert. Orders came down soon after. The division was ordered relieve the First Armored Division and elements of the Tenth Mountain Division without delay. Mount Luminasio and Mount Terranera lay dead ahead. Beyond—the primary objective—the Po Valley.

"Damn, I'm tired," Harry said. "All we've done is move from one part of the line to another for the past week."

"That's because we're in reserve for a change—so they have to put us where we can plug a hole in the line if they need us," Aaron said. "Captain Atwell said he'd rather be spearheadin' the attack—"

"Easy for him to say," Art said. "We've been the point of the spear enough—I'm fine with some of the other units gettin' kissed. I don't mind marchin' from place to place. Beats getting shot at."

"Hey, we've done our part on this little jaunt—we took those towns the 337th bypassed. And we got shot at plenty doin' that," Worth said.

"Yep." Aaron added. "Took a lot of prisoners, too. The Germans know they can't win. Ever since we crossed the Po River it's been a rout—the smart ones are givin' up."

"Like the Kraut colonel that surrendered his whole outfit to you when you took a patrol to check out that village yesterday," Harry chimed in.

"Yeah—but he made me mad. When he surrendered, he gave me his pistol. It's a nice pistol—I'm keepin' it. But then he said—in perfect English—'Isn't it interesting? I'll probably be sent to a POW camp in the United States. So I'll get to your country before you, Sergeant.' Damn wise guy."

"He may be that, but he's probably right," Harry said. "Hey— quiet—listen."

"What is that?" Aaron asked.

Harry cocked his head. "Sounds like somebody moaning. Where's it coming from?"

"Over here—on the left," Aaron whispered.

Aaron flicked the carbine's safety off. Harry did the same with his M-1.

Stepping cautiously off the roadway, Aaron peered into the foliage beside it. Two steps into the wooded area, he stopped.

Directly ahead in a small clearing lay a wounded German soldier. Blood covered the midsection of his uniform. His eyes found Aaron's. *"Vasser. Vasser,"* he said. His words were barely audible.

"Careful," Harry said. "It might be a trick."

Aaron moved closer. No weapon in sight. "It's not a trick. He's hit in the stomach. Looks pretty bad. The Jerries musta left him behind when they pulled out."

Aaron took his canteen and placed it to the German's lips. Blond and blue-eyed, the man was a prototypical German soldier. Aaron winced. They could easily be mistaken for brothers—under different circumstances.

The German drank from the canteen and then coughed and spit up blood. Aaron looked at Harry and slowly moved his head from side to side.

"*Danke, danke*," the man whispered. Sweat glistened on his face. His raspy breathing grew shallow. With a painstaking movement, he took his watch from his wrist and offered it to Aaron.

Aaron shook his head. "*Nein*—yours."

The German pushed it toward him. "*Nein*—you—you."

"Take it, Aaron," Harry said. "He wants you to have it—for giving him the water."

Aaron took the watch and nodded. "*Danke schoen*."

"I'll go get a medic," Harry said. "Maybe—"

"Don't bother," Aaron said. "He's dead."

They captured the city of Verona and then moved north toward Milan. Entering the city on foot, Aaron and Harry moved down a cobblestone street. Harry flicked the safety off his M-1. "Partisans told the advance patrol the Jerries have pulled outta here. Let's hope so."

"Yeah—remember Rome? They'd supposedly left there, too—then that machine gun opened up."

Approaching an intersection, Aaron sank to one knee next to the stone building at the corner. He poked his head around it and drew back.

"What?" Harry asked.

"Not sure. Lots of civilians in the street about a block up. Looks like something's going on—can't tell what."

"I hear 'em," Harry said. "Sounds like a celebration. Let's go see."

They stayed close to the buildings as they moved up the street, rifles at the ready. A huge crowd of Italians shouted and yelled, some shook their fists at something suspended from a rope in the town square.

"What the hell's going on?" Aaron asked.

An Italian man of medium height spotted them. He ran toward them, waving his arms and speaking rapidly. He pointed at not one but three items hanging from ropes attached to the overhang of what appeared to be an abandoned gas station.

"Il Duce! Il Duce!" he cried. "Looka, looka. No biga man now!" He spat and then smiled.

"Oh my God!" Aaron said. "Those things are bodies—but—oh God—no heads."

"*Si, si!*" The Italian pointed at the figures. "Il Duce, hisa mistress, and hisa driver. We hang up so everyone see—he's a dead! Pig!" The man spat again.

"Jesus," Harry said. "They don't even look like people—just like sides of meat or somethin'."

"Yeah—we better tell the captain. Hey—do you still have that camera you found?"

"Yeah—right here." He fished it from his pack and handed it to Aaron. "You take the picture—I don't think I can."

Aaron swallowed hard and then focused the camera's viewfinder on the gruesome scene. He snapped three photos. "Let's get outta here. I don't wanna stick around this place."


"It was Mussolini you saw," Captain Atwell said. "We just got the official word from regimental. The Italian government confirmed that he and his mistress and one of his henchmen were captured by partisan forces in Como and executed. They brought their bodies to Milan so more people could see the bodies."

Aaron shivered. "Damn—what an awful sight. I wish I hadn't seen it."

"Headquarters liked your photos—they made copies for you." Atwell extended an envelope toward him.

Aaron took it. "I'll send them home to my older brother. He's a schoolteacher—into history and stuff. He may want them. I don't."

Atwell shrugged. "Fine. Now saddle up. We're movin' out again."

Two days later Worth called Aaron to his side.

"Burnitz got it," Worth said.

"That stinks," Aaron said. "How?"

"He and Davis and a couple others were on a patrol—ran into an ambush. Davis carried Burnitz back. Guys said Patrick cried like a baby."

"Burnie's the only guy Davis ever buddied up with. I'm sure he did take it hard."

The battalion continued its push into the Po Valley. The Germans fought delaying actions, but the writing was on the wall. The Allied Forces had them on the run. Prisoners by the hundreds poured into the American lines.

"How can there be so many of 'em left?" Aaron asked. "I thought we'd killed most of 'em—boy was I wrong."

"You can say that again," Gibbs said. "If they had enough supplies and some air cover, they could hold out for years."

"We're beating 'em though," Rollins, a new replacement, said.

Gibbs glared at him. "Let me tell you somethin'. We've outproduced them and we've outsupplied them, but we have *never, never* outfought 'em. They're the best infantry in the world. They just happen to have a maniac for a leader."

"Can you believe this?" Worth asked Aaron. "We're actually on the high ground for a change. They're down there in that valley, and we're up here lookin' down on them."

"And in the morning we'll go down there and push them out. Have to wonder how long this can go on."

"Let's hope they don't decide to make a big fight of it. We're gettin' close to the end of this thing. Can't be takin' too many chances now."

Aaron nodded.

Patrick Davis stared into the darkness. He mumbled something unintelligible.

"Whaddya say, Patrick?" Aaron asked.

Davis stared at Aaron.

Even in the darkness his eyes looked fierce.

"I said, I'll fix 'em. I'll fix 'em good."

"Yeah, yeah, Patrick. In the morning. We'll take care of them then," Worth said.

"I ain't waitin' 'til mornin'," Davis said. He bolted from the foxhole and began to crawl down the hill toward the German line.

"Davis, get back here!" Aaron hissed, grabbing his boot heel. "You can't go down there alone!"

Davis turned and patted his Thompson. His face was set in a hard line. "Let go, or I'll turn this thing on you."

He jerked his foot free and disappeared into the darkness.

"What should we do?" Worth said.

"I'm gonna tell Gibbs," Aaron said. "Sit tight."

Before he could reach Gibbs, the sound of a Thompson firing full auto reached his ears.

"Damn, we gotta do something," Aaron said aloud.

The Thompson fired nonstop for the next twenty minutes. German fire rang out in response. Voices echoed through the valley as the Germans shouted orders and instructions.

"It's only a matter of time 'til they surround him," Worth said.

"Atwell said nobody's to leave their post. He's on his own," Aaron said.

The next morning, G Company moved down to the valley. The Germans were gone. There was no sign of Davis anywhere.

# CHAPTER FIFTY-SIX

"Who's the Dago talkin' to the Cap'n?" Worth said.

Aaron shrugged. "Dunno for sure. Gibbs said he's a partisan—claims to be a general or somethin'. Names Garibaldi."

"Whaddya think he wants?"

"Probably wants supplies or food—now the war's nearly over, he'd prob'ly like to impress his men by getting 'em some decent vittles."

Atwell motioned for Aaron to join him.

Aaron spoke over his shoulder as he moved toward the CP. "Maybe I'll find out what's up. Let ya know."

Worth nodded.

"Johnson, get battalion on the radio. General Garibaldi here's got some interestin' news."

Aaron rang up battalion. Atwell took the handset. "Colonel English, this is Captain Atwell. A partisan leader—a General Garibaldi—says he knows where the Germans are holdin' a bunch of political prisoners. He's asking us to head up there and liberate 'em. Yes sir, we can handle it. Well, we'll need enough trucks to get us there—he says it's about an hour's ride north. I'd like to take a few of the rifle platoons and a machine gun crew in case there's any trouble. Yes sir. We'll be ready to ride by the time the trucks get here. Thank you, sir. I'll contact you when we see what we're up against. Out."

Atwell returned the handset to Aaron and then turned to the sergeant. "Sergeant Gibbs, spread the word. Trucks will be here in an hour. We're gonna liberate some prisoners. Field packs, weapons, and ammo—we may get some resistance."

Gibbs saluted. "Yessir."

Aaron fiddled with the radio. Damn. Just when it looked like they might get a break, this Garibaldi palooka had to show up. Nobody wanted to take a chance on gettin' killed now that the fighting was almost over.

"Where is this place again?" Worth asked. The truck's noise caused him to speak loudly.

"Somewhere up near the Austrian border, accordin' to the map," Aaron said. "Not far from the Brenner Pass. Garibaldi told the cap'n the prisoners are bein' held at a former resort of some kind. Some German SS and Gestapo goons brought them there from a concentration camp."

Worth rubbed his chin. "Wonder why?"

"Beats me. Guess we'll find out when we get there."

Captain Atwell, Gibbs, and Garibaldi rode in a jeep at the head of the column. The trucks followed, laboring as they climbed the steep mountain road high into the Dolomite Mountains. In the distance the Italian Alps loomed, snowcapped peaks against a brilliant blue sky.

Rounding a bend, a large stone building several stories high appeared in the distance. Atwell raised his hand to halt the column. He gave the signal to dismount. Aaron followed Worth off the truck and joined the rest of the men as they spread out and moved forward on foot, weapons at the ready.

"See any sign of Jerries?" Aaron said.

"Not yet," Worth said. "Be ready, though—if they're SS, they probably won't give up without a fight."

Atwell raised his hand as they came within three hundred yards of the building. "Gibbs, send a few men ahead to scout out the situation. Tell 'em to stay alert—no firing unless they're fired on."

Jack Claytor reported back fifteen minutes later. "Sir—a number of the prisoners are milling around outside the building. Said the Jerries heard us coming and beat it."

"Alright, men, let's go see what we got," Atwell said, motioning the GIs forward.

A tall, lanky British officer ran forward, saluted, and then shook Atwell's hand. "Lieutenant Colonel Jeremy McGrath, RAF, and you are...?"

"Captain John Atwell. Colonel—what—?"

"We're so very glad to see you chaps. Things were a bit dicey for a while, as you Yanks might say."

"What's goin' on, Colonel? Why did the Germans move you people here?" Atwell said.

"Well, you see, we were at Dachau—and the SS boys got wind that the Americans were approaching. I gather they didn't want us liberated—staying true to the Fuhrer's wishes, I suppose. I guess they thought they could spirit us down here. Didn't count on you chaps showing up, however."

"What was so 'dicey,' as you put it?"

"Hmm—yes—became something of a standoff. The SS and Gestapo gents decided they were going to kill all of us—"

"How many of there are you?"

"A hundred and thirty-three altogether—we had to count off every evening. As I was saying, if it hadn't been for the Wehrmacht troops who accompanied us here, they might well have done it. But a quite decent Jerry officer told the head SS man that if they tried to kill us, he'd order his men to protect us. Got rather heated, I must say. Since the Wehrmacht officer had more men, the SS boys finally backed down. Then when one of the guards announced he'd spotted your convoy on the way, they all pulled out and left us. Thank God."

Atwell pushed his helmet back on his head and turned to Gibbs. "Sergeant, post some guards around the building and establish a perimeter. Don't want to have the Krauts changing their minds and sneaking back here. Then get all the prisoners together outside. See if any of them need medical care, food, whatever. Johnson, crank up the radio. I've gotta report to Colonel English."


A short, stocky man with a mustache and wearing a beret spoke rapidly, gesturing with his hands and arms as he did so. Aaron shook his head. "Look, mister—I don't speak French or Belgian or whatever. I'll try to find someone who does—"

"*Mais oui! Mais ouis! Vive la Americans!*"

Jack Claytor clapped Aaron on the shoulder. "He's just trying to thank you. Let me talk with him—I know a little French. Besides, the old man wants you inside on the double. Second floor. Said he needs your mechanical skills."

Aaron hurried inside. "Aaron, look at this place," Harry Klutz said. "It's a luxury hotel. And get a load of the lake out back—beautiful."

"Yeah, it's nice. I gotta find the captain."

Climbing the stairs to the second floor, Aaron spotted Atwell and Francis Furlong in the hallway to his right.

"You wanted to see me, Captain?"

"Yeah—darndest thing. One of the prisoners is locked in his room. The only one. I thought maybe you could pick the lock—be a shame to bust down this lovely door."

"I'll give it a try, sir." Aaron bent to one knee and studied the lock. "Any chance there's a key—"

"We already checked. The hotel manager said one of the Gestapo guys threw it in the lake out back—said Hitler had given specific orders to lock this guy up and throw away the key."

"Hmm—well let me see what I can do." Aaron opened the screw-driver blade on his pocketknife.

Atwell looked down the hallway. "Furlong, stay with Johnson in case he needs help. I'm gonna check out the rest of these rooms."

It took Aaron only five minutes to take the lock apart and push open the door. Inside a graying, middle-aged man of medium build rushed toward him and grasped his hand. "Thank you! Thank you!" he said in a heavy German accent. "I could see you men from my window but could not get out!"

Aaron sized him up. Good firm handshake. Spoke good English, despite the accent. So who was this guy that Hitler took such a personal interest in?

"What news do you bring? What can you tell me? Is the war over?"

"The Germans in Italy have surrendered—word is the rest of 'em can't hold out much longer."

"Hitler, Hitler—what about Hitler?"

"Rumor has it he's dead—committed suicide, supposedly."

The man's mouth fell open. He hung his head. "May God have mercy on his soul!"

Aaron took a step back. Had he really heard correctly? Mercy on Hitler's soul—after what he'd done to this man? Who was this guy?

"Umm—excuse me," Furlong said. "I need to get your name, sir—so we can account for everyone."

"I am Pastor Martin Niemoeller, from Berlin."

Furlong stepped forward. "Really? Pastor Niemoeller—I've heard so much about you. I can't tell you what an honor it is to meet you. Please, let us escort you downstairs."

Francis took the man's arm and guided him from the room. "Can I get you anything—food, water? And later, can I get your autograph?"

They proceeded a short way down the hallway. Niemoeller stopped and turned to them. "You want to know what I thought about while I was imprisoned? It was that when they came to take the Jews away, I didn't stand up for them because I wasn't Jewish. When they came for the communists, I didn't stand up for them—I wasn't a communist. The same for the Catholics, the trade unionists, and the gypsies. So when they came for me, there was no one left to stand up in protest for me either." He raised a finger and narrowed his eyes. "Remember what I'm telling you—never forget it."

Later Aaron caught up with Furlong outside the building. Niemoeller was nowhere in sight.

"So Furlong, who is this Niemoeller guy?"

"He's amazing. One of the few church leaders to openly oppose Hitler and the Nazis. Hitler threw him into prison for his troubles. It took real guts to take Hitler on like he did.

Aaron shook his head. "Wow. Hard to believe that madman Hitler let him live. I can't believe what Niemoeller said, can you? What he said when I told him Hitler was dead?"

"Furlong gazed into the distance. "Maybe—maybe I can."

Harry hurried to Aaron and Furlong. "Either of you guys seen Ferdinand?"

They shook their heads.

"Why?" Aaron asked.

"Nobody can find him. The captain's sending a search party to survey the area."

"But, the Germans left…"

"Captain's concerned maybe some of the Krauts came back and nabbed him—or worse."

"Let's go help look for him," Aaron said. "Where was he seen last?"

"He was going into the building to get some prisoners out. But that was over an hour ago. Nobody's seen him since."

"Let's check inside," Aaron said.

Aaron and Worth combed the building for the next forty-five minutes.

"This is the top floor," Worth said. "We've been through the lower floors stem to stern. No sign of him."

"He's gotta be here somewhere," Aaron answered. He stopped. "I hear something—down this hallway."

He moved down the hallway, carbine at the ready. Outside the third door on the right, the sound grew louder.

Aaron pushed the door open with the barrel of his carbine.

Art Ferdinand lay motionless on a bed in the room. Snoring away.

"Get the hell up, Art!" Aaron shouted.

Art leapt from the bed, wild-eyed. "What—where—what's wrong?"

"What's wrong is the whole durn company's been lookin' for you for over an hour. We thought something happened to you," Worth said.

"Oh geez—I'm sorry," Art said. "It just that it's been so long since I'd slept in a bed. After I got the prisoners out of here, I told them to go downstairs. I just couldn't resist this chance to get some shut-eye in a real bed."

Aaron smiled.

Worth chuckled.

"Well, you're gonna have to explain it to the captain. And I don't wanna be around when you do it," Worth said.

"Oh, I do," Aaron said. "I don't wanna miss this chewin' out."

# CHAPTER FIFTY-SEVEN

"Aaron, can you believe it? The war is over—it's over!" Art Ferdinand jumped up and down and slapped Aaron on the back at the same time.

"Yeah, yeah—it's great, Art. It is hard to believe. Thank God."

"I'll say. Here we are at this beautiful resort—a great hotel to sleep in. And home. Aaron—we'll be going home soon!"

"Let's hope so. Course, Japan isn't done yet. We may end up there."

Art stopped jumping. "Oh no! They wouldn't! Would they? We've done our part!"

"Captain Atwell says we better not get our hopes up too much."

"But *Stars and Stripes* says we're clobberin' the Japs now. They don't need us."

"Unless something really big happens, I got a feeling we're gonna be headed for the Pacific within the month."

Art's face fell. "Damn."

Aaron winced. Damn. Why did he say those things? He'd ruined Art's jubilation. It wasn't like he wanted to go fight in Japan. He wanted to go home. How long had it been since he'd seen Maggie? And Barry? Would things still be the same? No—things would probably never be exactly the same again. Maybe they would be better.

He'd found a postcard inside the hotel picturing the resort. He took it from his pocket and began to write.

> Hello Darling,
> This is where I was when the war ended. It was being used as a concentration camp. The mountains in the rear of the picture are still snow-capped.

"Johnson—the old man wants you," Harry Klutz said. He jerked his thumb toward the hotel. "He's inside—office just off the lobby."

Aaron scribbled a quick "Love, Aaron" on the card and stuck it in his pocket.

Captain Atwell sat behind a large wooden desk. One of the liberated prisoners, a tall, silver-haired man, stood ramrod straight beside him. He wore a suit—his prisoner garb no doubt replaced with clothing scrounged from somewhere in the hotel.

"Johnson, this is Kurt von Schuschnigg, former chancellor of Austria."

Schuschnigg bowed slightly.

Aaron stood stock still. Should he salute? Shake hands? Finally he nodded in return. "Umm—nice to meet you, sir."

"My pleasure, Sergeant," Schuschnigg said in a heavily accented voice.

Atwell appeared to be suppressing a grin. "General Clark personally ordered me to return Herr Schuschnigg to Austria immediately. You're going to drive him there—today."

"Certainly, sir. Should I check out a jeep—"

"Oh no. We found more suitable transportation in the hotel garage. I think you'll like it. It's all gassed up and waiting out back. Here are your orders—you'll need them to get through the checkpoint at the Austrian border. Herr Schuschnigg is ready to leave. He knows the way."

"Yes sir." Aaron saluted. "Sir, er—Herr Schuschnigg—if you'll follow me, we'll get under way."

"Excellent, Sergeant," Schuschnigg said. He fitted a monocle over one eye. "I'm eager to be in my country again."

Aaron escorted the man through the lobby and out the rear entrance.

A large, shiny black sedan was parked on the driveway. Charles Bradley leaned against one fender with his arms crossed. "I don't know how you managed to pull this assignment, Johnson. Here are the keys. Enjoy yourself."

Aaron gave a low whistle. What a beautiful car. No idea what make—but it was eye-popping. And the interior was just as grand. Large, plush bench front seat, roomy rear seat. Great looking upholstery.

Schuschnigg climbed into the back seat. Aaron crawled behind the wheel and started the engine. A deep, throaty exhaust sound hinted of power. Aaron smiled. He hadn't driven anything like this in his entire life.

"Ahem," Schuschnigg uttered. "We'll head north, Sergeant. Through the Brenner Pass. I will direct you."

Aaron maneuvered the high-powered sedan up the winding mountain road toward Austria. The sun shone brightly, the sky was crystal clear, and the view across the mountain passes and valleys was breathtaking. As they neared the Brenner Pass, snow covered the peaks of the Alps. They stood out majestically against the azure sky. The cool air barely hinted of approaching spring.

The car handled beautifully. Aaron accelerated into the curves, and the big car responded perfectly, hugging the road and whipping through the turns.

After powering through half a dozen S-turns, Aaron glanced in the rearview mirror. Schuschnigg, looking pale, sat in the middle of the seat, arms extended to either side to brace himself. He screwed the monocle into his face. "I say, Sergeant, don't you think you're driving a bit too fast?"

Aaron winced. "Sorry, sir." He eased off on the accelerator.

At the Austrian border, Aaron was halted at a checkpoint manned by American MPs. He presented his orders. When the MP saw the orders issued directly from Mark Clark, he did a double take. "Hang on a second." He stepped away to confer with his lieutenant.

Aaron fumed.

The lieutenant approached. "You expect me to buy these trumped-up orders, Sergeant? Who is this man?"

Aaron explained.

"Wait here." The lieutenant stepped to a field telephone. He spoke briefly. Moments later he stiffened. "Yes sir. Right away, sir."

He stepped back to the car and handed the documents to Aaron. "Sergeant, you've got some clout behind you today." He stepped back and waved Aaron through the checkpoint.

An hour later, Schuschnigg instructed Aaron through a series of highways until they reached a town. Following Schuschnigg's instructions, Aaron steered to a large square and parked near a fountain. His stomach tightened. Uniformed German troops walked the streets, rifles slung on their shoulders.

Aaron slid low in the seat and removed his helmet. Did these guys know the war was over? What would he do if they tried something?

"Wait here please, Sergeant. I will return shortly," Schuschnigg said. He exited the vehicle, walked across the square, and entered a two-story brick building.

Aaron sank even lower in the seat. Maybe the German soldiers would continue ignoring him.

In the car's side mirror, the figure of a fully uniformed and helmeted German appeared. He walked toward the car, his rifle slung over his shoulder.

Aaron took in a deep breath. Damn. What should he do? He loosened the flap on the holster of his forty-five and placed his hand on the pistol's grip. If he had to...

The German tapped on the driver's side glass. Aaron rolled it down slightly. "*Jah?*" he said.

"*Zigaretten?*" the German said as he placed two fingers to his lips. "*Zigaretten?*"

Aaron exhaled and then took a pack of Pall Malls from his field jacket pocket and handed them through the partially opened window.

The German smiled. "*Danke schoen! Danke schoen!*" he said, then turned and left.

Aaron sank back against the seat.

Moments later, Schuschnigg returned. "Come along, Sergeant. We've been invited to a luncheon with the burgomaster and his staff."

Aaron snatched his helmet off the seat and followed the ex-chancellor.

The first floor of the building contained what looked to be various offices. Richly paneled wood trim and heavy carpeting muted the sounds and gave an air of tranquility to the place. They were escorted upstairs by a man in a dark suit. Without speaking a word, he ushered them into a large dining room. A long table was set with china, silverware, and crystal goblets. Several opened wine bottles sat chilling in iced-down metal containers.

Aaron's stomach growled. He hadn't eaten all day. Something smelled wonderful.

At the head of the table a middle-aged man of average height, with thinning gray hair and a slight belly, stood dressed in a gray suit. His white shirt appeared to be heavily starched, and he smiled effusively when they entered the room. A number of other similarly dressed men were also present.

Schuschnigg said something in Austrian—or was it German?—to the assembled group. He waved a hand toward Aaron.

The gray-haired man walked rapidly to Aaron, his hand outstretched. "Welcome, Sergeant, I am Klaus von Schubert. I'm the burgomaster here. My wife and my staff are pleased to meet a member of the American Army and are delighted that you've returned our beloved chancellor to us and that you've agreed to join us for our meal."

"Umm—er—the pleasure is mine, Herr Schubert," Aaron said. "I apologize for my shabby appearance—Army fatigues are not really appropriate for an occasion such as this." Where had he come up with that line? Sounded like something he'd heard in a movie. No matter, it seemed to work okay.

Schubert wrinkled his brow. "Shabby?" He looked at Schuschnigg.

Schuschnigg said something, and the two laughed.

"Please be seated," Schubert said.

Food was immediately brought out from a door presumably leading to the kitchen. The aroma was surpassed only by the delicious taste of everything Aaron put in his mouth. Following the meal, Schubert toasted Schuschnigg several times, each time speaking in Austrian. Everyone downed gulps of wine with each toast. Aaron had no idea what was said, but he soon developed a rosy glow from the excellent wine.

"Sergeant, I insist you stay here tonight. We have guest accommodations waiting and will not take no for an answer," Schubert said.

"I would be honored, Herr Schubert," Aaron said. "You are too kind." The heck with driving back to Italy. If Atwell didn't like it, what could he do about it now? The war was over!

# CHAPTER FIFTY-EIGHT

The USS *Monticello* sailed from Naples on October 22, 1945, headed to Norfolk, Virginia.

"Man, it's great to be going home," Worth said.

Aaron leaned over the railing and gazed at the endless expanse of ocean. "Yes—yes it is. I almost can't believe it. I keep pinching myself. To tell you the truth, the way things went sometimes—I never thought it would happen."

Worth nodded. "I think we all felt that way."

"I mean, so many guys got hit. So many wounded—so many killed outright. Atwell said the division had almost seventy-five hundred casualties. That's half the division."

"It's really more than that when you figure only about a third of the division was actually in front line combat."

"It was just a matter of time," Aaron said. "No rhyme—no reason. Didn't matter how careful you tried to be. At some point your number had to come up. Like Bill Mauldin put it in the cartoon with Willie and Joe—I feel like a fugitive from the law of averages."

"That's what we are," Worth said. "It really hit me hard when we counted up how many of us were still around at the end."

"Yeah, of those two hundred and eighty-eight men who attacked hill seventy-nine—what was it? Only thirteen of us left at the end?"

"Somethin' like that."

"And of those only you and Furlong were never wounded?"

"A couple others—I don't think Ferdinand ever got hit. And Lieutenant Shingleton was never wounded, as I recall."

"But he rotated out before it was over—he wasn't there when the war ended."

"True. Still—the one who really stands out—"

"I know—Furlong."

"He never came close to being hit, did he?"

"Not that I know of. Never got sick—or even had a cold—"

"Or complained."

"Nope. Not once that I ever heard."

"Even when he stopped drinking coffee."

Aaron shook his head. "That affected me more than anything, I think. He never touched another drop."

"If it offends your brother, don't do it—that's what it says in the Bible, and Furlong meant to abide by it."

"And did."

"What're you gonna do when you get home?" Aaron said.

"Well—there's a couple of girls I've been writing. Think I'll look 'em up. See if I can take 'em out. Who knows where that might lead? How about you?"

Aaron smiled. "I'm not telling the first thing I'm gonna do—but the second thing I'll do is put down my duffle bag. It's been a long time."

"Bet she'll be glad to see you. And your son—"

"Barry."

"Right—how old is he now?"

"Let's see...he was born in January '44, so he'll be almost two years old."

"So he won't even remember you..."

"Right. I saw him for about ten days when I got out of basic. He'd just been born. Then I came overseas."

"That's gotta be tough."

"A lotta kids have it tougher—their daddies aren't coming home."

A dusty Model A Ford pulled to the side of the road. Aaron hopped out and shouldered his duffel bag.

"Thanks for the lift, mister."

"Anything for a GI—glad I came along."

"Woulda been a long walk here from Fort Bragg if you hadn't," Aaron said.

"Son?"

"Yessir?"

"I been wantin' to ask you the whole way. You said you was in Italy. Did you see a lot of action? I mean—was it rough?"

Aaron looked across the roof of the Model A. Then he peered in the window and locked eyes with the man. "Yeah—yes—it was rough. Saw stuff I hope to the good Lord I never see again."

The man nodded. He put the car in gear. "You take care of yourself. Git on home and kiss that pretty wife of yours. And have a great rest of your life. I think you earned it."

The Ford's tires crunched as the car pulled onto the highway and drove away. Aaron stared after it.

"Like I said," he said aloud. "Stuff I never, ever want to see again."

Things didn't look all that different. The red brick mill certainly hadn't changed. The unpaved road was just as dusty and potholed. The air was cool and the wind whipped around him. One mill-village house after another floated by on his right and on his left. Light from the windows, smoke pouring from chimneys. How long had it been? Two years and—what?—three months. Had she changed? Had he? Why hadn't he tried to call her? But he'd been in such a hurry to leave Bragg—the Army—all of it.

He crested the hill and continued down the road. Lloyd's house came into view. Someone was in the yard. Hard to tell in the near-darkness who it was.

He opened his mouth to call out, but didn't.

The person in the yard turned. Froze. Stared. "Aaron?"

"Hello, sweetheart." He dropped the duffel and quickened his pace.

She rushed to meet him. They collided in the middle of the street.

He hugged her tight—gave it all he had. "God, you're beautiful."

They kissed. A long, deep, passionate kiss. God, she felt so good. Smelled good. Tasted good.

"Why didn't you call—"

"I don't know—I just—"

"Momma? Who's that man?"

A tow-haired little boy stood in the yard, staring at them.

"It's your daddy!" Maggie said. "He's come home from the war!"

The boy shook his head. "Not my daddy. Lloyd my daddy."

Aaron and Maggie walked to the yard, each with an arm around the other. "No, Barry, Lloyd is *my* daddy. This is your daddy. Tell him hello."

"Come here, sport." Aaron scooped the boy up in his arms and hugged him. "I've been waiting a long time to see you. You sure are a big boy."

"Down! Down!" Barry squirmed and reached for Maggie. He began to cry.

"Oh, come here," she said, taking him from Aaron. "You'll figure it all out in a little while. Better get your bag and come in the house. It's getting chilly out here in the night air."

Aaron grinned. "Yeah—be right there."

He retrieved his duffel and headed for the house. Looking into the clear night sky, he focused on a bright star high in the heavens. He smiled. "God, it's good to be home. Thank you, Lord. Thanks for bringing me back."

# EPILOGUE

Aaron and his business partner, Arthur "Tab" Stikeleather, stood outside the entrance to the auto dealership they jointly owned. Bright sunlight reflected off the windshields of the cars on the sales lot.

"Well, Tab. Looks like we've made it through another day. Johnny sold one today and one yesterday. You've sold three this week. Things are lookin' up. Say, I've got to get home. Almost forgot—got a deacon's meeting tonight."

The squeal of brakes and the sound of two vehicles colliding came from the intersection at the bottom of the hill. A man—apparently the driver of one of the cars—stood looking at the damage.

Aaron squinted. "I know that man."

Tab smiled. "So? You know everyone in this town."

Aaron walked at a fast pace toward the scene. As he neared the group of people surveying the cars, the man he said he recognized looked up.

"Aaron?" he said.

"Charles Bradley. Long time no see. It's been over twenty years. I knew it was you the moment I saw you."

"I can't believe it—after all these years—"

A police car pulled to a stop beside them, and a uniformed officer exited.

"What happened here?" he said.

Charles turned to him. "I ran into this man's car, officer."

Aaron looked at the two vehicles. He turned to the driver of the other car, a thin man wearing a ragged denim shirt, khaki pants, and a porkpie hat. The brim of the hat was turned up on all sides.

"Sonny, it doesn't look like your car has any damage," Aaron said.

The driver shrugged. "No—his car got the worst of it. My bumper isn't even scratched."

The policeman cocked his head. "Hello, Mr. Johnson. You know these guys?"

"Yes, J.T. I know both of 'em. There's not much damage here to either car."

"How much would you say?" The officer pulled a small notebook from his shirt pocket. "If it's under fifty bucks, they can work it out between 'em."

The driver of the second car fidgeted. "Look, my car's not hurt. I just wanna be on my way."

The officer looked at Aaron. "How much to this other car, then?"

"Oh, it's definitely less than fifty bucks. My body shop can fix this damage in an hour."

"Okay. You folks get these cars out of the way. I'll direct the traffic 'til you're clear." The officer blew his whistle and waved waiting vehicles around the accident scene.

Sonny immediately jumped in his car and drove away.

Charles turned to Aaron. "Do you really think fifty bucks will fix my car?"

Aaron smiled. "Heck no. You're looking at a couple hundred at the least. But there was no need to get all tangled up with the law over it."

"Why didn't the other guy say somethin'? I ran that light sure as everything."

Aaron laughed. "That was Sonny Shiflett. He's a little shady. I doubt he's even got a valid license or registration for the car he's driving—he didn't want anything to do with the cops."

"Well, thanks. Can you believe runnin' up with each other like this—after all these years? Do you work at that dealership?"

"Yes—own half of it. Come meet my partner. Pull your car up to the lot. I'll get my guys started on it, and I'll show you around. I might even sell you a new car. And you're spending the night at our house this evening. Maggie will be happy to meet one of my Army buddies. And I want you to meet my two boys."

# About the Author

After retiring from a thirty-year career with the Government Accountability Office, Craig,, or Lynn, as he is known to family and friends, set out to write about his father's experiences in WWII Italy. He lives in Virginia Beach, Virginia, with his wife, Glenda, and his son, Wes. His daughter, Christy Chattleton, is married and lives in Manhattan. When he isn't writing, he can usually be found at the skeet range or working on a wood-working project at home.

6669311R0

Made in the USA
Charleston, SC
21 November 2010